Heart Wounds
(A Miranda and Parker Mystery)
Mystery)
Book 2

Linsey Lanier

Edited by

Donna Rich

Editing for You

Gilly Wright
www.gillywright.com

ISBN: 1941191096
ISBN-13: 978-1-941191-09-5

HEART WOUNDS

The popular Miranda Steele stories from Linsey Lanier continue in a new series!

Fulfilling your destiny…one killer at a time

Miranda Steele probes the British upper crust in the second Miranda and Parker mystery.

In the London Museum of Antiquity, a heart-breaking event occurs. Someone steals the priceless, newly acquired Egyptian dagger used by Marc Antony to kill himself over Cleopatra. Beside himself, the museum director calls in Parker and Miranda to investigate.

Miranda realizes someone could kill for a relic valued at over five million pounds. And that the first victim might be—her. The threat sets Parker's nerves on edge and he doesn't hesitate to show it. And Miranda doesn't hesitate to flare up.

Can the detectives work out their issues before the theft escalates to murder?

THE MIRANDA'S RIGHTS
MYSTERY SERIES

Someone Else's Daughter
Delicious Torment
Forever Mine
Fire Dancer
Thin Ice

THE MIRANDA AND PARKER
MYSTERY SERIES
All Eyes on Me
Heart Wounds
Clowns and Cowboys
The Watcher
Zero Dark Chocolate
Trial by Fire
Smoke Screen
The Boy
Snakebit
Mind Bender
Roses from My Killer
The Stolen Girl
Vanishing Act
Predator
Retribution
Most Likely to Die
Sonata for a Killer
Fatal Fall
Girl in the Park
(more to come)

WESSON AND SLOAN FBI THRILLER SERIES
Escape from Danger
Escape from Destruction
Escape from Despair
(more to come)

MAGGIE DELANEY POLICE THRILLER SERIES
Chicago Cop
Good Cop Bad Cop

For more information visit store.linseylanier.com

"Happy families are all alike; every unhappy family is unhappy in its own way."
Leo Tolstoy

CHAPTER ONE

If all went as planned, it promised to be a most monumental day. Sir Neville Ravensdale sat on the wide rear portico of Eaton House in Surrey, England breakfasting with his wife of nineteen years. He was dressed in his best silk suit with an Ascot cravat of cobalt blue arranged carefully at his neck. A color Davinia once told him made his eyes sparkle.

He had barely touched his croissant or his single poached egg. He hadn't heard the warblers singing in the hawthorns or smelled the fragrance of the blossoming bluebells or noticed the neoclassical design of the hedgerows, which he greatly admired.

All he could think about was the dagger.

It was Egyptian, just as his years of study told him it would be. The gleam of its ornate hilt flashed in his mind just the way it had when he'd first seen it two years ago on the excavation site, the foreign dust in his throat, the sun's heat forming sweat beads on his brow, his heart racing madly with excitement of the discovery and trepidation of what might lie ahead.

Just the way it did now.

He rested his fork across the Eaton china plate and picked up his teacup. "Positively everyone will be there, Davinia. I do wish you'd come."

Not even a flinch.

Wearing a pale chiffon morning dress, her dark hair pulled back in an artful chignon at the nape of her swanlike neck and looking as graceful as the statue of Artemis in the Louvre, his beloved wife stared out at the gardens and studied her climbing roses with an empty gaze. They had bloomed too late for Chelsea but would be in time for the Hampton Court Palace flower show.

But Davinia probably wasn't thinking that far ahead. No, she was thinking of how she'd show off the flowers during her Wildlife Rescue Charity meeting tomorrow.

At any rate she wasn't giving a thought to what was before him today. For the hundredth-and-first time in what seemed like so many years, he forced himself to admit the truth.

The love of his life no longer cared for him.

"I still can't believe my good fortune in acquiring such a find. Imagine. The very dagger Marc Antony used to do away with himself in 30 BC. And this morning, the museum shall have it on display."

Again, Davinia's only response was a sip of tea.

What did he expect? She hadn't taken an interest in any of his projects in years. And why should she? She had been Lady Eaton before the Earl passed. She'd been born the daughter of a duke. Why she had chosen a lowly museum curator as her second husband, he'd never know.

He was far beneath her.

"Don't you agree that the excavation in Alexandria was a godsend? Think of it. The very instrument the Roman leader used to commit suicide. Found right in Cleopatra's mausoleum. It will bring the museum to the public's attention once again." The institute had suffered from financial difficulties in recent years. After today that would change. "Can't you share in my enthusiasm just a little?"

Davinia sat up. "Oh. Yes, very nice, dear."

She hadn't heard a word. Her look of sheer boredom was as painful as what Marc Antony must have felt from that dagger when he sliced open his own abdomen.

To be sure, they'd fallen in love when they'd met. Deeply, passionately in love. But after three or four years of marriage the fervor had died away. The only explanation he could think was Davinia had come to regret having wed a mere commoner. And now with her at fifty-seven and him at sixty-two, there was little hope for rekindling any romance.

Pushing away his breakfast, Sir Neville rose to his feet. "Well, my sweet. I must be off. Cannot be late, you know. Not today."

He strode across the terrazzo floor to give her a peck on the cheek.

She smiled thinly, her first natural response to him this morning, and lifted her hands to straighten the Grand Cross pin on his lapel. His knighthood several years ago was a poor substitute for real noble blood. "Do make sure you look your best, Neville."

His best. Of all things in life Davinia cared most about keeping up appearances. He returned her lean smile. "Yes, dear. I'll do that."

And with that, he left and headed out for the car.

The drive to London was uneventful and when the chauffeur dropped him off at the museum's rear entrance and Sir Neville stepped out of the car, his heart swelled.

He inhaled a deep breath of city air as he smiled up at the tall ionic columns, the Greek Revival gables and cornices, the expansive wings of the sprawling building. The London Museum of Antiquity. This place was much more of a home to him than Eaton House. That was Davinia's domain.

The museum was his. And today would be his greatest coup to date. The acquisition of a dagger worth millions of pounds, though its historical significance was much more important than money. The story of Antony and Cleopatra, the two star-crossed lovers, had been revived in the media and all the country was abuzz with anticipation.

This was something he would be remembered for.

His dreary home life forgotten for the moment, he hurried up the steps with a spring in his gait.

Inside, the first person to greet him was his Chief Collections Manager, George Eames.

"Sir, I'm so relieved you're here."

The man was as much a friend as a colleague, ever since their days at Cambridge together. He had a sturdy frame some people would call big-boned. Taller than Sir Neville with a heartwarming rounded belly stretching the waist of his worsted wool suit, he had the deep-set eyes and heavy jowls of an old English bulldog.

His thinning brown hair was neatly combed, his brows trimmed, his suit pressed. But he looked tired. Well, he'd been working late here last night.

Sir Neville wished he could have been with him. He should have been here last night. But Davinia had insisted on going to the philharmonic and as usual, he'd given in.

"Everything in order, George?"

"Yes, yes. Of course. The reporters are assembled in room seventeen, the designers, the security staff, everyone is there. We've just been waiting for you to check everything out before the presentation."

"Excellent." He followed his man through the labyrinth of corridors, down two short flights of stairs, and into the holding area of the storeroom.

There in the center of the large expanse, among other deliveries, stood a cart covered in black velvet. Perched atop it was a small crate.

"Is that it?" Sir Neville whispered with reverence.

Toby Waverly, a young intern with longish, curly red hair nodded with his broad, friendly smile. "It is indeed, sir." He looked very smart this morning in his dark vest and crimson necktie.

A woman in a severe, dark blue skirt suit consulted her clipboard. "The plan is to roll the crate out first, then you'll be introduced, sir." The pleasant hint of her Indian accent under the crisp British reassured Sir Neville of the efficiency he relied on.

"Very good, Emily." Sir Neville gave the nod and followed his staff through the large double doors and inside the lift. When it opened, two workers rolled the cart across the Great Hall and into Room Seventeen, the Special Exhibitions room.

He waited at the door and peeked inside.

There among the hieroglyphics, the ancient coins, the busts of assorted pharaohs, and the newly constructed replication of Cleopatra's mausoleum, stood a crowd of people.

Friends, patrons, and reporters. Everyone from the BBC to the *London News.*

Excitement coursed through his veins as George made some introductory remarks that were far too flattering. Then George gestured to him, and Sir Neville entered the room to loud applause.

The press of the crowd combined with the smell of artifacts made him feel a bit dizzy. No, it was what that crate held that was doing that. The most important acquisition of his career. If only Davinia were here to share this feat.

"Thank you," he said, smiling brightly. "On behalf of all of us on the museum staff, thank you all for coming today. As you know, it's been over a year and a half since the artifact we're receiving today was first discovered."

Briefly, he detailed the difficulties of the excavation, the tedious negotiations with the government, the rivals who demanded the piece be put up for auction. "But in the traditional British spirit, we have carried on and weathered those storms. Thus, we stand here today about to put this historic find on display for all to see. And so, without further ado, I give you, Marc Antony's dagger."

Emily handed him a hammer, and he worked the claw against the metal braces of the crate, loosening them one at a time. One, two, three. His heart soared. He thought of the Roman legions, the ships of ancient Egypt. Antony and Cleopatra at the helm, then the lovers being driven into a tomb.

He could feel antiquity at his fingertips as the last brace came loose. He handed the brace and the hammer to Emily and lifted the wooden lid.

The container was filled with Styrofoam peanuts as was usual. Emily showed him a plastic bag she was holding up. He nodded and began to scoop the peanuts into the bag. One handful. Two. Three. When he'd emptied half the crate, he stopped.

The dagger should have been in the middle of the crate encased in bubble wrap for additional protection. He shot a frown of concern to George. His brow was always furrowed but just now, the creases were deeper.

Perhaps the packers weren't exact. The dagger must be somewhere. He scooped out more peanuts. More. More. He could see the bottom of the box. Surely, he hadn't missed it.

Emily handed the peanut bag to Toby and began frantically searching her clipboard. "The bill of lading is right here," she whispered, showing it to Sir Neville.

He scanned it. Everything looked intact.

And then his heart stopped as he realized what had happened. The troubled excavation, the rivals, the publicity. Spasms of confusion and panic and embarrassment reverberated up his legs, into his torso, through his chest.

Merciful heavens, was he having a heart attack?

The crowd began to murmur as he reached for the side of the box to steady himself. He gasped for air.

George rushed to his side. "Sir, are you all right?"

Sir Neville reached out for the man's hand and whispered in his ear. "Call Scotland Yard. The dagger has been stolen."

4

George's eyes went wide with shock, but he knew it was true. "Take care of the crowd," he said to Emily and began to lead Sir Neville out of the room.

She nodded and turned to the crowd. "Ladies and gentlemen, it seems there's been a slight mishap."

As Emily's voice rang in Sir Neville's ears and his head spun wildly with bewildered dismay, another thought stuck him.

By the time they had crossed the Great Court he knew, in addition to the police, he had to make another call to an old friend. To his friend's son, actually.

Wade Parker.

CHAPTER TWO

Miranda Steele leaned against the boards of the high-domed skating rink in Marietta, Georgia, watching a young fourteen-year-old girl go round and round on the ice, her skates making measured slicing noises.

The girl wore a simple lime green skirt over a black leotard and had her long dark hair—which was now streaked with golden highlights—pulled back in a ponytail. With one leg extended behind her, she glided along gracefully, her breath soft wisps in the cold air.

Wendy Van Aarle had come a long way since Miranda had first met her. But then so had she. And though she shivered in her lightweight coat and work clothes, Miranda couldn't suppress the warm glow in her heart as she overheard remarks of approval from some of the parents who were watching. Why shouldn't she be proud?

She'd once thought Wendy was her daughter.

Movement caught her eye and Miranda turned and smiled at the figure coming toward her from the spot along the rail where she'd been shouting coaching advice.

Another girl of the same age, dressed in solid black skinny jeans, ankle-high boots and a dark suede jacket. Her thick, almost black hair hung in soft waves to her shoulders, and she had a teal angora scarf around her neck that brought out the color of her eyes.

She walked with a slight limp from her injury eight months ago. Wounds she'd received the same time Miranda got hers. They were both on the tail end of recovery. Physically, anyway.

As she neared, Miranda's heart went from a warm glow to a tight clench—an almost painful mixture of joy and anxiety—as the pretty young girl who was really her daughter reached her side.

"Hello, Mother." She smiled back and gave her a peck on the cheek.

"It's good to see you, Mackenzie." Miranda let herself embrace the girl a moment, then let her go. It had been over eight months since she'd discovered this girl was her daughter—almost as long as she'd carried her. But the fact that she'd found her after searching for thirteen years still made her head spin. And their relationship was still…gelling.

"I'm so glad you could come."

"I decided it was about time." Miranda hadn't been to the rink in months, but today she'd ditched work early to come here. She nodded toward the ice. "Wendy's doing great."

Mackenzie smiled sweetly. "She needs to work on her crossovers and her sit spins really need improvement." Same move Mackenzie had had trouble with even when she was in her prime.

"Do you have to be so critical? Wendy hasn't been skating as long as you." Mackenzie had started when she was five or so, Miranda had been told.

"We've got to get her ready for the Atlanta Open. It's a tough competition." She drew in a mature breath, as if she were reining herself in. The people who had raised Mackenzie had ensured she had good manners. "But you're right. She's really come a long way."

"Under your expertise."

She nodded, a tinge of sadness on her face. The memory of what had stalled her skating career and changed the direction of her young life was still fresh for both of them. "Mother…"

"What?"

"Do you remember…I don't know how to say this."

Miranda watched her pretty face, the brows twisted with teenage stress. Probably something about a boy. Miranda had been dreading the time when either Wendy or Mackenzie might ask her for advice on the opposite sex. There wasn't much help she could give them in that department.

But she straightened her shoulders like a good mother and said, "Just spit it out. We don't have to hold things back from each other after what we've been through."

"I'm glad you said that." She picked at one of her fingernails. "Do you remember the first time you came to see me?"

Miranda frowned with apprehension. Why would she want to talk about that? The day Miranda had gotten into the Chatham mansion by posing as a skating coach? The day they'd both screamed at each other? The day Mackenzie had denied with all her being she was related to the likes of Miranda Steele?

"Sure, I do," she said, trying not to show the tension in her throat.

Mackenzie rubbed her arm and stared at the ice. "Do you remember what you told me that day?"

Primarily that Miranda was her mother. "I…guess I said a lot of things." That day was horrible. She'd been doing her best to forget it. "What are you getting at, Mackenzie?"

The girl inhaled and put her hand to her lips. "You told me…about my father."

Miranda sucked in the cold air so hard she thought she might choke. She'd forgotten the little detail that had slipped out when she'd been too angry to think straight. The girl had challenged her. And in trying to keep her safe from untold harm, she'd had a choice of telling Mackenzie her father was a crazed psycho or a rapist.

She'd opted for the truth. Or rather, she'd blurted it out. "I was raped," she had said.

She'd give anything to have that moment back. She wouldn't make the same mistake twice.

"I've been thinking about what you said. A lot."

"I…wish you wouldn't." It wasn't something a young girl should think about at all.

"I've been wondering…what it means. I mean, how it's going to affect me."

Affect her? Miranda's mind raced. Mackenzie had been a little snot when she'd first met her.

But the girl was different now. She'd had a real change of heart after coming close to death. Was she worried she'd turn into the nasty little shrew once again? Whether she'd become a criminal herself when she grew up? Disease?

Maybe all of it. But none of that would happen. Miranda knew it in her bones. Her daughter was a good kid. She had been raised by one of the best families in Atlanta. She'd turn out to be a model citizen.

What could she tell her? Memories of a dark snowy alley outside Chicago came back to her. Struggling. The sense of being held down against her will. Her skin meeting the frozen air as her clothes were ripped off of her. The smell of wool and aftershave.

"It's probably best not to dwell on it," she blurted out, rubbing her arms against the cold of the ice rink. Not a satisfying answer, she supposed, but avoidance was the only way Miranda could deal with it after all these years.

"You don't understand. I want you to find him."

"What?" Miranda gasped. The girl's words made her feel lightheaded. She must have misheard her.

"You're a private investigator. I want to hire you to find my father."

Now Miranda laughed out loud. "I'm a PI, not a magician."

"So?"

She let out an exasperated breath. "I—I never saw my attacker. He wore a mask that night. I didn't report it. There's no record of it.

Mackenzie turned to her, her deep blue eyes moist with tears. "Are you saying you can't do it?"

Miranda couldn't believe she was having this conversation. If she'd known, she wouldn't have come here today. "That's exactly what I'm saying. On many levels."

"I see."

She watched the girl fight for control. Whether of her temper or her disappointment, Miranda wasn't sure.

At last, she shook her head. "I'm so sorry. I didn't realize how painful for you this would be. I—I wasn't thinking. I'm sorry." And she turned and hurried away to the restrooms.

Miranda didn't follow her. She wouldn't know what else to say to her. But she had a feeling if Mackenzie had as much determination about finding her father as she'd had about ice skating, this wouldn't be the end of it.

When at last Miranda reached the drive of the southern castle in Mockingbird Hills that was now her home, she decided she made a lousy mother. She should have been comforting. She should have soothed Mackenzie's concerns with some wise, maternal words. The kind that could make even the worst problem seem small.

Trouble was, she didn't have words like that. Not for her daughter. Not for herself.

She'd have to leave that job to Colby Chatham. But Miranda had a feeling Mackenzie's adoptive mother wouldn't be hearing about her desire to find her biological father any time soon.

Better to leave it that way and not get involved. After all, what could Mackenzie do? There was no way to find the man who'd attacked her mother on a dark Chicago street fourteen years ago and caused her conception.

Best to let sleeping rapists lie.

She turned off the car and stared at the shadows of the oak trees dancing across the stone balustrade that bordered the ten-bedroom estate. The Parker mansion had been in the family for generations, but it had been Parker's real estate mogul father who had remodeled the place and turned it into a comfortable dwelling for his family.

And now it was her abode.

She'd always felt it was too much house and too much ritz to suit her. But after her encounter with Mackenzie, it felt like welcoming arms. Maybe that was because of the arms that were waiting for her inside.

Parker's.

Suddenly eager to feel them around her, she got out of the car and went inside.

The massive entrance hall was quiet as a church, its crystal chandeliers glittering mutely off the mirrors and edges of the classy furniture below and making the marble tile of the floor gleam.

There was no scent of anything yummy being cooked up. She wondered if Parker wanted to dine out tonight when her gaze traveled over the tall oil paintings on the high walls to the ornate mahogany staircase.

Parker appeared at the top, still in the deep blue suit and blood red silk tie he'd worn to work.

He began to descend, the usual debonair saunter in his stride, and she took in the form of the agile body beneath that suit that made her heart race. As he went, he pushed back a stray strand of his neatly styled salt and pepper hair that fell just over his ears. He caught her gaze with his gunmetal gray eyes, and she drank in that to-die-for face that every woman in Atlanta lusted over.

Her heart soared.

How did an ordinary former construction worker who'd never had a lot of money wind up with the likes of him? All she knew was she was the luckiest girl in the world to be married to this man. Not because of his wealth or his impossible good looks or even his unmatched investigative skills.

Because of his heart of gold.

"I was just about to call you," he said in his low, aristocratic Southern accent that was as rich as his bank account. "You left work early."

"I went to the skating rink."

"I thought as much." He could always guess what she was up to.

He reached her, took her in his strong arms.

Relishing the comfort of his embrace, she leaned her forehead against his shoulder and ran her hands up his biceps, drinking in the feel of the expensive fabric of his suit jacket and the well-formed muscles beneath it.

He lifted her chin with a finger and kissed her lips.

She reveled in the touch of his mouth, his heady, masculine scent. An image flashed through her mind of tearing each other's clothes off and getting it on right there on the marble floor under the bold light of the chandeliers, until he pulled away.

"Are you all right?" His handsome face was creased with concern. He was reading her mind again.

She opened her mouth.

She couldn't tell him about what Mackenzie had asked her to do. He'd only worry about her, and he'd done enough of that lately.

She just shrugged. "You know how teenage girls are."

The concern on his face relaxed into a smile. "I do." He'd raised one himself. Or he and his wife had. The wife he'd lost three years before Miranda came along. She knew that loss had almost been the end of him. "I have something to discuss with you."

"Oh?"

"Let's talk over dinner." He took her hand and ushered her toward the hall that led to the kitchen.

"Without even changing?"

He shook his head as his pace picked up. "There won't be time."

CHAPTER THREE

They ate in the kitchen at a small round oak table tucked away in the alcove, which they'd been using for awhile instead of the fancy one in the dining room.

Eating here suited them both, and Miranda was glad for the homemade chicken pot pie their cook, Emily, had left them.

Comfort food. Just what she needed tonight.

"So what do you want to talk about?" she asked after downing a savory forkful of the gooey concoction.

Parker took a sip of the coffee he'd opted for over beer or wine as his expression turned pensive. "Late this afternoon I received a call from an old friend of my father's."

"Oh?" She wondered what that had to do with them.

"It seems he's had some serious trouble."

She reached for her own cup and eyed the dark liquid that smelled as rich as Parker himself. Of course, it was that expensive brew he always had imported from St. Helena. She didn't want to admit she was getting hooked on it. "Go on."

"He's the director of a museum and one of its recent acquisitions has been stolen."

Acquisitions? "Okay."

"He'd like us to investigate."

She put her cup down without taking a sip, despite how good it smelled. "A museum case?"

"A friend's case."

Uh huh. They'd just started a new venture together, which they'd decided to call simply Parker and Steele Consulting. As an adjunct to the already thriving Parker Investigative Agency, they planned to take on cases anywhere in the world from anyone who'd ask for help. They were supposed to be difficult cases. Cases that had stumped the locals, the cops, or even the FBI.

So far, they'd only had one case. And just because things got a little dicey at the end, Parker had wanted to put restrictions on the operation.

They'd been arguing about it since they'd gotten back from Vegas. Parker kept using words like "safety" and "precautions" and "defensive measures." Miranda had interpreted those words as "repression" and "smothering" and "paranoia."

Okay. She understood where he was coming from, how he felt. He'd suffered losses. Terrible, painful, crushing losses that would bring most men to their knees. He didn't want to lose her, so he didn't want her taking "unnecessary risks," as he called them.

But what was she supposed to do? Stuff herself in a straitjacket and lock herself in a closet?

And what about that dream or vision or whatever it was she'd had in the hospital? She'd seen her life flashing before her, as they say, and her dead brother told her she had a destiny to fulfill.

So now Parker wasn't going to take on a challenging case that might pose some danger? No, he was going to play it safe and have them hunting down some stupid museum piece.

"Sounds pretty boring," she said flatly and watched his gray eyes turn dark with flame.

Parker's grip tightened on the porcelain coffee cup in his hand as he fought back his temper and studied his stubborn wife's face. The lines in her brow were twisted into knots of anger and her deep blue eyes with their fringe of long black lashes glowed with defiance and seemed to accuse him of being too obtuse for words.

She gave her wild dark hair an irritated flip over her shoulder and despite her attitude, the movement tinged his mood with arousal. Her feistiness always aroused him as much as it infuriated him.

She wore a simple blouse in the dark colors she preferred trimmed with a deep red piping that reflected her bold spirit. The spirit he adored. The spirit he could not live without.

He eyed the spot near her heart where the bullet of a madman had pierced her flesh over eight months ago. She was well and strong now. Or so she claimed. But he had almost lost her. He would never take that risk again.

Calmer now, he sat back with a casual air. "Boredom is often in the eye of the beholder."

Ha. Miranda gritted her teeth and met Parker's steady, penetrating gaze. Did he think he could pull those suave tricks of persuasion on her? "So what would we be looking for? Some ancient statue of King Tut? Or a painting? Maybe a nude?"

He smiled as if he thought he was making progress. "It's a dagger."

Miranda's brows rose. "You mean something you stab people with?"

"That was its intended use. It's an ancient Egyptian dagger."

She ran her tongue over her teeth. "Why would anybody want to steal that?"

"It's priceless. It was found in Cleopatra's tomb, which was discovered a few years ago. It's supposed to be the instrument Marc Antony committed suicide with. You remember the story."

Antony and Cleopatra? She remembered the movie with Liz Taylor and Richard Burton. She'd seen it on The Late Show at a friend's house when she was a kid. "Wasn't Cleopatra the one who killed herself with a snake?"

"An asp, so the legend goes. Her army was defeated by the Romans, and she had no other choice."

What a wimp. Miranda pushed her plate away. "So how would a thief fence a thing like that?"

"Many ways. Black market, Asia, the Middle East."

It could already be gone without a trace. But criminals always left clues behind. Even the good ones. Maybe this would be a challenging case. Wait a minute. She drummed her fingers on the table. "Where exactly is this museum?"

Parker gave her an I-thought-you'd-never-ask look of triumph. "London."

She bit back her surprise. "As in London, England?"

"I don't believe they have a museum with ancient artifacts in London, Minnesota. You have updated your passport, haven't you?"

She had to think a minute. She vaguely recalled filling out the forms, taking the photos and going to the post office with her friends Coco and Fanuzzi, who were dying of curiosity to know where Parker was taking her. When she told them it was just business, they didn't buy it. That was a few months ago.

"Yeah, I think everything's kosher."

Parker got to his feet and reached for the dishes. "That's good because I've booked us a late flight."

"We're leaving tonight?"

"Unless you still think it's too boring a case and want to stay home."

She rose, picked up the remainder of the pot pie and strolled over to the counter with it, tempted to toss it in Parker's face for stringing her along. But he was too dignified for that and besides, she'd only end up licking it off, and they'd miss their flight.

She cocked her head thoughtfully. "Well, tracking down a blood-thirsty dagger thief doesn't sound as exciting as tracking down a blood-thirsty killer…" she paused to let him stew a bit. "But I suppose I can tag along."

Parker set the dishes in the sink and stepped up behind her. He pulled back her hair and planted a deep kiss against her neck. "I was hoping you'd see it that way."

Just as she was sucking in her breath and closing her eyes, he added. "And by the way. This time, I'm in charge."

CHAPTER FOUR

Okay, it was the agreement.

They'd each take turns being in charge and last time she had been lead. If you didn't count Parker's pulling rank at the end.

She got it. It was fair. But Parker's glib announcement still made her grumpy. By the time they'd packed, hurried to the airport, and caught the ten-hour flight to Heathrow, she was in a foul mood.

Dressed ready to go to work as soon as they landed in her dark slacks and jacket, she tossed and turned, if that's what you called it when you were trying to sleep in an airline seat. Okay, it was first class and reclined almost all the way back. But Parker's remark and Mackenzie's request nagged at her the whole time, and she ended up with only about three hours of shut eye.

It seemed more like ten minutes when Miranda felt Parker shift beside her and opened her eyes to discover they were landing—and that she had a massive headache.

"Jet lag?" he asked, gentle concern in his voice.

"Uh," she grunted as she finger combed her hair and eyed him up and down.

In his unwrinkled traveling suit, he seemed rested. And he must have snuck off to the restroom already. He was shaved and groomed and as handsome as ever.

How did he get off looking so good? He couldn't have slept more than she had.

A delicious smell teased her nostrils, and a flight attendant handed them both coffee. Miranda grabbed her paper cup and slurped down half of the rich, delicious liquid in one gulp. She was feeling almost human again when she noticed Parker watching her, amusement in his eyes.

"Hmpf." She turned away with a half smirk and used a finger to lift the blind on the window, feeling a bit like a vampire avoiding the sun. She peered out.

No sun. All she could see was clouds. "Is that real London fog?"

"The genuine article," Parker grinned.

And they were supposed to slog through that vapor in search of a missing dagger like Sherlock Holmes? A bell dinged and the pilot announced they were on approach for landing.

Miranda buckled her seatbelt. "Who is this client, anyway?"

"Sir Neville Ravensdale."

"He's a knight?"

Parker nodded. "He was bestowed the honor a few years ago for his museum work. Cultural advancement."

She should have known he wouldn't be a chimneysweep. "And here I thought they only did that for men who slew dragons."

Parker indulged her with a smile.

"How does Mr. P know him?" Mr. P was Miranda's nickname for Parker's father.

"They met decades ago at a London auction. I believe my father was thinking of investing in land here. We sent Sir Neville and his wife an invitation to our wedding."

"We did?" Parker's daughter, Gen had handled the guest list.

"He wasn't able to come. I'm sure he'll be happy to meet you now."

"So he already knows we're married."

"Yes. Is that a problem?"

Letting a client know they were a husband-and-wife team had been a sore spot on their first case. They'd decided not to reveal their marital status to clients in the future. It provoked too many personal questions.

But it was too late in this case.

"Guess I'll just have to deal with it this time." As well as prove she was an investigator in her own right, and not just tagging along with hubby for the fun of it.

The plane landed and they disembarked, waded through customs and caught a black square-shaped taxi into town.

Miranda bolted upright when the driver swung into the lane and was about to shout, "Look out!" until she remembered they drove on the left side here.

Wait, he was also sitting on the right side of the front seat. That jet lag had really done a number on her. Scowling at Parker's amused look, she settled back in the seat.

It was raining, as the view from the plane had indicated, and the windshield wipers swooshed back and forth monotonously while music and strange ads played softly on the radio.

The cab had the leathery smell of public transportation mixed with an exotic, foreign scent Miranda couldn't place, and the scenery outside the windows was as monotonous as the wipers. Except for orange signs and flashing numbers she assumed were the speed limit, the curvy route looked a lot like the stretches of interstate around Atlanta in the rain. Concrete road barriers giving way to acres of tall brown grass dotted with trees along the highway.

Parker handed her the local newspaper he'd bought in the airport. "You might want to see this."

She took it and unfolded it.

"Marc Antony Dagger Snatched from Museum." The story had made the front page. An elderly gentleman with a head of neatly groomed, pure white hair stood gaping at the open crate before him. Surrounded by what she assumed were museum personnel, he wore a dark suit with an Ascot at the neck over a thin body that seemed a bit frail.

The look of shock and dismay and sheer mortification on his face instantly tore her heart out.

"So this is our client?"

Parker nodded grimly. He was feeling the man's pain, too. He glanced at the cabbie's back.

Right. Not good to talk about business in front of a stranger.

She nodded and scanned the story. It didn't say much they didn't already know. The dagger had been recovered last year from the mausoleum of Cleopatra, which in turn had been discovered a few years earlier in northern Egypt. The artifact was said to be priceless but on the black market could fetch upwards of five million pounds.

No small potatoes. A figure some might kill for.

As the legend went, the dagger had been a gift from the Egyptian queen to the Roman leader. But when Cleopatra's armies were defeated in battle against Antony's rivals in Rome, and he heard a rumor that his lover was dead, he used the dagger to kill himself.

Still alive, he reached her sanctuary and died in her arms. Later the queen followed suit with an asp at her breast.

Pretty serious love affair, Miranda thought, closing the paper and handing it back to Parker. And it had seemed everyone wanted the dagger ever since it was uncovered. The Egyptian government, collectors, other museums. The mild-looking Sir Neville must have had to fight tooth and nail to keep it.

She thought of the lost look on the elderly gentleman's face and felt that familiar resolve swell inside her. *Well, Sir Neville Ravensdale*, she decided. *I don't know if I can recover your dagger, but I'll give it all I have.*

Miranda looked up to see Parker giving her a knowing look tinged with an air of victory. He'd read her mind again.

"Headin' into town now, sir," the cabbie announced as they came to a halt at a traffic light.

She peered out the window. Beyond the masses of other vehicles, they were surrounded by shiny moving billboards and towering structures made of shimmering glass looking like they were put up yesterday standing right beside huge buildings of ancient stone, broken out with windows and arches and parapets, as if they had a case of architectural hives. The gaudy structures seemed to ooze centuries of history. You could almost feel the past encased within its stones.

Before them a noisy hoard of pedestrians in coats and sweaters and boots swarmed the intersection. Three bicycles rolled past the front of the cab, one with a child on the back. There were more people and bicycles on the sidewalks on either side of them.

Miranda blinked in surprise. Atlanta could get crowded, and the traffic was awful, but she'd forgotten what it was like in a really big city.

"Guess we're here," she exhaled. No turning back now.

"Just starting out, m'um," the driver grinned, pointing out the window. "'Round the corner is Hyde Park. Beyond is Buckingham Palace. Then there's Westminster Abbey, River Thames, the Tower—"

Parker leaned forward. "I'm sorry. We won't have time for sightseeing just now. We're in a bit of a hurry to get to our destination." With his aristocratic Southern accent, he almost sounded like he was born here.

"Of course, sir. Whatever you say." The cabbie adjusted the black beret he had on, straightened his shoulders under a dark blue pullover, and turned his radio up a tad to hide his embarrassment or maybe his feelings toward foreigners who hadn't come here to be awed by his town.

After an ad that was either about detergent or beer, the news came on. "Metropolitan police tell us they're following up all leads in the case of the invaluable dagger stolen from the London Museum of Antiquity yesterday...."

The cabbie shook his head and muttered to himself. "Never 'eard of anything so cheeky in all me born days. Imagine stealin' a priceless piece of antiquity right out from under the museum director's nose. Terrible. Just terrible."

Miranda shot Parker a troubled look. The news was all over town. And the police had been called in—of course. It wouldn't be easy for a couple of American PIs to make any headway. Besides, the thief could be anybody. Any one of the thousands of pedestrians in any of the thousands of city streets. Or he could be outside London. Or in China. Or India.

They zigzagged through the traffic, past monuments and gardens and red double-decker buses and ended up at the Queensbury Hotel near Tottenham Court Road. At least that's what the signs said.

Parker ran inside to check them in and get a bellhop to take their bags up while Miranda sat in the cab and studied a weathered fountain with a half-naked winged man atop it. He certainly wasn't dressed for the weather.

After a few minutes Parker returned.

"Where to now, sir?" the cabbie asked brightly, having regained his hospitable spirit.

"The London Museum of Antiquity, please."

"Oh, I am sorry, sir. The museum's closed today. Due to the tragedy and the police investigation and all that."

"I think they'll let us in."

The cabbie turned around, his eyes wide. "Are you two American reporters come to cover the story?"

Parker only smiled at the man. "Something like that."

CHAPTER FIVE

The traffic was worse than Atlanta and New York put together, but after what seemed like another hour, they'd traveled the two kilometers—or whatever it was—and reached Guilford Street and the Museum.

Still not convinced they'd get in, the cabbie offered to wait for them, but Parker waved him on.

Miranda got out and while the cab whooshed away behind her, she eyed the wide gray stairs, sitting like a giant stack of concrete pancakes before her. Above the stairs rose dozens of thick columns topped by a row of Greek figures along the roof staring down their noses at all who dared enter.

Friendly place. And downright huge. The size of the wings sprouting out from the main building promised plenty of walking. As she started the climb, she was wishing for her jeans instead of business attire. But at least she had on comfortable shoes and was back in pretty decent shape.

The rain had turned to a mist and by the time they reached the top, their skin and clothes were coated with moisture. Went right along with the chilly greeting awaiting them.

As they approached the huge entrance, a tall police officer, maybe in his late twenties, in white shirt, tie and jersey barred their way. "I'm sorry sir, m'um," he said, acknowledging Miranda with a curt nod. "The museum's closed to visitors."

Parker gave him his most patient smile. "We're not visitors, Officer. The director sent for us."

The man's thin blond brows rose to the brim of his peaked cap. "The director, you say? Sent for a pair of American tourists?"

Miranda eyed the short downy blond hair under his hat, his oversized ears, the badges on his shoulders. She couldn't decipher his rank, but he seemed too young to be more than a rookie. A rookie rule-follower. Her first inclination was to remind him they were guests, not colonists, maybe with the knuckles of her fist for emphasis. But she held back and let Parker handle it. Since he was in charge.

As if he were doling out a donation to the policeman's ball, Parker pulled out a business card from his back pocket and handed it to the man. "We're from the Parker Investigative Agency. We're here to look into the matter of the missing dagger."

The officer put one hand behind him and rolled back on his heels. "Really now? I'm sure Inspector Wample will be thrilled two American tourists have come to help him conduct his investigation." He handed the card back without budging.

Miranda watched Parker's jaw tighten. Then he smiled again and returned the card to the young man. "If you'll speak to your inspector as well as to Sir Neville Ravensdale, I'm sure all will be made clear to you."

Good one, she thought, stifling a grin.

Realizing they weren't going away, the officer snatched the card, turned on his heel as if falling into formation, and disappeared inside.

Miranda pulled her jacket around her, glad Parker had picked out something on the warm side for her to wear. "Looks like this one's gonna be a piece of cake."

Parker's dark brow rose, and he regarded her, the battle with frustration written all over his handsome face. "Once we resolve the authority issues, we'll be fine."

If "fine" meant they'd reached the haystack they were to start looking for Marc Antony's dagger in, she guessed he was right.

As they paced back and forth in the misty rain a loud bell clanged in the distance. It played a familiar ditty then went bong, bong.

"Is that what I think it is?" Miranda asked.

Parker nodded. "Big Ben. It rings every hour on the hour."

"Nice." Kind of a communal alarm clock for the entire city.

Big Ben stopped clanging and another ten minutes went by. No sign of Officer TightAss.

Miranda peered through the tall glass doors. "He might have gotten lost in there."

"You could be right," Parker said.

She put her hand on the tube-shaped handle and gave it a yank. It opened with ease. "Well, look at that. It isn't even locked."

His eyes twinkling with pride, Parker strode toward her and opened the door wide. He gave her a sly grin and a ladies-first gesture. "It is a public institution, after all."

"It is, indeed." She grinned back at him and stepped inside.

They stepped into a dark hall filled with squarish columns that led to a huge, wide-open white space flooded with light from a glass ceiling. It was good to be out of the rain, but the dampness from outside seemed to seep in through the walls. The air had a fresh, citrusy smell, probably from cleaners, and the entire area was silent except for the sound of their shoes on the tiled floor.

They strolled around the room, past thick stones covered with hieroglyphics, dramatic statues of nymphs and poets, busts of ancient pharaohs, mummified cats. They veered off into another hall where there were long cases filled with spears and arrowheads and pottery. The arched doorway at the end of it opened to another vast space. In the corner was the display that must have been intended for the dagger.

A golden rectangular structure covered in hieroglyphics sliced in half to give the illusion you were looking inside. A colorfully robed mannequin of the Egyptian Queen lay across a divan, a gold mesh headdress covering her long black hair, golden discs around her neck. The figure of a wounded Roman soldier in tunic and breastplate leaned against her, his head in her lap. His arm was raised as if he were about to stab himself. But of course, his hand was empty.

"There," Parker murmured.

Miranda watched him head for a tall marble staircase that wound around a wide circular pillar in the center of the room. She followed him to the foot of the steps and saw what he was going for.

About halfway up the stairs sat a lone figure in a rumpled dark suit, elbows on his knees, face buried in his hands. If he had been an exhibit, he would have been labeled "Despair."

Parker reached the foot of the staircase. "Neville?"

The man raised his head, his eyes wide. "Russell? Is that you?"

Miranda was surprised the man called Parker by the same name his father used for him.

"Yes, we're here." Parker hurried up the steps.

Miranda followed.

"Oh, thank heavens." The man rose and ran a hand over his white hair, then attempted to straighten his clothes. He seemed to have lost the tie he'd worn in the picture in the paper, but the suit was the same. He must have slept in it.

Parker reached him and the man took both of his hands. "Thank you so much for coming so quickly."

"We left as soon as we could."

"I do so appreciate it on such short notice." He turned to her and reached for her hand, still holding onto one of Parker's. "And this must be Miranda. I'm so glad you're here, my dear. Both of you. Though I wish we could have met under happier circumstances."

His touch was gentle, his skin soft and aristocratic. His face was round and almost childlike, a contrast to his thin body. His white hair had a faint angelic glow in the backlight, enhanced by the earnest expression of his well-groomed matching brows. His accent was posh, but warm and friendly. Not stiff and cold, like you might expect from a Brit.

And the look of kindness mixed with desperation in his crystal blue eyes melted her heart into a buttery pool.

"We're here to help, sir," Miranda told him. "We'll do all we can."

He closed his eyes, pain distorting his innocent expression. "And I need your help so desperately. I don't know what to do. They've taken George."

"George?" Parker asked.

"George Eames. My Chief Collections Manager. My friend and colleague. They took him in for questioning this morning. They think he's a suspect in this horrible matter."

Miranda looked at Parker. He seemed as bewildered as she was. "The police have already made an arrest?" she asked.

A door opened and footsteps echoed below. "There they are, sir."

Miranda turned and saw three men scurrying toward the staircase. One tall and thin. One short and round. The third one was Officer TightAss. The other two were in gray slacks, ties, and long dark coats that billowed out as they ran.

The officer waved an arm their way. "Sir, I apologize these imposters have broken in and—"

Sir Neville's whole body stiffened. Eyes flashing, he held out an arm in a protective gesture, looking like one of the mummified cats suddenly come to life to fight its captors. "They most certainly are not imposters, Officer. And I'll thank you to pay them their due respect. These are my friends from America. They're private investigators. I've hired them."

"You've what?" said the man in a coat who towered a good four inches over the officer.

Sir Neville started down the stairs. "I've hired them to help with this investigation, Inspector."

"I haven't authorized—"

"As director of this museum, I have the right to hire anyone I see fit to aid in this matter, Inspector. If you have a problem with that, perhaps I'll have to speak to your superior."

Miranda snuck Parker a look of surprise. The old gent wasn't as helpless as he seemed.

Parker sauntered down the steps with his characteristic air of ease and extended a hand. "Good morning, Inspector, gentlemen. As I told your officer here, I'm Wade Parker of the Parker Investigative Agency, and this is my associate, Miranda Steele." He turned back and gestured to her as ingratiatingly as if he were introducing her at a dinner party. "We intend to give you our full cooperation."

As if it took all the strength he had not to slap a pair of handcuffs onto Parker's wrist, the inspector took his hand and gave it a single, curt shake. "I'm Special Inspector Clive Wample of the Metropolitan police, and these are Assistant Chief Officer Vincent Ives and Officer Tadsworth." He waved his free hand toward Officer TightAss and the small, rotund man between them, the shortest one of the three.

Miranda scuttled down the steps and joined in the handshaking.

Wample and Ives. Sounded like a brand of bourbon. No, it was Wample, Ives and Tadsworth. More like a law firm or maybe a British boy band.

Inspector Wample put a skinny finger under his thin crooked nose and sniffed. "I was about to tell Sir Neville we've almost finished our examination of the key areas on the premises. You should be able to open again in the morning."

Sir Neville's mouth opened in alarm.

Parker descended the last step. "Well, then, Inspector. You shouldn't mind if we have a look at these key areas."

The inspector's eyes flashed, but one glance at Sir Neville told him he'd be in hot water if he didn't comply. "Very well, Mr. Parker. However, I insist we escort you."

CHAPTER SIX

Sir Neville led them back to the hall where the Antony and Cleopatra exhibit was.

He explained what had happened that day, the same details Miranda had read in the newspaper. He'd used a cart to bring in the crate that was supposed to have held the dagger, and when he opened it up—it was empty.

His voice broke and his face went pale as he retold the story, but since the crate, the cart, and of course the dagger had been removed, there wasn't much to see there.

The party moved upstairs and reluctantly Sir Neville led them to a hidden elevator that went to the apartments on the third floor where some of the staff lived.

George Eames's rooms were a cramped little space with a tiny kitchen and bedroom. The rectangular-shaped living room had a small window overlooking a park, and its walls were crammed with musty old books on archaeology and ancient history.

The inspector paced up and down the narrow space while Miranda and Parker looked it all over. "We've already gone through everything thoroughly, Mr. Parker."

Parker pulled a book from the shelf and examined it. "And did you find the dagger?"

"Not a trace of it, sir," said Officer Tadsworth.

Miranda heard Wample wheeze out an exasperated breath. "He lived here alone?"

"Why, yes," Sir Neville said. "He never married. His mother lives in Devonshire. He goes to visit her on the weekend. Oh, dear. She's going to be devastated."

Feeling sorry for both of them, she strolled over to the desk in the corner. Its surface was crowded with papers, pens, periodicals, open books. George Eames might not be neat, but he was definitely studious.

"George was working on the Battle of Actium. It was to be our next exhibit."

Must be what the chicken scratches on the notepads were. "Did you find any mysterious letters or notes about the dagger? A telegram? A diary?"

This time the inspector replied. "No, nothing of the kind."

Didn't sound like they had much of a case.

Parker turned to another shelf where there was a photograph. He studied it. "Who's this?"

Miranda came over and gave it a look. Four young men stood in front of an old church dressed in—what was that, cricket uniforms? They all were grinning and had their arms around each other like the best of chums.

Sir Neville peered over Parker's shoulder. "Oh, that photo's from Cambridge. The four of us all went to school together. We were good friends." He pointed to the two figures on the left. "That's George and myself. We, of course, were mad for archaeology." He moved to the next young man, the tallest one. A sturdy, broad-shouldered fellow with dark hair and features. "That's Trenton Jewell. He went on to be a barrister. He practices here in London." He pointed to the last figure, a slight fellow with a hairline that was already receding. "That's Cedric Swift. He's on the faculty now. Teaches computers." He smiled sadly. "Can you imagine? Back then we were inseparable, but now we've gone our separate ways."

"Except for you and Mr. Eames," Parker pointed out.

"Yes. Though I do see Trenton occasionally at social events. George was considering the academic life and did teach for a while. About ten years ago he came to me and said he wanted to work for the museum, so of course I hired him. He was eminently qualified."

"I see." Parker put the photograph back on the shelf.

His face was bland, but Miranda could tell what he was thinking. The same thing she was. Could the motive behind the theft of the dagger have been professional jealousy?

Parker turned to Inspector Wample. "We'd like to see where the dagger was received."

Back down the hall to the elevator the entourage went, Sir Neville at the lead. Then back across several rooms on the main floor to another elevator, down into a dungeon-like hall below the building.

At the end of the hall stood aluminum double doors. Sir Neville punched numbers into a pad on the wall to disengage the security system and opened the doors.

Inside, it was nothing like a dungeon. Bright with fluorescent overhead lighting, the huge space was almost friendly. Roomy tables and stools. Rows and rows of shelving units holding various shaped crates. Rows and rows of long drawers full of objects of antiquity, so Miranda supposed.

It was cool and the dampness she'd felt everywhere else in the building was gone. A unit hummed in the background. Probably responsible for environmental control. Still, the faint smell of ancient things hung in the air.

Sir Neville gestured to a small cart that stood about waist high. It was covered with a black velvet cloth and a narrow crate sat atop it. "That's where the dagger was supposed to have been."

"It was delivered in that crate?" Miranda asked.

"Yes. George received delivery at 17:55 two nights ago." He strode over to a countertop where a computer screen sat and pressed a few buttons on the keyboard. "There. See for yourselves."

Miranda went over for a look with Parker beside her. They bent together to examine the data on the screen. "Looks like the barcode was scanned at the time you said, Sir Neville."

"Yes, of course it was."

Miranda ran her tongue over her teeth and thought a moment. "Any chance there was a breach in security in the delivery? Before the truck got here?"

Sir Neville's eyes grew round. "Certainly not. We've been using that company for years and have never once had an incident."

There's always a first time. But she decided it was better not to voice her thought just now.

Parker put his hands in his pockets and began to stroll around the room, giving it a once over, with a nonchalance Miranda knew was driving the cops nuts. She loved watching him twist the guts of people who took the easy way out of solving a crime.

He turned back to the cart and studied it a moment. Then he reached into the front pocket of his jacket and drew out a small thin rod. He clicked the end of it and a beam appeared.

Flashlight. How'd he get that through the airport? Miranda wondered.

"We've printed everything already," Wample said. That was obvious from the gray powder splotches everywhere. "Except the things that will be bagged and taken to the lab."

Parker bent down alongside the cart and lifted the black velvet to peer inside. Miranda joined him. Stainless steel, two wire shelves, wheels. Nothing on the shelves but more fingerprinting dust.

Parker rose again and ran his flashlight over some of the crates on the shelving units along the walls.

Wample danced fitfully from foot to foot. "Honestly, Mr. Parker. There's nothing more you can do here. What on earth do you expect to find?"

"Now I can't tell you that until I find it, can I?"

Miranda couldn't resist grinning at the inspector. The truth was, as an ace investigator, Parker had found a lot of things the police had missed. And she had uncovered a few items herself, for that matter.

"In my 'umble opinion, we should call it a day and go 'ome." The opinion came from the short, rotund Assistant Chief Officer Ives. It was the first words he'd spoken since they'd met, and he sounded like a Cockney frog. A very tired Cockney frog.

Miranda could empathize with him on that score. She'd hardly had any sleep and was battling a case of jet lag. But nothing energized her more than an unsolved case. Apparently, even if there wasn't a murder involved.

Parker ambled around a little more, then looked up at the ceiling. "No security camera here."

"We use motion sensors in the storeroom itself," Sir Neville explained.

"Hmm." He focused on a spot just over the cart. "Now that's interesting."

Miranda followed his gaze. A large ceiling vent was suspended right above the crate. Someone with the right knowhow could climb onto the roof, crawl through the duct work, loosen the vent and…what? Shimmy down a rope to get the goods?

"You say there are motion sensors when the system's on?" Parker asked.

"Yes, most assuredly." Sir Neville gestured, drawing lines in the air. "They crisscross every meter. It was quite an expense, but one we felt was necessary. Now it doesn't seem as if it was enough. Perhaps we should have installed more cameras."

Cameras or not, with all those laser beams ready to sound an alarm at the slightest touch, getting in here would have been pretty tricky to pull off. You'd have to be a professional.

Parker ran his beam along the lower portion of the shelves, then along the floor under the units. The light fell on empty flooring, and Miranda was about to agree with Ives when she saw a flash.

"There."

Parker stopped. "Where?"

"Right there." She pointed. He was at a different angle and hadn't seen it. She crouched down, got on her knees and peered under the two inches beneath the lowest shelf. "There's something down there."

"Indeed there is." Parker was right beside her. He switched his light to the other hand, pulled a handkerchief out of his pocket and reached underneath.

"You should let us handle the evidence, Mr. Parker." The inspector really sounded annoyed.

Ignoring him, Parker rose again with the treasure in his hand. He held it out for examination.

"What is it?" Ives wanted to know.

"Looks like a button," Miranda said. It was a round, silver bead, engraved with a cross and rose.

Sir Neville came over to study it. "Why, that's from the staff uniform. Someone must have lost it."

Wample reached out and took the handkerchief right out of Parker's hand. "We'll take that now. It'll go into evidence." Parker could have stopped him, of course, but he was going to turn it over anyway.

"Evidence?" Sir Neville said, his blue eyes round. "Just because someone lost a button? What are you going to do, Inspector? Arrest my entire staff?"

"Now, calm down, sir. It's been a long day. This is just routine. I'm sure it's nothing." Wample shot Parker a nasty glance. "All right, Mr. Parker, Ms. Steele. I'm calling a halt to your 'investigation' here. It's time for us to get back to the station."

"Excellent," Parker grinned. "We're finished here. And next we'd like to speak to your suspect, so that's just where we'll be heading."

CHAPTER SEVEN

Sir Neville offered his car for transportation, complete with chauffeur, and they all piled into the nicely upholstered backseat.

Parker eyed Miranda carefully as they took off. Since her injuries last fall, he'd vowed he would ensure his wife was well taken care of and here she was going on little sleep after a long flight. And she hadn't eaten.

"Would you prefer to go back to the hotel? You must be exhausted." He spoke softly, knowing it was a sensitive point she wouldn't want shared with strangers. But Sir Neville was staring out the window, lost in his own thoughts.

Slowly she turned her head to him. Her lip started to curl in her tigress snarl that amused, aroused, and irritated him all at the same time. Then she thought better of it and simply shook her head. She stared past the driver and through the windshield.

It wasn't as if he had expected her to say yes. "Aren't you hungry?"

Her head snapped back, her eyes flashing a "lay off, buster" warning.

"Never mind," he murmured and stared out his own window. Apparently he was still having trouble finding the delicate balance between business partner and husband, he thought with irritation. Perhaps he never would.

Gritting her teeth, Miranda focused on the sound of the second set of windshield wipers she'd watched today as they swept away the rain that had started up again. How could Parker even think of dropping her off at the hotel while he went on to question the first suspect? How could he cut her out like that?

She drew in a breath, fighting with her temper. Okay, he had a point. She was tired. And hungry. And irritable. But so was he, although he didn't show it. She could see the weariness in his eyes. Yet he was determined to help his friend. She respected that. Why couldn't he respect the same determination in her?

Well, he did. He'd told her often enough how much he thought of her talents, her dedication. He was just looking out for her the way he had ever since she'd met him. She guessed she should be glad she had a man who cared if she ate or not. Leon wouldn't have cared if she'd had to eat dog food off the floor.

Okay, maybe she was being a bitch. She reached over and squeezed Parker's hand. "Maybe we can find a vending machine or something at the station."

He turned and studied her, both surprise and suspicion in his expression. At last, all he said was, "Good idea."

They zigzagged through the traffic, went through a roundabout, then onto a street called Whitehall, until they reached a tall glass building with a revolving sign labeled New Scotland Yard.

The driver dropped them off at the front and they hurried through the glass doors into a labyrinth of halls and offices and reception desks.

Currier and Ives, or rather Wample and Ives, were nowhere to be found. They managed to find a vending machine, and Miranda wolfed down some peanut butter chocolate thing that was supposed to be a candy bar but tasted like bland mud.

Then they moved on to the next reception desk. And the next. And the next.

After turning up the charm full blast and jumping though more hoops than a circus tiger, Parker finally got them in to see George Eames.

A constable led them down a set of elevators, which they called "lifts," descending into the lower bowels of the building where you could almost feel the weight of the massive structure pressing down on you, about to cut off your air.

They were ushered into a dank little room and had to wait almost half an hour before the suspect was brought in.

Miranda instantly recognized the figure in the photo she'd seen in his rooms, though he had aged several decades.

George Eames was a large man. Taller than Sir Neville and huskier, older looking, too, with a belly that was round and somehow gave him a friendly but distinguished air. Miranda thought of the photo in his rooms. He might have been athletic once. Might have been a football player in his day. Or maybe rugby over here. But today, like Sir Neville, he looked broken and beaten and was still in the suit he must have put on yesterday. It was as rumpled as his worn face.

And yet he broke out in a smile as soon as he caught sight of his friend. "Neville. You came at last."

"Of course, I did."

The two men embraced each other in a hug that seemed to light up the dreary room with the warmth of their longtime friendship. And then Sir Neville introduced Miranda and Parker and there was more handshaking.

"How have they been treating you?" Sir Neville wanted to know as soon as everyone was settled around the tiny table and perched on rickety wooden chairs.

"As well as can be expected, I suppose, given they think I stole the dagger."

Miranda was silent, studying the man's pear-shaped face with its heavy jowls sagging with sorrow. The emotion seemed genuine, but maybe he was just sorry he got caught.

He closed his large eyes and shook his head. "I've never been so humiliated in my life."

"I know. This is dreadful, George. Simply dreadful," Sir Neville crooned.

"But how are you holding up, old friend? How's Davinia?"

Sir Neville patted his hand. "We're doing just that, George. Holding up. But it's you I'm concerned for."

Miranda popped out of her chair, its legs scratching against the concrete floor as she pushed it back. It was too crowded around the table, and she preferred standing when she interrogated people.

She decided to cut to the chase and save Parker the distress of starting the uncomfortable questions. "Mr. Eames, why do the police suspect you?"

He spread his large hands over the table, the corners of his wide mouth turning down. "Because I was the last one in the storeroom, m'um. I checked in the crate when it arrived. I set the alarms. Guess it's reasonable to think I could have done it. But why would I do such a thing? The museum is my life. And I'd never betray Neville."

"Of course, you wouldn't." Parker gave him a comforting smile, but Miranda knew he was faking it. He wasn't any surer this man was innocent than she was. "Can you remember anything unusual you saw, Mr. Eames?" Parker asked. "Anything suspicious?"

The collections manager's thick, curly brown brows furrowed as he tried to think back. After a moment, he shook his head. "No. As I said, I had a late dinner in my rooms. The lorry came around ten o'clock. I received the package, set all the alarms—"

"Wait." Parker held up a hand. "Did you check what was in the crate?"

Eames gave a Sir Neville an unsure look.

"Go on, George. Tell them."

The man nodded. "It's routine, you see. The crate has a metal brace on all four corners. They're easy to loosen with a hammer or a crowbar, and then reuse."

Miranda folded her arms and resisted the urge to tap her foot. "And so?"

"And so that's what I did. I opened the crate to ensure what was delivered."

"And what did you find?"

Eames swallowed and pulled at the neck of his shirt as if he wished he had a glass of water. "The dagger was there. It was encased in packing peanuts and bubble wrap. I saw it. I…touched it. With my own two hands." He stared down at the table and the cramped little space became as quiet as a tomb.

Parker broke the silence. "Did you open the bubble wrap?" It was a trick question. Designed to see if the suspect had to think before replying.

But Eames answered without hesitation. "Oh, no, sir. I meant I could see it through the bubble wrap. That's as far as I went."

Miranda strolled to the corner. Might as well ask the inevitable. "What happened then?"

"Then? Why, I put the packing peanuts I had removed back, replaced the braces on the crate, and set the alarms as I said. I double-checked them, as I do every night, then went out for a walk."

"A walk?" Miranda kept her expression bland to hide her suspicion.

"It's my habit." He closed his eyes wearily. "The inspector told me they have me on video leaving the building. Of course, they do. It's one of our own cameras."

"Where did you go?"

"Round to Princess Louise and back."

"It's a pub in the vicinity," Sir Neville explained.

"It's my exercise. My habit. There would be a video of me leaving the building about that time every night."

But maybe this night he'd gone to meet a black market fence for a stolen dagger. No wonder Wample was so sure he was right about this arrest.

"I was going to have a spot of pudding at Louise, but it was too crowded, and I was all aflutter about the big day on the morrow. So I went home, had a draught of brandy and went to bed. The next morning, I was as excited as a schoolboy. The press arrived, everything was ready. Neville arrived and we rolled in the cart with the crate to unveil the dagger. And…it was gone. I have no idea what happened. I feel as if this is all my fault, but I didn't take it. I followed protocol."

Parker leaned forward with a stern look in his eyes. "Mr. Eames. I need you to remember if there was anyone in the storeroom with you last night. Anyone who might have followed you in."

Eames blinked at Parker as if he was speaking Dutch. "No. Toby usually helps me receive, but he had a date and I told him it was all right, I'd take care of it myself. I wish I hadn't. At least I'd have a witness."

"Toby?"

"Toby Waverly," Sir Neville supplied. "He's an intern. He started at the museum two months ago."

Parker's brows furrowed. "You let an intern help receive priceless artifacts?"

"Not all of them are so valuable. There are usually other staff members there. Several. But it was a weeknight, and we had an early day the next morning. I sent everyone home."

"When the Marc Antony dagger was being delivered?"

With a groan Sir Neville put his palms against his temples. "This is all my fault. I should have been there. But the lorry service has always been impeccable. Our security system is first rate. We've never had a single incident before. I never thought—" His voice trailed off.

Parker reached over and patted him on the arm. "We have to all stay calm, Sir Neville. We have to think. Mr. Eames, I'm sorry, sir, but I don't have enough to get you released yet. Tonight I want you to concentrate very hard and try to remember who on your staff has been acting strangely within the past week or so. Who might have been in the storeroom when he or she wasn't supposed to be. Anything out of the ordinary you can recall."

Looking worried, Eames shifted in his chair, making the old wooden slabs creak. "I'm not sure what I can come up with, but I'll try."

"We'll get you counsel, of course." Sir Neville said.

"No need. I already have someone."

"Really?"

"Well, when the inspector started tossing accusations around, I thought I had better. I spoke to Trenton Jewell."

Sir Neville blinked several times as if confused. "Trenton? We haven't been close since Cambridge."

"I see him now and then. Actually, he called me."

Parker shot Miranda a look of concern. "How did he know you were in here?"

"Is the news of Mr. Eames's arrest in the media?" Miranda wanted to know. She hadn't heard it, but she'd only seen one newspaper.

Eames looked from Miranda to Parker to Sir Neville. "I—I don't know. Trenton hears things in his profession, I suppose. Anyway, he offered to defend me pro bono."

Sir Neville sat back, a look of shock on his gentle face. "That's wonderful, George. Very generous of him."

And strange, Miranda thought. But what did she know about old college friendships? She'd never made any real friends until last year. You don't form attachments in the school of hard knocks.

Parker rose and the other two men got to their feet, weariness in their movements. After everyone said good-bye, Parker called the officer to take Eames back to his holding cell, and the three of them shuffled back down the hall.

"We'll do as you said, Russell," Sir Neville murmured almost to himself. "We'll figure out who did this. All of us together."

They had better. Or Sir Neville would be looking for a new chief collections manager soon.

CHAPTER EIGHT

As they climbed back into the limo, fatigue began to hit Miranda hard. She leaned back her head, closed her eyes and listened to Parker and Sir Neville chatting.

"If it's not out of the way, your driver can drop us off at the hotel."

"Hotel? Oh, no, Russell."

"I think we need to get some rest at this point."

"Oh, of course you do. And neither of you has had a decent meal, either. What a bad host I am."

"You're not a host, Sir Neville. You're a client. You've had a very bad happenstance."

Happenstance? Miranda thought. Parker was sounding more British by the minute.

"Nonetheless, you are both my guests. And as such, I can't let you go to a hotel. You must stay at Eaton House."

Miranda's eyes popped open. "Eaton House?"

"Our estate in Surrey. Well, technically Davinia's estate."

Parker nodded. "Oh, yes. I recall now."

"It's just an hour's drive. I promise to make you comfortable."

"Are you sure it won't be any trouble?" Parker asked.

"Oh, no. There will only be Davinia, and Lionel and his wife."

Parker frowned. "Lionel is your son, correct?"

"My stepson. His father was the late Harry Halsing, Earl of Eaton. Lady Gabrielle, daughter of the Marquis of Camden, is Lionel's wife. They haven't been married very long."

Parker turned to Miranda. "What do you say?"

All she wanted was a nice meal and a cozy bed. But it might be smart to get to know Sir Neville's family, even with all their crazy names and lineage. One of them might have had access to the museum. Or they might have a better idea of who Sir Neville's enemies were.

She nodded. "I'm game."

Sir Neville smiled for the first time since she'd met him. "It's settled then."

They turned a corner and once again stopped at the hotel to check out and get their bags. Then Sir Neville told the driver to head home.

CHAPTER NINE

By the time they reached Surrey, the rain had stopped, and a magnificent sunset flooded the rolling hills on the horizon with dazzling color. A rainbow stretched over a hill and ran behind a clump of trees, adding to the splendor.

But even the gorgeous landscape's impact paled next to the grandeur of Eaton House.

A huge estate of weathered, ornate stone that must have been constructed centuries ago, it stood with its turrets and spindly, sharp spires pointing majestically to the sky, while its hundred or so windows looked snobbishly down their noses at the peons entering below.

If the Parker estate was too rich for Miranda's blood, this place was diabetic coma level. In fact, Parker's whole house would barely make a nice garage here.

The chauffeur opened the limo door, and Miranda stepped out into fresh air tinted with the scent of flowers and the sound of birdsong. "Nice digs," she murmured under her breath to Parker.

It made him smile.

But Sir Neville shook his head at her reaction. "It is rather ostentatious, isn't it? But Davinia loves it, so here we are."

The chauffeur hurried up the stone steps and opened the massive front door, and their host ushered them through a narrow, medieval-looking passage and into a grand hall at least three times as large as the Parker mansion foyer back home.

Its floor was covered with a huge red-and-gold carpet with a gaudy design, its walls were filled with even gaudier tapestries of men in tights under willow trees, and above and between the hangings were rows and rows of tall gothic arches and high windows that let in the receding sunlight.

"As magnificent as I recall it," Parker said.

"You've been here before?" Miranda asked.

Parker nodded. "When I was a boy."

"A very curious boy, too, as I recall," Sir Neville added.

While they stood there gawking, a female voice rang out from one of the halls "Neville, is that you?" She didn't sound very happy. A moment later a statuesque woman stepped through one of the arched doorways and stopped short. "There you are. Where on earth have you—? Oh."

She looked to be maybe in her mid-fifties, though she wore her age well. She had her dark hair caught up in a stylish chignon at the nape of her neck, and she wore a rosy dress that went well with her flawless complexion. The skirt was cut to accent her long legs. She might have been a dancer in her heyday.

Sir Neville stretched his arms to encompass everyone in the room. "Davinia dear, this is Wade Parker's boy, Wade Russell Parker and his wife Miranda Steele from Atlanta, Georgia. Russell, Miranda, this is my wife, Lady Davinia."

As if programmed for good manners, Davinia stepped stiffly forward, hand outstretched. "Good evening, Mr. Parker, Ms. Steele."

"Good to meet you," Miranda said, not sure that it would be.

"Wade Parker. Why yes, I remember your father. You're visiting from America?" She cast a doubtful glance at her husband. Obviously, she wanted to know why he'd dragged these two near strangers home.

"They're private investigators, Davinia. They've come to help find who took the Marc Antony dagger."

She blinked, her gaze going back and forth from her husband to her new houseguests, as if he had just spoken in Japanese. "But isn't Scotland Yard handling that?"

"Of course, but Russell has an outstanding reputation. Well, his whole agency does. He's solved cases that have stumped the authorities. I thought the museum deserved the best."

"Oh, yes. Such a dreadful business. I…heard about it on the news." She placed a hand on his arm. The first gesture of affection Miranda had seen between them. "I'm so very sorry, Neville. You must be devastated."

"Yes. Yes, I am. Shaken to the bone, in fact. But never mind me. Russell and Miranda are in want of a good meal and a quiet night's rest. I hope we can provide that for them."

Her eyes glowed as her mouth opened in dismay. "Have you forgotten the dinner party tonight?"

Now Sir Neville's mouth opened and shut again. For a moment, he looked as if he wanted to argue with Davinia. Instead, he shook his head. "Yes, I did forget what with…what happened at the museum. I suppose it's too late to cancel it, even though it could prove…discomforting."

Davinia turned a tad defensive. "Of course, it's too late. I didn't know what to do. I wasn't sure you would even be here, Neville. I thought it would look worse to cancel. This way you can show you're handling the incident with grace." She waved a hand at Miranda and Parker. "Why, you've even brought in your own investigators. I'm sure all will be set right in a matter of days."

Talk about living in a glass tower. This lady didn't know much about chasing down ruthless criminals, did she? And Miranda couldn't help catching a hint of resentment in her tone.

Apparently, Sir Neville hadn't even spoken to her since the theft. There was trouble brewing in River City and that was the last thing they needed. And to top it off they had to go to a dinner party? They should have stayed at the hotel.

Lady Davinia turned to them with a magnanimous smile. "Mr. Parker, Ms. Steele, would you be so good as to join our party for dinner?"

Parker cleared his throat and straightened his tie. "I'm afraid I haven't brought a tux, Sir Neville."

"It's to be small, rather informal," Lady Davinia answered for her husband. "Loungewear."

Miranda frowned. They were supposed to come in PJs?

"Suits and ties will do for the gentlemen. Cocktail dresses for the ladies."

Now it was Miranda's turn to feel awkward. "I don't have—"

"I packed one for you," Parker interrupted. "The blue one you wore to the Governor's mansion this spring."

Miranda glared at him. How could he know they'd need evening wear? Besides, she'd been hoping to go over the case with him tonight. Not hobnob with some highbrow Brits.

Satisfied Lady Davinia gave them a dismissive, thin-lipped smile and turned to go. "Very good, then. Dinner is at eight. I'll have Geoffrey show you to your rooms."

"Have him take up the bags," Sir Neville called to her. "I'll show them up."

She paused in the archway to turn back for a moment. "The corner chamber room will be comfortable, I should think."

Sir Neville nodded. "That should suit them well."

"Until tonight then." Lady Davinia nodded graciously at her new guests and left the room.

"Well, then. Shall we?" Sir Neville gestured the way, and they followed him through another arched doorway and into another huge hall.

This one was littered with statuary and antiques and had fancy columns around the walls that led to a high ceiling covered with paintings done centuries ago. But the artwork was dominated by an alabaster staircase leading to the stories above—a maze of parapets and more arches.

Sir Neville ushered them to the stairs. As they made their way upward, he pointed out the Chinese vase from the Ming dynasty, the statue of Minerva hugging a large candle holder, the portraits of this or that aristocratic ancestor hanging from the vast walls.

As they rounded a corner, Miranda nearly jumped at the life-sized knight on horseback guarding the landing.

"Saint George can be rather intimidating," Sir Neville chuckled. "I apologize if he startled you."

"Saint George and the dragon?" Miranda asked.

"The very one. I was fascinated by the treasures in this house when I was first invited here. It was one of the things that attracted me to Davinia. We used to discuss them for hours." His face grew taut.

Sounded like they didn't do much of that anymore.

They went down a long, winding hall under a series of cream-colored arches and finally arrived at a tall paneled door.

"Here we are," Sir Neville said, opening it. "I hope you'll be comfortable here."

Miranda stepped inside and saw a large room with a row of tall windows hung with heavy brocade curtains on either side of a huge, inviting bed. The thick spread was decorated in a busy purple-and-gold octagon pattern while stripes of fleur-de-lis in matching colors formed a dome over it on the ceiling.

The scent of flowers came from fresh cut lilies that sat in a vase on a table. In the opposite corner stood an antique oak table that looked like it came from France.

Their bags sat at the end of the bed. The mysterious Geoffrey had come and gone unnoticed.

Miranda had the sudden urge to leap over the bags, sink into the downy covers and fall asleep.

"You have a private bath. It's over here." Sir Neville crossed the carpet and opened a side door. "Towels, soap. Everything seems to be here. Do let me know if you need anything."

"We will," Parker told him.

Sir Neville crossed back to him and took his hands. "Thank you again for coming, Russell. I know you'll solve this case." He turned to Miranda. "Both of you."

"We'll do our best," she told him.

"I'll see you in a few hours." And with that he left them alone.

As soon as the door closed, Miranda kicked off her shoes, scampered over to the bed and sank down onto it.

Parker loosened his tie, studying her wearily. "Aren't you even going to take off your clothes?"

"Uh," she answered numbly.

He draped his tie over the back of a chair, pulled off his coat and laid it across the arm. Then he followed suit, removing his own shoes and taking his place on the opposite side of the bed. "Good idea."

"Uh huh," she said, her eyes closed.

"I know this place is out of the way, but I thought it might help the investigation to get to know those who are close to Neville."

"My thoughts exactly." She rolled over and threw an arm across his muscular chest. But all she had the strength for was to smile at the sensation.

Parker moved under her, going for his pocket. He pulled out his cell. "I'll set an alarm for an hour."

"Sure," she said, opening an eye to scowl at him and wishing they could sleep until morning. And that they could beg off going to that dinner.

But before she could even suggest it, her eyes fluttered closed again and she was fast asleep.

CHAPTER TEN

An hour later, Miranda's eyes popped wide open at the sound of the rooster crow ringtone she'd given Parker as a lark last Valentine's Day. That would teach her to play games.

Groggily, she reached across him, groping for the thing.

Parker grabbed her wrist and pulled her on top of him.

"Cock-a-doodle-doo!" the phone buzzed.

"Turn that thing off. It's making my jet lag worse."

He chuckled, found it on the nightstand and hit the button. Relief.

He brushed back her hair and fixed her with a lusty gaze in his gray eyes. "I've never made love in a castle before."

Raising a brow, Miranda affected a British accent. "Oh, haven't you now?"

Grinning with delight he pulled her to him and kissed her hard. He could really get horny when he was sleepy. He rolled her over and dipped his tongue into her mouth, making her groan with delight and temptation.

She closed her eyes and let him work his way across her cheek and down her neck before she stopped him. Before she lost the ability to speak. "We've got to quit. Party."

He stopped kissing her and rested his head against her shoulder. "What we sacrifice for others."

"So true." She couldn't resist reaching down and giving his butt a tweak before she rolled over. Of course, he was still in his dress pants so it wasn't as much fun as if he'd been naked. But he felt it.

"I will return that favor later," he said in a low, lusty voice.

"I was hoping you would," she laughed and headed for the suitcases. It took her a minute to realize they were empty. "Someone's either already unpacked for us or stolen all our clothes." She looked around the room. "Where's the closet?"

"Try the wardrobe." He gestured toward the corner at a beautifully carved piece of furniture with a mirror on the front of it.

She tiptoed over to it and gingerly opened the door. Their clothes were hanging neatly inside. "Cool," she grinned.

Parker got to his feet and stretched. She caught the sight of his delicious, well-formed body in the mirror and was starting to think twice about ditching that dinner party.

He had other ideas. "Do you want the bathroom first?" No cozy shower together for them. At least not yet.

With a sigh, she turned back to the wardrobe, digging for the dress he said he'd brought for her. "No, I want to try this on first."

"All right. I won't be long." He grabbed his shaving kit off the dresser and headed for the adjacent room.

It took a while to paw around in the roomy wooden container, but the smell of cedar and lavender from a sachet inside it was nice. At last, her fingers landed on something.

Here it was. She pulled out the hanger and held the dress up to herself. It was a satiny thing in ocean blue she remembered Parker had said brought out the color of her eyes. It had a twisty bodice and waist and a sheer neckline embedded with jewels.

Fancy, but she guessed she'd fit in wearing it tonight. More than if she sashayed in with her jeans and a T-shirt, which would have been her first choice.

While the sound of running water came from the bathroom, she pulled off her slacks and blouse, tossed them onto the foot of the bed and slipped the delicate outfit on.

After zipping it up, she turned to look at herself in the mirror.

Bummer. It looked okay, but she'd lost weight since she'd last worn it. Since her long hospital stay and rehabilitation.

What was she going to do? It was the only dress she had. She reached behind her and pulled the fabric together. Quickie alteration? Maybe Sir Neville had a tailor stashed away somewhere in this castle.

She spun on her heel and headed into the bathroom. She gave the door a quick knock. "Parker? I don't—"

The bathroom was round and lined in big gray stone blocks, like a mediaeval tower. Surrounded by stained glass windows, Parker was lying back in an old-fashioned tub, his arms and torso glistening, his dark hair plastered on his muscled chest.

She couldn't help grinning as her libido spiked. "Well, well, well. What have we here?"

He turned his head and eyed her with a mixture of annoyance and lust. "There doesn't seem to be a shower. Not unusual in a home of this age."

"Guess not." She sauntered over to the tub, pulled up a wicker hassock and sat down, hiding a snicker as she greedily took in his naked body under the water. She didn't know what he'd put in the water, but he sure smelled delicious.

He raised a dark, wary brow. "I thought we had agreed to attend the party."

Playfully she splashed her fingers in the water, just over a man's most cherished part, and made a little wave. Cleopatra wending her barge up the Nile in search of Marc Antony.

"Miranda," he warned.

She pursed her lips. "I'm rethinking blowing it off."

He took her hand in his wet one, turned it over and gently kissed her palm. "As much as you're tempting me, we can't leave Neville alone tonight. We promised we'd be there."

She sighed and leaned back. Yeah, they did. "You just can't say no to the old guy, can you?"

The lines around his eyes creased as he took on a faraway look. "I was thirteen when my father brought me to London to meet his friend Neville Ravensdale. He thought it would be a good, cultural experience for me."

"Mr. P took you to Eaton House?"

"Neville was living in London at the time. He was simply Mr. Ravensdale then. I believe Lady Davinia's first husband was still alive. But Neville was acquainted socially with both of them, and we came here for some outdoor party or some such."

"Oh, yeah. Sir Neville said Davinia was married to the Earl of…someplace."

"Eaton. As in Eaton House. Her son inherited the estate, but she has use of it for her lifetime, as I understand it. And she's Lady Davinia. Sir Neville isn't a peer."

"A what?"

"A peer. Peerage is the system of hereditary titles in the United Kingdom. Our host is addressed by 'Sir' because he's been knighted by the Queen. Lady Davinia is a daughter of a peer as well as the widow of one. She has her own title."

She waved her hands in the air and got to her feet. "Forget I asked."

The designations of English lords and ladies wasn't something she wanted to know about. Her world had always been mere survival. Getting through a tough day laying brick, and an even tougher night of bad dreams and longing for her daughter.

That made her think of Mackenzie and her request yesterday. Surely the girl had forgotten about that by now.

Parker wasn't finished. He reached for her hand. "Miranda, when my mother died, Neville came to Atlanta to be with me and my father for a time. We had some long talks. He was very comforting."

Parker had lost his mother at sixteen, and Miranda knew it had put a strain on his relationship with his father at the time. No wonder Sir Neville meant so much to him.

"Okay, I get it." She sat back down. "So what about this case, Parker? I hate to say it, but it looks to me like George Eames is in pretty hot water." She dangled her fingers in the bath to emphasize the point.

Parker drew in a frustrated breath, his brow creasing.

She dangled her hand in the bath water again and went on. "Eames admits he was the only one to see the dagger. He was the one who set the security system in the storeroom. There's no video to prove otherwise. All the evidence points to him."

"It does. But we both know it's circumstantial. It doesn't prove conclusively he did it."

That was true. But it was also true Parker didn't want Sir Neville's friend to be guilty. "So how do we disprove it? What's our next move?"

"What do you think?"

"I thought you were in charge here."

The corner of his mouth turned up. "I want to hear your thoughts."

Was he really picking her brain or just testing her? But maybe she should come at it from a different angle. "Eames had opportunity and means, but if you believe what he says about his loyalty, he doesn't seem to have motive. Other than money."

"A man who lives in a museum working with precious artifacts doesn't seem to be the type to steal for money."

She shrugged. "Maybe he's gotten tired of that. Maybe being around all those priceless things finally got to him."

"Is that what your gut tells you?"

Her shoulders sagged. "No." Her gut said the man was innocent, but she liked Sir Neville, too. Maybe they were both too biased for this case. She gave the water another splash. "And so, the only thing we can do is hunt around for someone who does have motive."

Parker's face turned determined. "And that's what we'll do at this party."

"It's a start, I guess." She eyed the water.

"All we have for now." Parker took her hand and lifted it out of the tub. "And we'd better get ready if we're going to make it on time."

With a sigh of longing, she got to her feet and dried her fingers on a nearby towel. "Oh, you made me forget why I came in here. This dress doesn't fit anymore."

"It doesn't?" He eyed her with concern.

"The waist is too loose. See?" She put her hands on either side of the garment and shifted it back and forth.

Parker scowled. "You haven't been eating enough."

She rolled her eyes. He had to get bossy, didn't he? "I could eat a horse tonight if I had something to wear to dinner."

He thought a moment. "Call down and see if Lady Davinia has a needle and thread."

She dropped her arms at her side. "And what will I do with that?"

"I'll sew the dress."

She let out a laugh. "You can sew?" Parker was handy, but he was used to having a staff to perform a lot of menial tasks for him.

He looked offended. "I've sewn my own wounds at times. It shouldn't be that much different."

"Okey-dokey." She had to see this. Suddenly feeling more awake, she turned and stepped back into the bedroom.

There was no phone in the chamber, so Miranda decided to go downstairs herself and find her hostess or maybe a servant.

She found her way through the maze of halls to the big stone staircase, recognizing the dude in armor on horseback and hurried down the steps. At the bottom, she wasn't sure which way to go, so she headed across the huge space and into the halls on the other side. After following a path this way and that, she was wishing she'd dropped breadcrumbs behind her when she spotted a door that was ajar.

It was imposing in the darkened hallway. Twice her own height and made of thick paneled oak. But light was streaming through the opening, so there had to be somebody in there.

Miranda put her hand on the elaborate brass knob and was about to push the door open all the way in when she heard a voice.

"What on earth were you thinking, Neville." It was Lady Davinia.

She heard Sir Neville mumble something back but couldn't make out the words.

"You couldn't pick up your mobile and call me?"

Miranda blinked in surprise. The woman's accusatory tone was biting. She was really mad.

There was a creaking sound and a slam. "I was rather preoccupied, Davinia. Didn't you hear what happened? The dagger—"

"Of course, I heard. It's all over the news. I would think you'd want to come home straight away after such an embarrassment."

"I'm sorry if I couldn't save face for you." There was another slamming sound.

Wow. She'd almost walked into a hornet's nest. Maybe she should go, but her investigator's nose kept her where she was. They were supposed to find out more about the people around Sir Neville, after all.

"What are you looking for?" Davinia snapped.

"Your grandfather's Cornish whiskey. I need a drink."

"We used it up at New Year's. All the guests had some and there was nothing left after midnight."

Sir Neville's weary sigh was audible.

"You haven't told me why you didn't come home." Now Lady Davinia's voice was a plea.

The sound of it made Miranda feel as sorry for the woman as she did for her husband. She must be lonely way out here in the country while her husband was getting accolades for his work in London. Though he sure didn't get any yesterday.

"What could I do?" Sir Neville said, irritation bubbling in his voice. "The police were at the museum all night. They've arrested George Eames."

"George? No." Her tone went from pleading to concerned.

"I'm glad at least you can see that he's innocent."

"Why wouldn't I? Of course, he is."

"Scotland Yard doesn't think so."

There was a long pause. Then Davinia spoke again. This time with tenderness. "How dreadful. What are you going to do, Neville?"

"I don't know. My only hope is that Wade Parker and Miranda Steele can help."

Uh oh.

The next few words were muffled then the door opened. Instinct had Miranda stepping behind one of the nearby pillars before she could be seen.

Davinia appeared in the doorway, dressed in the same rosy outfit she'd worn earlier, her face looking pale and shocked. Holding a lacy handkerchief at her mouth, she took off down the hall in the opposite direction. Miranda decided not to bother her.

She'd find her way back upstairs and use safety pins for her dress.

CHAPTER ELEVEN

They were late.

By the time Miranda got out of the tub, fluffed up her unruly hair that the weather had made even more of a mess, and managed to get her dress together with some pins, it was almost a quarter after.

Making the best of it, she waltzed down the stairs on Parker's arm, both of them all decked out in evening finery, her head high and Parker looking his debonair self.

They found the other guests had already arrived and were chitchatting away in the great hall, their British accents echoing to the tapestry and arches above. There were plenty of couches and chairs, but everyone was standing in the middle of the antique carpet, and they all turned to stare as Miranda and Parker stepped through the doorway.

For an instant, Miranda wondered how this party would go with the host and hostess at each other's throats half an hour ago, but Lady Davinia floated over to them with her game face on—or maybe it was her aristocrat face—to act the role of gracious hostess.

Taking Miranda's arm, she introduced them, tactfully presenting Parker as the son of Sir Neville's old friend and Miranda simply as his wife. So despite its being a top news story, the theft of the Marc Antony dagger would be off limits as a conversation topic.

"So much for our plans," she murmured to Parker under her breath, meaning the plan to find someone other than George Eames with a motive for taking the artifact.

"We'll have to use the circuitous route," he replied so low only she could hear him. She was better with the direct approach.

Miranda said her how-d'ye-dos to Lord and Lady Lovelace and their young daughter, Eunice. They lived in Hindhead, wherever that was, and were tall, thin and had matching receding chins. Next in line was Her Grace, the Duchess of Oxham who was dressed all in lavender and silver brocade, her dark gray hair piled atop her head and accented with a demure tiara, no doubt the woman's interpretation of "loungewear."

She curled her nose at Miranda as if she were a dead animal as she gingerly shook her hand. But the grand lady claimed she was delighted to meet her.

Last but not least was Lady Gabrielle Eaton, Davinia's daughter-in-law, a young woman maybe in her mid-twenties with big shimmering green baby-doll eyes and a laugh like sparkling champagne. She had a head of hair thick with short red-gold curls artfully styled to frame her sweetheart face and she wore a deep red, low-cut cocktail dress with lots of shiny bling around the neck.

She was married to Lady Davinia's son, Lionel, Lord Eaton, a nice-looking young man who seemed to be in his early thirties. He had dark coloring and a closely trimmed Van Dyke beard, which made him look exceptionally British with his navy blazer and slacks.

They were about to head for the dining room when the butler brought in a late arrival.

"I'm so sorry to be late," a deep voice bellowed.

Sir Neville spun toward the door and started. "Trenton! I—I had no idea you were coming tonight."

"Nor did I." Lady Davinia's polite tone hid her sudden distress.

An imposing figure stood beside the butler, towering a head over him, with a girth twice as large. Trenton? Trenton Jewell? Was that the third young man in the photo in George Eames's rooms? If he was, like Eames, he'd aged a good bit since then.

He was dressed all in black. His iron-colored hair was combed to the side of his large head and slicked down in an old-fashioned style. A foreboding crease, probably earned from endless hours of peering into law books, divided his brow in two. Along with his large, sharp nose it gave him the look of a hawk about to seize its prey.

Appropriate for an attorney.

With a frivolous laugh, Lady Gabrielle daintily scampered across the carpet and took the man's hand. "Hello, Trenton. So good of you to come." She turned back. "I invited him, Mother. Mr. Jewell is an old friend of the family." She gave him a wink as she let out another giggle. "He's gotten me off all those silly citations I got in the city. You know, after I had imbibed a little too much?"

Recovering from the surprise guest, Lady Davinia straightened her shoulders and crossed to Jewell, hand extended. "It seems like ages since you've been to Eaton House, Trenton."

"And so it has." Jewell shook the hand in a delicate gesture that made Miranda wonder what his past relationship with Davinia had been.

Davinia gave her daughter-in-law a scolding scowl whether for not consulting her or the comment about the drinking, Miranda couldn't tell. Then she turned to the butler. "Tell the cook we'll be eleven."

"Very good, m'um," he nodded and disappeared into the hall.

From her corner, the Duchess of Oxham nodded. "Good to see you, Trenton."

"And you, madam. The duchess is also a client of my firm," he explained to the room.

Sir Neville took his old friend's arm and led him toward one of the sofas. "Trenton, how good to see you. It's been ages."

"Hasn't it though, Neville. Or Sir Neville, I should say."

"Nonsense. Old friends shouldn't hold with formalities." As they passed by, Miranda heard him whisper, "Any progress?"

The crease in his forehead growing deeper, Jewell shook his head. "I'm afraid not yet."

After a few more minutes of meaningless social chatter, a servant came and whispered something in Lady Davinia's ear. She put on a broad smile. "Everyone, it seems we're ready now. Shall we go in?"

They formed a sort of processional, with Jewell escorting the duchess at the lead and Lady Davinia and Sir Neville taking up the rear, they marched down a winding hall and into the dining room, as if putting on their own little parade.

After navigating through another maze of arches, Miranda and the group stepped into a rectangular shaped room with a long oak table in the middle with high-backed, elaborately carved chairs. It was set with fine china and glassware and dotted with long candles in silver holders and crystal vases of fragrant blue flowers. Three small chandeliers hung from the ceiling, which was lower than the halls but still way up there.

Needed to be, Miranda thought, to make room for the huge paintings along the walls. Images of ladies in fancy silk and lace gowns and bearded gentlemen in brocade on horseback in darkened backgrounds. People who must have lived centuries ago, some of them perhaps Eaton ancestors.

They sat at the places marked for them in a boy-girl-boy-girl pattern with Lady Davinia at one end and Sir Neville at the other. Miranda found herself near Davinia's end sandwiched between Lord Eaton and Lord Lovelace. Parker wound up near the other end.

She didn't care for that. Not that she couldn't hold her own with the upper crust. She'd had plenty of practice doing that since she'd met Parker. But he was always so much more at ease in ritzy social situations.

But when a door opened and delicious aromas of fancy food began to fill the room, she forgot all about her uneasiness. She remembered all she'd had all day was that awful imitation of a candy bar at the police station and started to salivate like a mad dog.

Servants placed steaming bowls of something green in front of the guests. Miranda eyed hers carefully when it came. It had leafy things floating in it and looked a little gross, but it smelled wonderful.

After figuring out which spoon to use, she dipped it into the thick liquid and ventured a taste. Pea soup? Zucchini? With a light kick of spice. Yum. She didn't care what it was. She was tempted to pick up the bowl and slurp the whole serving down in one gulp.

But since she might want some answers from these people, it was best not to offend them. She glanced over at Parker and caught him watching her with a look of amusement as if he were reading her mind.

She knew he was glad she was eating. He cared about things like that. And maybe if she kept her ears peeled, she'd learn something that would help with their investigation.

While the two Lords on either side of her chatted away about the real estate business Lord Eaton seemed to own, Miranda attacked the soup and finished the whole thing just before the next dish was served.

It was salmon. Flaky and delicate in a creamy, rich-tasting lemon sauce dotted with capers. Miranda dove in. She was halfway through it when Lionel turned to her as if he'd just noticed her. "So sorry, Ms. Steele. We do go on about our business."

She paused, fork nearly to her mouth and blinked at him, surprised he was addressing her. "Oh, no. That's fine. I don't mind."

His brown eyes twinkled. "Lovelace and I are on the board of a real estate firm," he explained. "We do luxury properties. You wouldn't be in the market for a small estate in the country, would you?"

She decided to play dumb and innocent. "Oh, you'd have to talk to my husband about that."

He chuckled. "I'll take that as an invitation."

On the other side of her, Lord Lovelace uttered a very British laugh. "Eaton, you're such as salesman. Can't you give it a rest?"

"You never know who your next customer is going to be, now do you?"

Lovelace shook his head. "I apologize for him, Ms. Steele. And for our weather, too. I know it's frightful to most Americans." How smoothly he switched to a neutral topic.

"It's not so bad." She smiled before scooping up the last bite of salmon and putting it in her mouth.

Lionel reached for his wineglass as the next dish was served. Some sort of poultry leg in a thick brown sauce. "It's rabbit," he whispered when he saw her staring at it.

Miranda picked up her knife and fork and grinned as if she ate it every night. "My favorite." She took a bite and tasted garlic, red wine and shallots over lean, fresh meat. Delicious.

Lionel studied her for a long moment as he set his glass down and picked up his own fork. "It must be sunny in—where is it you're from? Atlanta?"

"Yes. It's starting to get hot this time of year." Unlike this conversation. She really wanted to ask him what he knew about his stepdad's dagger. "Sun, sun, sun," she laughed.

He leaned in closer, his Van Dyke beard nearly touching her shoulder. "I know it's a forbidden topic, but my mother isn't listening right now."

Lady Davinia was engrossed in a conversation with Trenton Jewell, the lawyer, her face tight and drawn.

"I understand you're a private investigator?"

Miranda swallowed the bite in her mouth and reached for her wineglass. "Yes, that's right." Sir Neville must have told him.

"How intriguing." His gaze roamed over her face then descended to her cleavage. "It must be very exciting work."

Miranda swallowed a sip of wine and laughed as she set down the glass. "Sometimes. Hours of boredom interrupted by moments of sheer panic." Something Parker had said to her once.

"Nonetheless, interesting enough to draw the attention of an attractive woman such as yourself." His gaze remained between her breasts. Was he coming on to her?

Her instinct was to belt him. Not only because she didn't take that kind of shit, not even from an English duke or whatever he was, but because he dared to do it at a table with both of their spouses present. This guy was a cad.

But causing a scene wouldn't get information out of him, so she shifted her weight, picked up her wineglass again and took a slow sip as she studied him right back until he moved his gaze. "If the case is interesting, like this one."

His narrow brows rose. "Indeed?"

"A priceless artifact stolen from right under the museum director's nose? I wonder if you have any theories."

Lionel's gaze narrowed as it moved to the far end of the table where Sir Neville sat, head down, silently picking at his food. The poor man looked miserable. "Theories?"

"Ideas about who must have done it?"

"None, I'm afraid. But isn't it your job to come up with theories?"

"Guess so." She took a sip from her glass and swirled the wine around in her mouth before swallowing it. "You don't know the staff at the museum very well, then."

"Not really."

"But surely you must visit the place. You probably have your own private key."

His eyes narrowed sharply. He knew exactly what she was implying. "No, I don't. I'm not really interested in the place. It must be years since I've been there."

Well, this was going nowhere.

Lady Davinia must have caught a few words. She turned her head and gave her son a passing scowl, then addressed the older woman to her right.

"Duchess, have you heard about the Countess of Shefordshire's daughter?"

The woman nodded graciously. "I have. She's getting married."

"She must be so excited. I remember how thrilled I was when Lionel and Gabrielle were planning their wedding." Davinia's smile seemed forced.

Lionel decided to join the discussion. Probably to avoid any more of Miranda's questions. "Oh, Mother. How can you say that? You and Gabby argued for days about the bridesmaids' dresses, and I was caught in the middle of it."

Lady Davinia laid her hand against her breast as if horrified. "She was insisting on a bold red silk."

From the far end of the table Lady Gabrielle's girlish laugh rang out. "I'm just a free spirit, Mother. But the dusty rose we compromised on was quite beautiful. I'm lucky to have a mother-in-law with such good taste."

Lionel raised his glass to his youthful wife. "And I'm lucky to have gone down the aisle with the Marquis of Camden's daughter." He took a sip and gave a casual laugh. "I married up, as everyone knows."

Guess that meant Gabrielle outranked him in the aristocrat hierarchy.

"Then they don't need to be reminded, do they, my love?" Gabrielle smiled back at him, but there was a bite to her grin.

Miranda didn't know if it was her imagination, but it seemed like there was a whole lot of subtext going on here. Secrets hidden under the smiles and laughter. Things that were not very polite at all.

"They've already decided on a December wedding," the duchess continued as if she hadn't heard Gabrielle or Lionel at all. "In the evening. Candles and ermine and all."

"Sounds lovely," Davinia said. "Speaking of weddings, I'm so sorry we couldn't attend yours and Wade's, Miranda."

Miranda swallowed the bite of roast lamb in her mouth, the course that had been delivered a few minutes ago, and thought of the way her gown had looked when she'd hobbled down the aisle in a nearly empty church.

Wouldn't have gone over big with this group. "I'm sure it wasn't as grand as your son's."

The hostess smiled and nodded and went on with other local gossip.

As Miranda concentrated on her food, she caught the twinkle in Parker's eye and felt a swell of triumph. She was getting pretty good at not sticking her foot in her mouth at uppity social get-togethers.

Too bad she wasn't getting much information on the stolen dagger.

A few more courses were served, and the conversation turned to more talk about people she didn't know. Jewell went on for a while about his boyhood in a town she'd never heard of and how he'd taken up law to follow in his father's footsteps, although the profession was far from his first choice.

By the time the meringue with strawberry sauce was served and the meal ended, Miranda didn't know whether she was more bored or frustrated. But at least she was as stuffed as the roast lamb.

As she rose Lionel held her chair. His demeanor seemed to have switched from flirtatious playboy to a serious businessman.

He leaned close to her shoulder and whispered. "I won't pry into your investigation, Ms. Steele, but I do hope you'll wrap this case up soon. It's such an embarrassment to the family." He glanced down at the far end of the table and watched Sir Neville get to his feet.

Lionel's eyes glinted with fury. And if she wasn't mistaken, Miranda could almost feel the hatred for his stepfather radiating from him.

CHAPTER TWELVE

The party relocated back to the great hall for after-dinner digestifs, but after several more long moments of fruitless chitchat, Parker strode over to their hostess.

"I'm so sorry to be a wet blanket, Lady Davinia, but my wife and I have had a very long day. I'm afraid we'll have to say goodnight."

Miranda wanted to jump into his arms and plant a big sloppy kiss on his mouth right in front of everyone. Instead, she nodded. "He's right. It's been lovely, though."

"Perfectly understandable," their gracious hostess replied.

Before they could say good night to Sir Neville, Gabrielle's voice rang out. "But you are coming to the match tomorrow, aren't you?"

"Match?" Miranda regretted the question as soon as it was out of her mouth.

"The Ashton Downs Polo Match."

"Lionel will be riding in it," Lord Lovelace offered. "And the weather's supposed to be smashing."

The young woman scampered over to Miranda and took her by the arm. "It's for charity. You simply must come. Both you and Mr. Parker. You will, won't you?" Her pleading bottle-green eyes gleamed like gems and her red-gold curls shimmered around her pretty face as she gave a little childlike pout.

But from the odd twist at the corner of her lips and the vice grip on Miranda's arm, she guessed the child could turn into a hellcat pretty fast if she didn't get her way.

And why was it so important to her that they be at some sporting event? Maybe she longed for female companionship. Maybe she wanted to flirt with Parker.

Miranda usually didn't like Parker to rescue her, but she was glad when he reached for the woman's wrist and eased it off his wife.

"We'll have to see in the morning, Lady Gabrielle."

They said their goodnights and left quickly.

As they made their way up the grand staircase in the neighboring hall, Miranda whispered to Parker. "The only thing we got tonight was good food."

He gave his head a slight shake. "Along with the meal we were treated to a good serving of tension and resentment."

So he'd sensed it, too.

Upstairs, she'd wanted to discuss the case. Maybe over a lovemaking session but as soon as they pulled off their clothes and climbed into bed, Miranda's eyelids shut of their own volition. After going twenty-four hours with jet lag and a few hours sleep, she was finally losing it.

She snuggled against Parker's shoulder. "I think Lionel Eaton hates Sir Neville."

"I got the same impression," he murmured in a weary voice. So they were on the same page.

"Could be a motive for taking the dagger. You know, to destroy him?"

"Could be." Parker slipped a strong arm around her and pulled her close. She felt his breath in her hair.

But why would Lionel do something he found so embarrassing to the family? Or was that just an act to throw off the American detectives? She didn't know and her thoughts were blurring together.

She wanted to say more, but before she could, she fell fast asleep in Parker's embrace.

Lionel pulled off his tie and sank into a chair, too furious to even undress.

He'd drunk too much sherry after Neville went off somewhere with Trenton Jewell and the detectives went to bed. He'd been left with the ladies, listening to female prattle about shopping or some such nonsense and thought he needed it to settle his nerves.

The drink hadn't calmed him a whit.

He got to his feet, stomped across the bedroom floor and slung the tie over the wooden valet. All he could think of was that damned dagger. "This incident is going to bring even more reproach on this family than when Mother first took up with that museum curator," he grunted under his breath.

"Lionel, you're boring me." He spun around and glared at Gabrielle who was stretched out on her stomach on the big bed, examining her nails.

"How could Mother think of marrying someone who wasn't one of us? He doesn't understand our ways. He never will."

Gabrielle shook her head without looking at him. "You're only repeating all the same things you've said over and over for years."

"It bears repeating over and over until he's gone from our lives. How long will it take before Mother grows tired of him?" He pulled off his coat, slipped it over the wooden form, then did the same with his trousers. He grabbed his pajamas and headed into the bathroom.

When he'd finished, he returned and found his wife nestled under the covers, a sly look on her pretty face. She crooked a finger at him.

God, no. She didn't want sex. "Not now, Gabby. I have a match tomorrow."

She pouted as he crossed to the bed and got in, ready to turn out the light.

Before he could, she pulled him close and kissed him on the cheek. "Not to worry."

He scowled at her.

She was lovely with the glow of the lamplight giving her golden red hair an ethereal look. And her round breasts were always tempting. He'd married her for her position first, but her looks and her bosom had been tied at second. Still, he had little in common with her in the way of interests. Often he found her conversation nauseating. He'd had to find that sort of companionship elsewhere, and it was usually accompanied with enough sex to satisfy his physical needs.

"What are you talking about?"

She cocked her head and gave him that schoolgirl smile that had first drawn him to her. "I'm just saying you might get your wish soon."

She was confusing him. "How do you know that?"

"Neville and your mother have been arguing since he got home from the museum."

"They've argued before."

"Not like this. You don't understand." She lowered her voice to a whisper. "The theft of the Marc Antony dagger has completely devastated Neville. You know how he is. He'll fret and obsess over it until it's found. And it probably won't be found. Your mother will grow so tired of his ruminations, she's sure to leave him."

Her words made him turn over and lift a brow. "You've thought a good deal about this matter, haven't you?" More than she usually thought about anything but parties and clothes.

"Well, it's what you want, isn't it?"

Her words startled him. He was so used to Neville being about and complaining about his being part of the family, it was strange to think of him gone. And what would that do to his mother?

He'd had enough of this conversation. Gabby was being silly. He was riding tomorrow. He needed sleep.

He turned over and shut off the light.

Gabby's voice was like a sadly tolling church bell in the dark. "You didn't answer me, Lionel."

He lay his head on the pillow and heaved a sigh. "Yes, of course it's what I want. But I don't expect to get it."

She bent over him and pecked him on the cheek once more. "Oh, you might be surprised."

Then she turned over and pulled the covers up, thank God. But as he drifted off to sleep, he couldn't help wondering…could she be right?

CHAPTER THIRTEEN

Too agitated to sleep, he paced back and forth in the cold, narrow room, the dank air seeping into his bones.

No one understood. No one knew what this shell of an existence was like for him. Year after year of agonizing disappointment. The memory of loss compounding year after year. Watching your rival achieve anything he wanted with hardly any effort at all. While you labor away striving, working, hoping...only to lose to him again.

And then the one thing comes along. The culmination of all your desires. The single person who could turn it all around and make your life worth living once again. And he snatches that away as well.

Damn him.

He thought of the coin.

The small silver disk stamped with Julius Caesar's image. A genuine Roman denarius. How he'd coveted it. But Professor Kent had given it to his prize student instead of him.

And so he watched him after that, a rotting seething burrowing deeper in his bowels year after year, as Neville Ravensdale achieved more and more and more.

And now there was the Marc Antony dagger.

It had reminded him of the coin when he first learned of its discovery. Rare and ancient and beautiful. And in that moment, he'd vowed to have it. Or rather that Neville would not have it. And he didn't have it.

But now?

He sank down on the bed and raked his fingers through his hair. He'd known the risks of this scheme, but he hadn't let them stop him. Perhaps he should have thought things through more. He'd gotten in over his head. He might have to pay too dearly for what he'd done. He might be paying for a long while.

Had it been worth it? Guilt scratched at the edges of his heart. He scoffed at the sensation. Of course, it was worth it. Just the look on Neville's face when he opened that box in front of all those cameras was worth it.

How the great Sir Neville had fallen. Humiliated and disgraced before all.

No, everything would work out. He'd figure out what had gone wrong. He'd fix it. He'd fix everything.

Just now all he had to do was bide his time and keep quiet. Two things he was very good at.

As he lay back on the narrow mattress a thin smile spread across his face. Yes, everything could be fixed. And after a time, all would be well.

CHAPTER FOURTEEN

Miranda awoke to faint birdsong and shafts of light streaming in on either side of her through the narrow arched windows surrounding her bed.

No rain. Too good to be true.

She pulled Parker close and gave him a big healthy kiss on the mouth. "I feel a lot better now," she grinned as she came up for air.

"And so do I." He kissed her back, hard and feral, turned her over and nestled between her legs.

"Hmm." Yielding to that wonderful mushy feeling, she arched her back to meet him and relished the delicious sensation of his warm skin against her body.

His lips left her mouth and were just making their way down her neck, headed for nether regions when there was a sharp rap on the door.

"Sir? Madam? Breakfast in ten minutes," a servant informed them.

"Damn." Parker's head sank against her shoulder.

Not even time for a quickie. "Rain check," she said, hoping the words wouldn't jinx the good weather.

Dutifully he rolled over and got to his feet.

She pulled herself to the side of the bed and eyed his bare butt as she ran her fingers through her tangled hair. "So what's the plan for the day? Are we going to this polo pony shindig?"

His brow creased, his whole beautiful body in perfect investigator work mode, even though he was still stark naked. "If we do, we might be able to pick up some more information about the stepson."

"Maybe. But he's riding in the match. We might not pick up anything."

"What do you suggest?"

She raised her palms. "Go back to the museum and dig around some more? Talk to some of the staff?"

He considered that a long moment then drew in a breath. She knew he was as frustrated as she was with this case. "Let's see what Neville has in mind."

Breakfast was something of a repeat of last night's dinner, except with bacon, sausage, eggs done several different ways, and strong tea. And everyone was dressed more casually.

Miranda was surprised to learn that all the guests except Trenton Jewell had spent the night. She assumed the attorney wanted to be at Scotland Yard early this morning to get George Eames released.

"I'm afraid I'll have to beg off the match today," Sir Neville announced. "The museum's reopening and I need to be there."

Lady Davinia set down her cup with a sour expression. "Oh, Neville. Can't you ask someone else to do that? It's Lionel's big day."

Lionel had already left for the grounds so there was no chance to watch him close up in the light of day. At least not right now.

"He often plays polo," Sir Neville said. "I can catch him another time."

Davinia glared at him. She looked tired and worn out as if she hadn't slept much. "It's the summer tournament."

Sir Neville studied the muffin on his plate, looking very uncomfortable.

Miranda's heart went out to him. She wouldn't say he was henpecked—a term she despised—it was more like Davinia was his jailor, constantly reminding him of the prison of his social obligations.

The Duchess of Oxham took a tiny sip from her teacup and daintily set it back in its decorative saucer. "I understand today will be a match not to be missed. They're playing New Zealand."

Davinia's look turned to pleading. She was obviously using her social calendar to avoid dealing with her husband's too public problem.

Sir Neville sighed. "Very well." He tossed his napkin and rose, giving Parker and Miranda an apologetic look. "I'll give Emily a ring." But before he left the room, he leaned over Parker's shoulder and whispered. "We'll break away at the first opportunity and head for the museum."

Trying to look as if she hadn't heard anything, Miranda stared down into the bottom of her cup. She didn't need tea leaves to tell her with the undercurrent of stress, the polo match was bound to be loads of fun.

CHAPTER FIFTEEN

The attire for the match was "smart casual," which in this case meant summer dresses and flat shoes for the ladies and seersucker or blazers with no ties for the men.

The women seemed to think hats were required, and since Miranda didn't have one, Gabrielle loaned her one. A big, floppy brimmed thing with a deep red ribbon to match her red-and-white dress—another item Parker had snuck into her baggage.

"Now you'll look very smart," Gabrielle giggled, as she fixed the hat atop Miranda's head.

And just as inconspicuous as any self-respecting investigator would want to be. Whoopie.

It was late morning when they arrived at the polo ground a few kilometers north of London.

Nestled among a deep green forest of trees that might have been there since King Arthur's day, a huge playing field was sectioned off with narrow boards. Outside the perimeter cars were parked here and there, and people were setting up lawn chairs and blankets. There was a large scoreboard and two goal posts, as you might expect.

On the opposite side, a wide, white building with a green roof dominated the sidelines. Colorful tents were pitched on either side of it. Spectators were gathering under them as well, their cheerful chatter filling the air.

Davinia's party, of course, had reservations under the porch roof of the clubhouse, and they all sat at a large round table, a light breeze cooling their skin, sipping drinks and munching from a fruit basket the hostess had brought along.

Almost as soon as they'd sat down, Sir Neville excused himself, saying he needed a long walk. Poor man. Miranda related to his need to get away and be alone with his thoughts.

She toyed with the peppermint concoction she'd ordered and wished she could escape herself. With a sigh she gazed across the big field with its emerald grass so green it must have come from Ireland. Horses with short manes and wrapped-up tails were being walked around the sidelines at the far end to warm them up.

Beside her, Lady Gabrielle chatted away with all her animated zest. She had on a sleeveless safari print wrap-around with a cute little hat that matched the dress and made the color of her eyes a more exotic green.

Wondering if she had her own dress designer, Miranda watched her dip a strawberry into her daiquiri and take a dainty nibble. "The object of the game is to hit the ball with the mallet until you get it through the goal posts," she explained to Miranda, gesturing to either side of the field. "Each team has four players, numbered one through four. Lionel plays number three because he's the best on his team."

Not at all as airheaded as she'd been last night, Miranda thought. "You seem to know a lot about it."

She smiled almost shyly. "My father used to take me to the matches when I was little. It's where I met Lionel."

"So he's played a long time?"

Her green eyes danced with enthusiasm. "Oh, he loves the game. He says it's the most exhilarating thing in the world. Well, other than sex."

Davinia scowled at her daughter-in-law. "Gabrielle. Really."

Gabrielle only giggled. "Oh, Mother. What a prude you are."

Davinia looked away and suddenly seemed uncharacteristically rattled. She quickly recovered. "I need a walk," she said. "Please excuse me."

She rose, as graceful as a ballet dancer. Under a discreet chiffon hat with a narrow brim, her dark hair had been fashioned into an elaborate knot at the nape of her neck, and she wore a pale blue print dress in a breezy fabric that complimented the refined lines of her body.

She murmured an apology to her guests and strolled off, head high.

The woman was in a lot of pain. The air was thick with it even after she left. Maybe she'd find Sir Neville and they'd make up. Miranda hoped so.

Music began to play over the loudspeaker, and everyone rose to a rousing chorus of *Rule Britannia!* Then an announcer introduced the players, and the eight riders belonging to each team and two officials gathered in the middle of the field.

Several pairs of binoculars had been placed on the table. Miranda snatched one up to watch.

An official threw in the ball, and they were off. Well, for a while they just batted the thing around among themselves. Someone broke loose. Then they were off. The ball came rolling out of the huddle, every horse and rider after it.

Back and forth the players went, turning the ponies this way and that, mallets whipping through the air, hooves pounding.

And so was Miranda's heartbeat. She leaned forward, every muscle taut as she inhaled the game.

"I've got to do that," she murmured across the table to Parker. Apparently too loudly.

Gabrielle gave her a nudge. "You like risk, Ms. Steele?"

Miranda lowered her binoculars and turned to the young woman. "What do you mean?"

Gabrielle grinned, her eyes sparkling, as if she knew all there was to know, not only about the game, but about her guest as well. "Polo is supposed to be one of the most dangerous sports in the world."

"Really?"

"But I gather you have a taste for danger, being a private investigator and all."

So someone had told her who she and Parker really were. Probably Lionel. But might as well find out. Miranda blinked at her as if startled. "Who said I was a private investigator?"

"Davinia, of course." She rolled her eyes. "And she says we're not to discuss it. But I think it's exciting. Are you working on a case?" Her babydoll eyes were round with innocence.

If Davinia told her she and Parker were investigators, she told her why they were here. Not that it would be hard to guess. So why was she playing dumb?

Miranda gave the young woman a big smile. "Can't a PI go on vacation?"

Gabrielle didn't miss a beat as she sucked in an excited breath. "And you chose London? How honored we are."

Sure, you are. And I'm the Queen of England. "Thanks," Miranda said and turned back to the game.

A horn blew and everyone stopped.

"That's the end of the first chukker," Gabrielle said.

"Chukker?"

"Divisions of the game. There are six in all. And the riders have to change ponies so as not to wear them out." Tapping the table, she glanced around nervously, then gave a little laugh. "Oh, there's Mr. Jewell. I must go say hello." She got to her feet and scampered off.

Jewell was here? Miranda wondered if he'd made short work of getting the police to let George Eames go. Maybe he was looking for Sir Neville to tell him so.

Miranda caught Parker's gaze across the table. His steady look told her he was thinking the same thing she was. There was something weird going on here. She was determined to find out what it was.

The next chukker started. Gabrielle wasn't back yet. Neither was Davinia.

Instead of watching the match this time, Miranda used her binoculars to scan the crowd. Along the far side of the field, groups of spectators were laughing and eating. Near a family seated on the grass, a little boy danced happily, holding up an ice cream bar.

A little farther on, several well-dressed young men and women leaned against the hood of a car chatting to each other. She spotted Gabrielle talking to them. Friends of Lionel's? Hard to say.

In front of the group a white picket fence ran the length of the next section where some of the ponies were being walked. She watched them for a while trying to spot the stepson, then moved to the stretch along the goalpost.

Bingo.

There was Davinia. And she was with someone.

Miranda adjusted her binoculars for a close up. A look of worry on her elegant face, Davinia seemed to be having a heartfelt conversation with the very good-looking young man beside her. Couldn't have been much older than Lionel. Sharply dressed in a lightweight casual suit, his wavy blond hair blowing in the breeze, he exuded youthful confidence.

Except for the crease between his brows.

Miranda cleared her throat. "Duchess."

"Yes, my dear."

"Do you know who that is with Lady Davinia?" she pointed in the general direction.

The elderly woman raised a gloved hand to the brim of her hat and squinted hard for a long moment. "Oh," she said at last. "That's Sebastian Fairfax. He's a good friend of Lionel's. They went to school together. He owns an advertising firm in the city. Very nice chap. Used to ride before he got hurt last year."

"Oh, that's too bad."

Maybe Davinia was concerned over his injury. Or something else.

She moved her binoculars to the right, following the line of the picket fence in the opposite direction. Past more picnickers and vehicles, another tent, into the woods. Then she saw him. He might have just finished his stroll under the trees.

Sir Neville leaned against the fence, his hand to his chest as if he were having a heart attack. His pale face was ghost white.

And he was staring straight at the young man and Davinia.

CHAPTER SIXTEEN

Miranda slapped the binoculars down on the table and spun around to Parker.

He'd been following her gaze and was already on his feet, making excuses and hurrying away to help. She did the same and they hurried through the crowd.

The third chukker began and with all the commotion, it seemed to take forever until they reached the fence where he stood.

Parker put a hand on the elderly gentleman's arm to steady him. "Are you all right, Neville?"

"What's that?" His crystal blue eyes looking dazed, he blinked at Parker as if coming out of a dream. "Oh, I—" He cleared his throat and straightened himself, pulling out of Parker's grasp. "I'm fine, Russell." He lifted his chin, clearly trying to hide his embarrassment under the famous British stiff upper lip. "A spot of indigestion, I believe. Too much rich food last night. Really, I'm perfectly fine."

"Are you sure?" She was worried he wasn't.

"Of course, I'm sure. I—I was just lost in thought. I was remembering this." He held out an open hand.

There in the center of his palm was a tarnished coin. Its edges irregular and worn with the passage of centuries, it bore a profile of a man with curly locks and a wreath around his head.

"It's a genuine Roman denarius from 44 BC. It bears the image of Julius Caesar himself. A favorite professor of mine at Cambridge gave it to me on a walk one day. I've been thinking about that afternoon." Sir Neville's eyes grew moist. "I didn't feel worthy, but he said I had a promising career ahead of me. Now look what it's come to. What I've come to." He shoved the coin into his pocket.

"Let's get him out of the sun," Parker said, taking one of Sir Neville's arms.

Miranda nodded and took the other arm.

"I'm fine, really," he protested. "At worst it was an anxiety attack. It's passed now."

"Let's just go over here, Sir Neville." She gestured toward one of the tents.

"Really, my dear, you're very kind but this isn't necessary."

She forced out a casual laugh. "If you don't need some shade, Sir Neville, I do."

There were also kind people under the tent who gave up a lawn chair so Sir Neville could sit down. Miranda watched their faces trying to guess if they recognized the museum curator who'd been in the news, but they seemed too preoccupied with the game and their own affairs.

They helped Sir Neville down, though he was still putting up a fuss.

"As soon as you rest a bit, we'll take off for the museum," Parker reassured him.

While they waited Miranda stared out at the ponies and riders battling around the field, though she'd lost interest in the game. It seemed Lionel's team was ahead by a few points.

At last, the horn blew to signify the chukker's end. She turned and studied Sir Neville's face. His eyes seemed clear now, but he still looked pretty pale.

"Maybe he should go home," she said to Parker.

Sir Neville reached up to take her hand and patted it. "No, no, my dear. I need to get to the museum. I can't leave Emily—"

"There you all are!"

Everyone turned in time to see Gabrielle scurrying over, the flare of her safari print skirt swishing around her shapely legs. "Where on earth have you been? It's time for the divot stomping."

"The what?" Miranda asked.

"Divot stomping, of course." Gabrielle stared at her as if she were crazy. "Come on, then. Everyone's out there already."

From his chair Sir Neville waved a hand. "You go on, Gabby. I'm too old for divots."

"Oh, Neville." She stuck out her lower lip, her babydoll eyes glistening.

"We need to keep an eye on Sir Neville just now, Lady Gabrielle," Parker told her in a firm tone.

She wasn't about to take no for an answer. "Well, Ms. Steele, then." She grabbed Miranda's hand. "We'll only be a few minutes. I'll bring her right back when we're finished." She gave her a yank that nearly pulled her off her feet.

Miranda heard Parker's low growl behind her and turned back with a do-I-have-a-choice? look as she hurried out to the field with her captor. If she wasn't trying to get information out of this prima donna, she might have slapped her.

Instead, she smiled as if she were excited. "So what do we do?"

"Oh, it's easy. We go about and put back the tufts of grass the ponies kicked up. Like this." She kicked at a clump of dirt at her feet, found an empty hole and pressed it into the ground with the toe of her shoe. "See?"

"Okey-dokey." Miranda found one and did the same. Only her press was more of a real stomp that made Gabrielle giggle.

The whole field was full of spectators now, everyone kicking at the clods of dirt and putting them in their places. Peppy music played from the loudspeaker and people were cackling and joking and having a jolly good time with the task.

Some of them had had a little too much to drink and Miranda thought Gabrielle might be one of them.

They made their way over the field, divot by divot.

Gabrielle spread her arms out to steady herself as she stomped one, trying to imitate Miranda's. She broke into peels of giggles. "Isn't this a lark, Ms. Steele? It's my favorite part of the game."

"Oh, yeah." Aristocrats doing manual labor for no pay? It did have a certain charm, but not one that appealed to Miranda. At least not at the moment.

Gabrielle hurried over to another clump with cute, mincing steps. "Davinia and I are going shopping after the match in Chelsea. Come with us?"

A shopping trip? That was where Miranda drew the line. Be polite, she reminded herself. "Oh, I'm sorry. I can't. I've got to be at—"

Her eyes went wide, and her lip quivered in that pouty expression again. "Oh, you must. You simply must."

Good grief. Miranda was really getting tired of this spoiled little girl telling her what she "must" do. She was about to tell her off when she had another thought.

Three women alone on a shopping spree in the city. What could be more intimate? What could be more inductive to idle conversation about their private lives? Maybe she could find out who that Sebastian dude was and why Davinia was hanging around him. Or better yet, what secrets Gabrielle was hiding.

"All right," she said. "But I've got another appointment first." At the museum. "Maybe I can meet you somewhere later?"

The pout turned to a smile of rapture. "Oh, that would be smashing. I'll give you my mobile number."

Mobile. That meant cell. Already regretting the commitment she'd made, Miranda pulled her phone out of her pocket. She gave the woman her number then keyed in the one Gabrielle rattled off. It was a weird pattern she wasn't sure she'd gotten right.

She read it back.

No answer.

She looked up. Gabrielle was gone. Where'd she go? Miranda sighed. What a spacey chick.

She stopped stomping and shielded her eyes with her hand, feeling like a hen looking for her lost chick. She was near the far edge of the field where riders were warming up their steeds for the next chukker. The crowd was dense and noisy. If she didn't find Gabrielle in a few minutes, she'd forget the divot stomping and the shopping trip and head for the museum with Parker and Sir Neville.

She tried to turn back, but she felt like a trout trying to swim upstream.

Suddenly a small blur of white blazed over the grass and jumped the low divider.

"Come back, Sissy!" a woman cried.

A cat.

Then there was a loud shriek. A horse's shriek. Miranda had heard that sound before.

"Lookout!" someone shouted.

"It's number three's pony."

There was the sound of galloping hooves and people started screaming and running every which way. Hunting for a spot where she wouldn't get trampled, Miranda spun around.

And froze.

The hazy image of a shiny chestnut coat with bridle and riderless saddle danced before her eyes. The loud whinny seemed to pierce her eardrums. The earthy odor of horse filled her nostrils. She blinked hard and the image cleared.

The animal was bucking and rearing up only a few feet from her. Its body lifted off the grass, forehooves pawing the air like a crazed orchestra conductor. She thought she caught the glint of a horseshoe.

The shouts around her became a dull muffle. She'd seen this before. But not this close.

The dancing hooves hovered in the air for what seemed like ten minutes. Right over her head.

Then down they came. Down. Down. Down. Closer. Closer. Closer.

Just before they reached her, she snapped out of her daze and instinct kicked in. She ducked and rolled as if she were avoiding a karate kick.

She kept rolling.

She didn't stop until she heard a man cry. "I've got him. It's all right now."

She raised herself up on her elbows and caught sight of Lionel's thin body in jodhpurs, boots and team jersey, holding his pony's bridle, his pointy beard bobbing as he reamed out some assistant on the other side of it.

The assistant led the animal away and he hurried over to her. "Ms. Steele. Are you quite all right?"

She glared up at the man.

She jerked her head to the sidelines where dozens of people were murmuring to each other and staring at her. Squinting into the crowd, she spotted Gabrielle patting the white cat in the flustered owner's arms while an official seemed to be lecturing her that pets were not allowed on the field.

Behind the spectators a host of riders stood. And behind them she saw Trenton Jewell, towering over them with his tall frame, a look of sheer horror on his face.

Angry suspicions flooded her.

She'd seen something like this happen on a case last year. Someone had killed somebody with a riled-up horse to make it look like a freak accident. And this time? It would have been hard to kill her on the open field. But if she were injured, she couldn't very well keep on investigating this case, or so someone might have been thinking. And that someone probably assumed Parker would be at her side and drop the case as well.

She took a deep breath. It was a theory, anyway. Nothing she could prove. Not yet, anyway.

She looked up and saw Parker pushing his way through the crowd.

He rushed to her side, alarm streaking his handsome face. "Miranda. Are you hurt?"

"I'm fine." Now she sounded like Sir Neville. She got to her feet. "Just a few grass stains on my dress." She looked a mess.

"Good Lord, what happened?"

Hell if she knew.

She waved her arms at the ground where she'd rolled. "But look at all the divots I packed down."

The people around her laughed at her joke, the way folks do when they discover a tragedy has been avoided.

Parker took her arm and gently led her away. "Would you like to go back to Eaton House?"

She shook her head. "Let's get to the museum. And let's get out of here before Lady Gabrielle tells me I 'must' stay for the second half."

CHAPTER SEVENTEEN

The vision of horse's hooves pawing the air still playing in her head, Miranda climbed into Sir Neville's limo and the three of them rode back to the museum in silence.

The driver dropped them off in the rear when they arrived and they went in through a back way just as Big Ben rang out, announcing it was noon. Inside they negotiated a winding, twisty path of narrow halls to a room that was his office.

Ever thoughtful, Parker had packed a bag with a change of clothes for both of them. How she loved that man.

After Sir Neville showed them to a small storage room next to his office and left them alone to change, Miranda dug into the bag, wanting to squeal with delight at the sight of a pair of comfortable dress slacks, even if they weren't jeans.

Parker leaned against an antique writing table and watched her wriggle out of her dress, a patchwork of mud and grass stains over the red-and-white fabric, her lean body framed against the background of dusty old volumes and maps behind her.

He shook his head.

His headstrong, adrenaline-junkie wife, who loved fast cars, roller coasters, and food three times as spicy as he himself could handle. Why, no matter where they went, did she always end up in some sort of danger? When would she ever stop giving him near heart attacks? What in the world was he going to do with her?

Miranda tossed her dress over an old chair and pulled on the white cotton blouse Parker had packed. She buttoned it up and was about to step into the charcoal slacks when she looked up and saw him staring at her. "What?"

Slowly he shook his head. Uh oh. She knew that look. "Why did you let that woman drag you onto the field?"

She frowned at him. "Lady Gabrielle? I didn't let her drag me out there. I just let her think she did."

He inhaled in that strained way that let her know he was upset. "Very well. Why did you go with her?"

Her own temper rising, she waved her hands. "Why do you think? To get information out of her."

"And what did you get?"

He had her there. She'd gotten more out of her when they were at the clubhouse. She zipped up her slacks and reached for the matching jacket. "I don't know. She's a really good divot stomper?"

His gray eyes went dark. "You could have been killed. Or injured."

So that was it. Of course, it was. His overprotective side was rearing its ugly head again. "But I wasn't."

"Thank God you have excellent reflexes."

"Yes, I do." She pulled out shoes from the bag and slipped them on. "And you know, that's what I learned from going out on the field."

"What? That someone wants to hinder our investigation?"

If only his mind didn't go in the same direction as hers. She knew he'd rather leave the case unsolved than risk injury to her. Chivalrous of him, but she didn't think it was a good idea. "It might have been an accident. A cat ran onto the sidelines and spooked Lord Eaton's horse."

"Or it might have been orchestrated."

As she put her ruined dress in the bag, she thought of the faces she'd seen along the sidelines. Lionel, Gabrielle, the cat owner. And after all, Gabrielle had loaned her a hat with a big red ribbon that the horse might have seen as a target. Still…

She shook her head. "Gabrielle's not as dumb as she lets on, but I don't think she's capable of something like that."

His eyes narrowed as he grew thoughtful. "It wasn't a very successful attempt."

"You mean if someone was trying to injure me?"

"Yes."

She cocked her head at him with a grin. "They weren't counting on my excellent reflexes."

He didn't smile back. "But they will next time."

Did he really think there'd be a next time? He could be right. Or it could have been an accident.

She handed the bag to him. "If someone was trying to stop our investigation—"

"Then we won't let them," he finished, taking the bag from her.

She was glad to hear that.

"But Miranda," he reached for her, held her by the shoulder, his grip gentle but firm. "From now on, I want you to be very careful."

Parker finished dressing and opened the door.

Miranda stepped into Sir Neville's office and found him at his desk, a heavy piece of furniture that must have been made two centuries ago. It was covered with clutter. On the parquet floor before it lay a dark rug with an elaborate floral pattern. A few potted plants sat in the windowsill.

The walls were polished wood with more bookshelves filled not only with old tomes, but also with small replicas of ancient things from the Middle East. Tarnished vases, cat figures, a small sphinx, and a figure of a winged beast with a man's head.

She turned to their client.

He sat in a big leather chair staring at the phone, looking wearier than ever. "I just got off the phone with Inspector Wample. George hasn't been released."

Miranda looked at Parker. His brow creased, probably with the same thought she had. What was Trenton Jewell doing at the polo match when he should have been getting Eames out of there?

"Have they charged him yet?" Parker asked.

"Apparently they're about to."

Miranda thought of Parker's advice for Eames to try to think who on the staff had been acting strange lately. If he'd thought of anyone, he'd have contacted Jewell, who would have told them. Right? Or he would have called Sir Neville.

She wondered how many phone calls you got when you were being held by Scotland Yard. They could go down there and talk to him again, but if any of the staff had been involved in the theft, it would be better if she and Parker talked to them soon.

Parker had the same idea. He strode over to the desk and laid a soothing hand on the old gentleman's shoulder. "Sir Neville, Miranda and I need to speak to your staff."

His silver white brows knitted together. "What's that, Russell? Who?"

"As many as are in today. It may take a few hours. And if we may use your office, I'd greatly appreciate it."

Good move. Be a lot more intimidating to be in the director's office.

"It's noon. Don't you want some lunch?" He was avoiding the request.

Parker looked at Miranda. "Are you hungry?"

She shook her head.

"We'll eat later."

Sir Neville got to his feet with a huff and strode to the window. "You can't be thinking anyone had a hand in this dreadful business with the dagger."

Parker's voice was gentle. "We have to eliminate them ourselves. Someone may know something. May have seen something. They wouldn't necessarily be involved."

He almost had her convinced.

Sir Neville's narrow shoulders rose with a heavy sigh. "Very well. I don't suppose you'll be needing me here then. I'll go check on the silk paintings Imogen and Graham are setting up." He glanced at his watch. "I usually lunch in the café on the main floor. Perhaps we can have something together when you're finished?"

"We'll meet you there," Parker said. "Do you have a list of staff members?"

Worry creased the poor man's gentle face, but he straightened his shoulders and nodded. "My administrative assistant can provide you with the names. I'll speak to her." He turned and left the room.

"He took that well," Miranda said dryly.

"He's loyal to his staff. I don't blame him for feeling offended."

"No, I guess not. Do you want to take them separately? I can go in the room next door."

He shook his head. "I want you with me."

She raised a brow. Did he want her professional opinion, or did he not want her to leave his side so some polo pony wouldn't come flying through the window and trample her?

He gave her a narrow look and read her mind. "I want us to do this together. We're a team."

"Okay." She'd take that as a peace offering of sorts. For now.

CHAPTER EIGHTEEN

Miranda never imagined it took so many people to run a museum.

Security people, guards, greeters at the entrances, clerks in the gift shop, maintenance people for everything from the plumbing to keeping the restrooms clean. Not to mention the registrars and managers, or the programs and exhibition designers and curators for the Middle East collection, the Ancient Asia collection, the Greek and Roman collection and, of course, the Egyptian collection.

"We'll never get through all these in a day, Parker," she sighed, scanning the long list the admin had given them. The police couldn't have questioned them all, either. They'd gone for the low hanging fruit of George Eames.

Parker's brow creased with concern. He always liked to be thorough, but there were only the two of them. "We'll take representatives from each department and focus on those with the highest security clearance."

That sounded reasonable and maybe even doable.

They checked off a dozen or so names and Parker asked the admin to bring them in one by one.

Parker took Sir Neville's chair in an obvious power play, while Miranda leaned on the edge of the desk, hovering like a bird of prey, while the interrogatee sat in a small chair on the other side of the carpet.

There seemed to be people of every race, hair color and body type, each with their own accent, each wearing uniforms or casual clothes with a name badge and a deep red necktie or scarf to identify them as someone who worked here.

They questioned each employee about their typical routine and where they were the evening the dagger was delivered.

The replies were what you might expect. The security guards made rounds and kept an eye on visitors. The gift shop people sold their wares and went home at the usual time. The restroom attendants cleaned the johns. Everyone had a reasonable alibi for the time span between the delivery and the presentation of the dagger.

It would take a long while to check each one.

Everyone knew the dagger was coming. No one claimed to know exactly what time. No one was on the premises at the time it had arrived except a few guards, who were in other parts of the building.

They worked their way down the list and finally got to Emily Chopra, the Curator of Egyptian Art.

The woman sat in the leather chair with an almost military posture, her gaze moving from Parker to Miranda and back again. "This is about the Marc Antony dagger? I thought the police had already made an arrest."

Parker gave her a steady gaze. "We've been asked to conduct a separate investigation."

She laced her fingers, unlaced them, laced them again. "Well, I don't think Mr. Eames is the thief if you want my opinion on the matter."

"Do you have any idea who might be?"

Her dark eyes went wide. "No, I don't." She had skin the color of cocoa and was small and delicate. Dressed in a severe black suit, her dark hair parted in the middle and twisted into a tight bun in the back, she could have been a cross between an Asian princess and a nun.

Miranda looked down at the clipboard with the names the admin had given them for effect. "Chopra," she said after waiting enough time to make anyone uncomfortable. "That's an Indian name, right?"

"Yes. Northern India." She spoke with a clipped, almost artificial accent. A British accent with just a hint of exotic.

"But you're English?"

She re-laced her hands again, tightly this time, her face strained. "Of course. I was born here. My grandfather was from New Delhi. But both my parents were born here in London, as was I. And if you're wondering about my loyalty to the museum, all I can say is that this institution is my life. Sir Neville Ravensdale can vouch for that."

Defensive.

Miranda slid off the desk and took a half step toward her. "You were with Sir Neville on the morning the dagger was to be presented, correct?"

"Yes, of course. I was waiting for him in the storeroom. He arrived a few minutes before—" she inhaled sharply. "Before we went up to present the dagger to the public and place it in the display. That didn't happen of course."

"No, it didn't," Parker said, his voice thick with sympathy. He was playing the "good PI" role this round.

As if she hadn't heard him, Miranda took another step toward the curator. "Ms. Chopra, did you have an opportunity to be alone in the storeroom with the crate that held the dagger?"

"That morning?"

"Or any time after it was delivered."

She jolted slightly at the implication. "No, I didn't. I left early the night before and came in early to make sure the designers were putting the finishing touches on the Cleopatra exhibit. I went down to the storeroom about ten minutes before Sir Neville arrived."

"Were you the only one in there then?"

"I just told you. Mr. Eames was there, and Toby Waverly came in a few minutes later."

"Toby Waverly?"

"He's an intern who occasionally helps us in the storeroom, as he was doing that day."

Miranda nodded slowly, gave the clipboard a tap. "Can anyone verify your whereabouts?"

"On that morning? Mr. Eames can, as I just said."

"What about the night before?"

Her mouth opened, then closed. She turned her head and stared out the window, robot-like. "I live alone. I went home that night, had dinner. I spoke to my mother on the phone for about half an hour, then I went to bed. Really. I resent your insinuations, Ms. Steele."

Miranda drew in a slow breath. She hated harassing the lady. She was probably telling the truth and had just been doing her job.

Parker rose and came around the desk. Now it was his turn to perch on the corner. "My partner is simply following protocol, Ms. Chopra. I apologize this is so trying."

She stared down at her hands and drew in a breath. "It's all right. I realize you're only doing your jobs."

"Is there anything else you can tell us that might help us find who perpetrated this horrible crime?"

"It is horrible. Whoever did this has no regard for antiquity. For beauty. For the preservation of ancient cultures. All they care about is lining their own pockets. That's how I know George Eames isn't guilty. He loves this place. But if I knew anything, believe me, I'd have already told the police."

So they were zero for eleven.

The last victim on the list was the Executive Director of Security, Arthur Yeats.

He came lumbering into Sir Neville's office, head down and sank into the chair, his lanky body overflowing it vertically. He had on worn jeans and a rumpled shirt. His longish brown hair looked like he hadn't combed it in a week and his five o'clock shadow might have been from yesterday.

"Mr. Yeats," Parker began. "We've asked you here—"

"I know why I'm here, Mr. Parker. I saw Emily in the hall." He raised his narrow, elongated head and pulled at his long nose in an agitated gesture. "I haven't been able to sleep since the…incident."

Miranda believed him. From the information they had, Yeats was a computer geek in his mid-thirties, but he looked like he'd aged twenty years.

"I've been over and over every detail of our security system ever since Thursday morning."

Sure, he had. He might lose his job and never get another one in the field.

"Of course, you could always do more if funds were unlimited, which ours definitely are not. But we have an exceptional system. My department is responsible not only for guarding the collections against theft, but also accidental damage, fire, flood and such." He let out a weary sigh, as if a natural disaster would have been easier to deal with.

"Tell us about your security measures," Parker asked.

Yeats sat up in his chair, eager to spill all. He began giving them a litany of technical details. The number of units, their strategic placement, the calculations for the sensors.

Miranda's skin started to crawl. This was getting them nowhere. "Mr. Yeats, all we need from you—"

He held up a hand. "Wait. Why don't I show you?"

She scowled at him.

"I have a theory." His sunken eyes pleaded with her.

Miranda looked back at Parker. He nodded.

CHAPTER NINETEEN

They followed Yeats's lanky frame down the tall marble staircase where they'd first seen Sir Neville, while he babbled about the problems of security and the details of electronic devices. At the bottom of the steps, they took a turn and crossed the huge open space into one of the smaller halls.

It was one of the rooms in the Ancient Asia collection, Miranda realized as she found herself surrounded by a breathtaking assortment of archaic doodads. Sandstone figures of Buddhas. Life-sized statues of emperors from long ago dynasties. Glass shelves filled with ivory and porcelain and jade, each object embossed with delicate patterns.

Yeats's athletic shoes trod steadily over the shiny tiles of the floor past a large tapestry of women in kimonos under flowering trees. "Many of the pieces have wireless sensors. The faintest touch sets off an alarm in the control room."

He came to a halt before a bronze statue of a naked woman, possibly some ancient goddess, her metallic hair piled two feet atop her head. "Here. I'll demonstrate." He pulled out a walkie-talkie. "Humphries?"

"Yes, sir," a rough British voice answered.

"Testing 12B4."

"Very good, sir."

He waved a palm close to the statue's bare navel and a beeping sound came over the radio.

"12B4 operational," confirmed the man on the other end.

"Thank you. That's all for now." Yeats disconnected.

Miranda peered hard at the statue. She couldn't see any sensor on it, then she lowered her gaze and spotted it. It was hidden on the white pedestal, its beam going straight up. No one could touch the thing without the control room knowing it.

"I'm impressed."

"Yes," Parker echoed.

"Thank you." A hand behind his back in a geek-military fashion, Yeats gave them a triumphant smile then turned and strolled into the next hall. "We have alarms on the windows, guards patrolling twenty-four seven."

They went through another door and made their way past walls covered with ancient maps and carvings and depictions of journeys over unknown waters. Finally, the space opened into the museum's entrance.

The place was open for business, all right. Visitors were coming in the doors, as if nothing had happened a few days ago, though the crowd seemed a little sparse. Friendly looking guards greeted each patron as they entered.

Yeats turned his gaze up and nodded to the thick square columns spread around the room. "Cameras at the entrances show us every face that enters the building. The film is observed by the guard you just heard in the control room as well as recorded."

"And you've reviewed the film around the time of the theft?" Parker wanted to know.

Yeats nodded. "The week before and the morning thereof. Haven't spotted anything suspicious." He waved a hand toward a small line at a table. "We also do a search of parcels anyone brings in."

Miranda saw one of the smiling guards searching a student's backpack. "It looks pretty thorough. But there has to be a hole somewhere."

Solemnly, Yeats nodded. "That's my theory. Follow me."

He led them back across the open space with the big marble staircase to a small hall where a set of locked double doors barred the way.

"Service entrances like this one are always locked. Only employees who have the correct clearance can enter. With a keycard." He showed them his card then swiped it through a box on the wall. The doors opened.

They stepped into an enclave where the service elevator was. Yeats pressed a button, and they went inside. He pressed another button for the basement. He was taking them to the storeroom.

Parker let out an audible sigh of frustration. "I believe we've already spoken with the staff members who have access to this area. And we've seen the storeroom."

Though it wouldn't hurt to see it again, Miranda thought.

Yeats raised a long finger in the air. "Bear with me. You haven't seen this."

The doors opened to a long hall with bare eggshell-colored walls. There was a solid wall to their left and the only way to go was right. They turned and trudged down the passageway, passing more secured doors that Yeats pointed out as closets or utility rooms or break rooms.

He came to a halt in front of the aluminum double doors to the storeroom and pointed to the pad on the wall. "Entrance to this area requires a special code. The code is issued to only a select few of the museum personnel. Myself, the storeroom supervisor, the collections manager. And the director, of course."

"Yes," Parker said. "We noticed Sir Neville using it when he brought us here."

"Others have to be buzzed inside by someone already there. The code is changed every other month, though people complain about it."

"A sensible policy."

"The museum cut the budget for cameras here, so we installed motion sensors inside the room that form an intricate pattern. That's also changed periodically. The last person out of the room in the evening uses the code to reset the sensors."

Now Miranda was getting irritated. This guy was wasting their time telling them things they already knew. "And so?"

Yeats eyed her down the length of his narrow nose. "And so, it would be very difficult for someone to enter the room with the sensors engaged. They would detect the person's presence, which would set off alarms in the control room, similar to what I demonstrated in the Ancient Asia collection."

"You're saying the sensors would have to be turned off," Parker said.

"Correct. And you can only do that by accessing this panel."

Which meant someone on the inside had to do it. Like George Eames. They were going in circles. Miranda watched Parker's eyes narrow as he gave the security man a hard look.

"And where were you Wednesday night, Mr. Yeats?"

The tall man grimaced, his lips twisting as he raised a hand to them while he studied the floor. "I was with my fiancée all night, I'm afraid. The police have already spoken to her."

But she might have lied to them.

Yeats turned back to the panel.

"We don't need to go inside," Parker told him flatly. "We've already seen it."

Yeats shook his head. "That's not what I want to show you. It's down here." He made a quarter turn and headed off down the hall.

They followed him, winding this way and that, up four concrete steps, up another set of five and finally came to another pair of double doors. They bore a green sign marked "Exit" with a picture of a stick figure going out a white opening.

Yeats gestured at the doors and stated the obvious. "These lead outside. They're always locked."

Miranda folded her arms and grimaced at the metal push bars. "And your point is?"

He blinked at her as if it should be clear. "There are no cameras here. But again, you need to swipe a keycard with the correct security clearance to enter from outside."

She blew out a breath. "What are you saying, Yeats?"

He waved a hand at the doors with exasperation. "That if someone with the codes to the storeroom wanted to, he or she could have let the thief in right here."

Miranda shifted her weight. He could be on to something. "And that's your theory?"

Yeats closed his eyes and nodded as if he were grateful he'd finally gotten through to these dense detectives. "Yes. It's an alternate explanation to Mr. Eames."

"Unless he was the one who let them in," Parker pointed out.

CHAPTER TWENTY

The crest-fallen Yeats escorted them back upstairs and left them in the Great Hall where the marble staircase was.

Frustrated, Miranda scratched at her hair and watched a group of schoolboys in uniforms pointing at one of the half-naked statues, their giggles echoing to the high ceiling. "We're coming up with zip, Parker."

Parker's face was hard with concentration. He wasn't paying attention to the kids or any of the other visitors roaming around.

Suddenly he turned and headed for the corner at a fast clip.

"Where are we going?"

"We need to find Sir Neville. There's one more person we need to question."

Who? she wondered as she trotted after him. They'd finished the list. But she thought she had an idea.

They found Sir Neville reading a book at the end of a long table in a cafeteria-like café on the far side of the Great Hall. It was a wide-open space dotted with planters, odd-shaped lamps and clean shiny surfaces, embellished with bronze. There were only a few other patrons at distant tables, all engrossed in muted conversations.

The smell of meats and cheeses and strange tangy sauces filled the air, and Miranda's mouth began to water. But she ignored it.

Sir Neville looked up guardedly as they approached, reached for a decorative coffee cup in a saucer before him. "Have you made any arrests?"

Parker grimaced, then held out a seat across from the gentleman for Miranda. "No, you'll be happy to know we've found nothing incriminating."

Sir Neville put down his cup without taking a sip and shook his head as if chiding himself. "I don't mean to be rude, Russell. It's just that this ordeal has been so trying."

Parker took a seat beside Miranda. "I know."

"I've just had a call from a representative of Buckingham Palace. We're partially state-funded so they're concerned, of course. The crown hopes this is all settled, and the dagger is found very soon. I didn't know what to say."

Miranda felt her throat clench. Now the Queen of England was involved in this case? "We're doing our best to wrap things up as quickly as possible, Sir Neville," she told him.

Though they weren't even at the making progress stage, let alone the wrapping things up stage. If they didn't find the thief soon, maybe the Queen would chop off their heads.

Parker gave his friend a steady look. "There's one more person on your staff we need to speak to."

"Someone else?"

"Ms. Chopra mentioned there was another person in the storeroom with you the morning the dagger was discovered missing."

Sir Neville frowned. He searched first Miranda's face then Parker's. "Do you mean Toby Waverly?"

Parker nodded. "Yes."

Miranda knew that was who Parker had meant.

Sir Neville's mouth opened in horror. "Toby? He's just a boy. An intern from King's College. They're one of the oldest universities in England. Extremely selective. They wouldn't send us a...a relic thief."

They had to keep the man calm. "We're not saying he's a thief, Sir Neville," she told him. "We just want to find out if he knows anything."

Parker patted the sleeve of the man's suit coat. "We'll probably find nothing."

Sir Neville sat back, his shoulders sagging. "Very well. I'll contact my assistant and have him paged. Would you like to see him here?"

Parker shook his head. "Have her send him to your office."

Sir Neville took out his cell phone. "In the meantime, why don't you have something to eat as guests of the museum?"

Parker turned to her. "What would you like?"

"Let's look at what they have." She got up and went to a counter filled with sandwiches and baked goods. She hesitated. It looked good from a distance, but who knew what was in those things.

Parker pointed to the menu board overhead. "They have a bok choi and shitake salad with free range chicken. Or a guinea hen sandwich."

"Hmm." Before she could decide, her cell buzzed. She pulled it out of her pocket and eyed the display. It was Lady Gabrielle.

After considering letting it go to voicemail, she whispered to Parker. "I think I need to take this." Ignoring his scowl, she turned and took a few steps before answering. "Hello?"

Familiar girlish laughter greeted her ear. "Ms. Steele? Where on earth are you?"

Since the woman wasn't here to see it, Miranda indulged in a grimace. "Still on that errand I said I had."

"Well, I wanted to tell you we left Chelsea. Now we're at Selfridges. It's on Oxford Street. You must join us. You simply must."

Must, huh? *No, I mustn't*, she wanted to reply. She really wanted to help question Toby Waverly. They could be close to getting a break. On the other hand, he might turn out to know as little about the night of the theft as everyone else around here.

As she rolled Gabrielle's demand around in her mind, Miranda felt a familiar sensation. Not anything big. Just a tiny tingle at the base of her neck. A feeling she'd had before.

The image of Lady Davinia strolling the polo grounds with that Sebastian dude came to her. She thought of Gabrielle's innocent face on the sidelines after the horse attacked, an expression Miranda was sure had been fake. She thought of the hooves of that polo pony pawing the air right over her head.

There was something up with these aristocrats. And if it had anything to do with the Marc Antony dagger, it was worth following up.

She took a breath and grinned into the phone. "I'll be there in a little while, Lady Gabrielle. Can you give me directions?"

Gabrielle explained how to get to the place and clicked off, and Miranda returned to Parker. He was at the cash register with a tray holding two artfully arranged dishes. He'd already ordered for her.

She eyed one of the plates. Some sort of melted cheese and meat on sourdough bread with an arugula garnish and chili peppers on the side. It looked delicious.

"Uh…" She pulled her fingers through her hair, shifting from foot to foot. "I'm not going to be able to eat that."

Parker's expression went dark. Big surprise. "What do you mean?"

She made a careless gesture with her hand. "Lady Gabrielle wants me to meet her and Lady Davinia at someplace called Selfridges."

His scowl grew darker. "That's a department store. A high end one. Are you having a sudden urge to go shopping?"

He knew she despised shopping and everything that went with it. "Gabrielle is. And she says I 'must' join her."

She gave a laugh and watched Parker's lip twitch. Every muscle in his beautiful body tensed beneath his tailored suit as his temper boiled over in that Mount Vesuvius way of his.

But he managed to control himself as he leaned near her ear. "Miranda, do you really think that's wise?" His voice was low and ominous.

He was still worried about her after the polo pony incident. Annoyance rising inside her, she shrugged. "Like you said. It's shopping. In a department store. What could happen?"

"Oh, I don't know. Any number of things. You could go out on the street and get pushed into oncoming traffic, for instance."

He had a point. If Lady Gabrielle was out to hurt her to stop this investigation, she could be planning something like that. But this time, Miranda would be on her guard. "I'll be careful."

"Careful enough?"

That was a low blow. "Do I have to remind you I can take care of myself?"

He eyed her up and down as if sizing her up for the first time. "Not in the slightest." He reached for her hand. "Do I have to say I don't want you to go?"

Now he was playing the tender card. She pulled out of his grasp. "I think I might learn something."

He didn't reply.

She poked him in the chest with her forefinger. "Tell you what. If something happens, I'll say you were right, and I should have listened to you."

He gave her a wry smile, tinged with fury. "That might be too late."

Her temper crackled inside her. She didn't want to make him mad. But they were supposed to be partners. Why couldn't he trust her?

She leaned forward and lowered her voice. "Look. We both think there's something funny going on with the family. Why not take this opportunity to dig under their facades?"

He didn't answer. He knew it was a good opportunity, but he didn't want to admit it.

She stepped close to him. "Well, you go follow up on your hunch about the intern and I'll follow up on mine." Despite her irritation, she rose on tiptoe to peck him on the cheek. "I'll meet you back here when I finish, and we'll compare notes."

His tone turned demanding. "Miranda."

She wiggled her fingers at him. "Bye."

He could have come after her. Pulled rank, forced her to stay. But that would have only caused a big scene. Instead, all he did was send her a furious scowl.

Anger pounding in her temples, she spun around and headed out the exit, leaving him fuming and her stomach empty.

Parker watched his headstrong wife march out of the café and head for the museum exit, his jaw as tight as a vice grip.

Why couldn't she listen to reason? Why couldn't she take some precautions? But she'd never been one to be cautious when she thought a clue was at hand. And she had good instincts. Most of the time they were dead on point. It would be counterproductive to keep her from following up on them. And as she said, it was only shopping.

Still, if anything happened to her…

He let out a long sigh and headed back to the table. This consulting business of theirs might prove to be the death of him.

He found Sir Neville staring off into space, dismay in his eyes.

Parker set down the tray and sat across from him. "Are you all right, Sir Neville?"

The man shook himself out of his reverie and frowned. "Oh, I suppose I am.

"Would you like a sandwich?"

"Miranda isn't eating with you?"

"No, she had an errand." Best his friend didn't know what that errand was. He picked up his sandwich and took a bite.

Sir Neville shook his head. "No, thank you, Russell. I had something earlier." His light blue eyes took on a faraway look again and his white brows drew together. "I saw Davinia with a young man at the match today."

Parker tensed. He'd seen them too and knew that's what had brought on the anxiety attack. "Oh?"

"He's a friend of Lionel's. Used to be a polo player himself. He's in advertising, I believe."

As the Duchess of Oxham had said.

"He's a very handsome chap." Sir Neville's upper lip began to quiver.

Parker stopped chewing.

"The thing is…"

"What?"

He watched his friend wrestle back the painful emotions that must have gripped him on the polo field earlier.

"She had that look in her eye. That glow. The one she used to have when we first met."

Parker put down his sandwich. He hadn't expected this. "Neville, I—"

"We used to talk for hours back then. We had so much in common. She was an art student in college and had an interest in the Etruscan period. Then we married and after a few years it all…disappeared. It was as if she woke up one morning and realized she'd been beguiled into marrying someone beneath her."

Parker thought of the problems Miranda had had because of the difference in their status. It had taken all the patience he had to convince her they had a future together. "I'm sure that isn't the case, Neville. All marriages go through ups and downs."

"Ours has been down for over a decade. It wasn't until today that I realized how far down it was." He turned to Parker, his blue eyes glassy. "Russell—I think Davinia's going to leave me."

"I'm so sorry." Parker felt as empty as his words.

This man had crossed an ocean to comfort him when he was a boy, and now he had nothing to offer in return.

They sat staring at each other for a long moment. "I'm afraid I don't have a magic elixir for marital woes." If he did, he'd take a dose of it himself right now.

Sir Neville wiped a hand across his aged face. "No, I didn't expect you to. And I didn't mean to burden you with my personal problems. You have enough to worry about with my professional ones. Finish your lunch and we'll talk to Toby."

Parker picked up the sandwich again though he had little appetite.

He hoped with all his being this intern gave him something he could work with so they could close this case soon. It was the best he could do for his old friend.

CHAPTER TWENTY-ONE

Following Lady Gabrielle's directions, Miranda made her way through the pedestrians on Gowan Street, past historic-looking buildings, a pizza shop, and a Starbucks until she reached the underground station to catch the Central tube.

She tossed a few coins Parker must have stuffed into her pocket into the turnstile, climbed aboard and flopped down on a blue patterned seat. After a minute or two, the train took off and zoomed along the tracks. It was a lot like the subway in New York, she thought. Only the crowd here wasn't as rough looking.

A group of older women in raincoats chatted away down the aisle, and across from her a thin, middle aged man sipped delicious smelling coffee from a Styrofoam cup. The scent made her mouth water again, which made her temper resurface.

As the car rattled noisily along, she stared out the window into the darkness of the tunnel and thought about how mad she was at Parker. Okay, he didn't want her to get hurt. She got that. And maybe the polo pony thing was upsetting.

But did that mean he was going to hover over her like a mother hen for the rest of this case? She couldn't work like that. How could he expect her to?

She was pondering that over when a female voice poshly announced they were at Bond Street. Her stop.

Without any more answers to her problems with Parker than to who stole the Marc Antony dagger, she got off and made her way back up the concrete stairs to the sidewalk and a street lined with more old buildings and filled with small cars, red buses, bicyclists and pedestrians.

She hiked a block west, then half a block north and found herself in front of the huge store.

The place had as many Greek columns decorating its facade as the museum. A humongous statue of a regally robed woman stood right over the entrance, as if warning those who entered, "You'd better have bucks if you want to come in here."

This was going to be interesting.

Miranda stepped through the revolving doors and was flooded with a cloud of exotic smelling fragrances and a sea of white counters. She began to inch past the sparkling surfaces filled with merchandise, everything made to entice and empty the wallet, wondering what kind of mercantile jungle she'd stumbled into.

Ignoring the beckoning clerks, she made her way to the second floor where a DJ was spinning old Elton John tunes. She wandered around for a while and at last spotted Davinia's elegant frame and Gabrielle's animated one—in the Women's Designer department, of course.

Her red-gold curls shimmering under the bright lights, Gabrielle acted as excited as a schoolgirl when she saw her. "Oh, Ms. Steele," she squealed. "I'm so very happy you've joined us at last. This is going to be so much fun."

Lady Davinia gave Miranda a perfunctory smile that lacked her daughter-in-law's enthusiasm. "I'm afraid we may have already reached our allotment of fun this afternoon, Gabrielle," she said stiffly. "I'm quite spent."

Gabrielle ignored her and turned to Miranda, big green eyes glowing. "What do you think of this Valentino?" She held up a bright red lace dress with a short scalloped skirt.

Hard to imagine what it might look like on her against the white silky dress lavishly decked with silver bangle-bling the woman had on. Apparently, she'd changed somewhere or bought the white outfit and decided to wear it.

Falling right into the role she was playing, Miranda took the hanger and held up the garment. That was when she got a glance at the price tag.

Holy moly. It might be in British pounds, and she didn't know the exchange rate, but she could tell it was still a whopper. She hoped Parker didn't pay that much for her clothes.

But then who was she to tell a member of the aristocracy how much she should spend on a dress? She handed it back to Gabrielle with a bright fake smile. "It's nice."

"How about this Pilotto?" Gabrielle pressed a luxurious piece of material with a bold print of pinks and blues and golds against her body. Its shape on the hanger was so weird she couldn't tell how it would be worn. The price on that one wasn't much better.

Giving up, Miranda raised her palms. "I really couldn't say. I'm not much of a shopper."

Davinia leaned over her shoulder. "I'm trying to get her not to spend everything in Lionel's bank account."

Before Miranda could reply, Gabrielle scoffed at the comment. "I believe a person ought to live their life to the fullest, don't you, Ms. Steele?"

Miranda opened her mouth, but Gabrielle kept talking. "We should buy Ms. Steele something, Mother. You know, to make up for her dress getting ruined at the match today?"

Feeling guilty about that, was she? Or was she just trying to remind the American investigator what she could do to her?

Miranda forced another grin. "Not necessary." The last thing she wanted to do was try on clothes. "Actually, I was hoping for something to eat." Now that was the truth.

She was hungry and eating with Ladies Who Lunch would be the best way to get them to relax and open up.

Lady Davinia glanced at the gold and diamond watch on her wrist. "It is almost teatime."

Teatime? Wasn't that around four? "Wow, I really got carried away with my errand. I haven't even had lunch."

Gabrielle opened her mouth as if horrified. "Oh, my. Then we must feed you, mustn't we, Mother."

"I suppose so." Davinia's elegant dark brows drew together in thought. "There's Dolly's downstairs. They have sandwiches."

"No, oh. Not in the store. We need to take her somewhere fabulous. Arbutus."

Davinia shook her head.

"High Tea, then."

Davinia considered that a moment, then nodded with a regal air. "Very well."

Miranda didn't care where they ate as long as she could wolf down a burger somewhere and get them talking, she'd be fine.

Miranda followed the ladies out of the store and discovered Gabrielle had her car. A tiny, shiny white Mercedes with a trunk so small it was a miracle it held all the packages the ladies stuffed into it.

They climbed inside and Gabrielle pulled onto a crowded street.

Miranda still wasn't comfortable with the riding on the left thing, and Gabrielle's driving was about as capricious as her thought patterns, so she focused on the four-and-five-story brick buildings lining the road. With their elaborate trim they looked like they must have been built in the seventeenth or eighteenth century. Back when people had nothing better to do than carve decorations into walls.

Cars were parked on both sides of the road, some spots marked "Disabled." The sidewalks were crammed with shoppers on their way to buy luggage or jewelry or yes, more clothes. They passed a hot dog shop that would have suited Miranda just fine. But no, not these ladies.

At Duke Street, they made a turn in front of an arch with a gold-trimmed gate and after spending longer than it took to drive here, found a parking spot a block away from their destination.

Miranda got out and followed her hostesses down a quaint cobblestone walkway and into a clean looking place done in mahogany and muted colors with shiny mirrors, spotless wineglasses and tabletops, and a staff with expressions that said they took the job of food service very seriously.

A stiff waiter in black seated them and handed them menus.

Miranda squinted at the offerings.

Pass on the pig's head. Likewise on the squid and mackerel burger. After hunting for a plain old cheeseburger without success, she settled on the Dorset crab with guacamole, peanuts and Provençal figs. Whatever that was.

The waiter brought drinks and she sipped tea and listened to the ladies sum up their shopping trip while she waited for the food to come. Best to let them settle in before she went to work on them.

At last, the food arrived. The waiter placed slices of some sort of cream cake in front of Gabrielle and Davinia, then set Miranda's order before her.

It was small and looked like it might have been plated by one of Picasso's offspring. She poked a fork into the crab and took a bite. Edible. Good, even. And loaded with tasty exotic flavors she couldn't begin to identify. It would do.

She waited until she was about half finished then decided it was time to pounce. In this situation, Parker would go for a subtle, suave approach. She went for direct.

"So, Lady Gabrielle. How do you know the woman with the cat?"

Gabrielle's eyes went wide, and her teacup froze halfway to her lips. "How on earth do you mean, Ms. Steele?"

Playing dumb, huh? Seemed to be her standard ploy. Miranda waved her fork. "You know. The woman whose cat got loose at the polo match? I saw you talking to her."

Her eyes got even bigger. The cup went down to its saucer as Gabrielle recovered with a girlish giggle. "Oh, yes. That was Ellen Quinn. I went to school with her. Haven't seen her in ages."

Somehow that didn't ring true. "Really strange that her cat jumped right out of her arms and headed straight for your husband's pony."

"Yes, wasn't it though? I would have thought Lionel would have better control of his own steed." She laughed at her own innuendo and toyed with her cake.

Miranda pretended to study a landscape on the wall. "I don't know. It just seemed as if it was orchestrated, didn't it?"

Gabrielle started blinking like a flashing traffic light. She reached for her tea again. "I'm sure I don't know what you mean."

Uncomfortable with the conversation, Lady Davinia cleared her throat. "Ms. Steele, I apologize for what happened today. You must send me the cleaning bill."

Miranda picked up her cup and waited a beat before she replied. "Good idea. I'll tell Parker to add it to our expenses."

Now it was the mother-in-law's turn to blink. Before she could come up with a polite response, Gabrielle's cell went off, playing an annoying synthesized tune in a funky, syncopated beat.

"Oh, that must be Lionel. Please excuse me." She hopped up, cell in hand, and hurried off to an alcove where the restrooms were for privacy.

Now that was an interesting way to escape uncomfortable questions.

Lady Davinia gave Miranda a look of distress. "I am sorry for Gabrielle's rudeness, Ms. Steele."

Miranda shrugged. "It's okay." She'd been talking to people who'd have liked to run away from her all afternoon.

Davinia stared at her teacup. "I did mention to Gabrielle the real reason you and Mr. Parker are here. I suppose she told you."

Nice of her to admit that. "Yes, she was curious about the case."

Lady Davinia kept her eyes on the liquid in her cup as if she wanted to say something else, then thought better of it. Now would be a good time to mention the guy she was with at the match.

Miranda was just about to when Gabrielle scampered up to the table.

Her face was pale and there was no trace of a smile on her lips now. "I have to pop around the corner to meet someone for a moment," she sputtered as if out of breath.

Davinia scowled. "Gabrielle, really? In the middle of our tea?"

"I have to, Mother. It's…an old friend. She's…run into a bit of trouble. I won't be long." She turned to go.

"Well, what are we to do?" Davinia called after her, a bit of temper showing.

Gabrielle turned back and rolled her eyes. "Just wait here. I won't be more than fifteen minutes." And with that, she scooted out the café door.

Miranda watched her, gritting her teeth to make herself sit there instead of following the flighty woman out the door.

Old friend, her ass. If that was Lionel on the phone, she could be meeting him around the corner to plan their next attack. Miranda thought about Parker's warning that someone might push her into traffic. She'd have to be careful when she went back out on the street.

Beside her Davinia let out a long sigh. "Again, I apologize for my daughter-in-law's lack of manners, Ms. Steele. She's so unpredictable. I try to give her guidance, but it's an uphill battle."

"I'm sure it is."

Davinia picked up a spoon and stirred her tea absently. "Gabrielle lost her mother at a young age and her father had no idea how to raise a young girl. He sent her off to boarding school and showered her with gifts. I'm afraid she's a bit spoiled."

That explained some of her behavior. But not all of it.

Miranda took a breath to steady herself and smiled warmly. "That's all right. It will give us a chance to talk."

"Yes, I've wanted to talk to you." Davinia's fingers caressed the handle of her china teacup as her expression took on that drawn, tired look. "I've been wondering how the case is going. Are you close to finding who took the dagger?"

Not the first question she expected out of this lady. But it was reasonable. She gave her a canned reply. "I'm not allowed to say much. We're making about as much progress as usual at this point." If she could catch Gabrielle at whatever game she was playing.

"Poor George Eames."

"Yes," Miranda said allowing sympathy into her voice. "His lawyer hasn't been able to get him released yet."

"Such a pity. And Trenton is one of the best barristers in the city."

"Is he?" He didn't seem to be doing much for his client.

"He courted me after my first husband died."

"Trenton Jewell?"

She nodded. "He was very ambitious, always talking of big plans he had. Pipe dreams, really."

Let her talk, Miranda decided. She mirrored Davinia's movement, stirring her tea and waited.

"He even proposed marriage. But I chose Neville instead, of course." Her lips turned in a sad smile. "Lionel didn't approve of either of them. He was only a teenager then. The type who could be very vocal about his opinions. I thought he'd get used to the idea. But to this day, he resents Neville. He feels I married beneath my status."

Now they were getting somewhere. "I got that impression at dinner last night."

"Oh, Lionel doesn't hold back his feelings." Davinia took a sip of tea.

Which meant Gabrielle knew about his feelings. Probably got the brunt of his complaints. So they team up to steal the dagger? Why? To embarrass his stepdad? Make Davinia see what a fool she married? Didn't seem worth going to prison but maybe they thought they were above that. And was Lionel's friend Sebastian a part of the scheme?

Davinia's heavy sigh brought her out of her thoughts.

The woman was wringing the napkin in her lap and fighting the moisture that had suddenly appeared in her eyes. "The truth is, Ms. Steele…Neville and I haven't been happy for a long, long time."

Miranda didn't know what to say to that. She had guessed as much, but she didn't expect the lady to come out and admit it. Not to her.

"I think Neville stopped loving me years ago."

"Oh—I'm sure that's not true."

She shook her head. "All he cares about is his museum, his artifacts, his precious relics. The only time we spend together is at social gatherings. If it weren't for those, I wouldn't see him at all. We never talk. Not really. Not like we used to. Oh, dear." She took her napkin and dabbed her eyes. "I apologize. I didn't mean to unburden my soul like that."

Miranda stared at the lovely woman, suddenly feeling as sorry for her as she did for her husband. She was the last person to hand out marital advice, but she dared to reach over and touch the Lady's hand. "It's all right. I wish I could say something to help, but I'm just the investigator here. As I told your husband, Parker and I will do all we can to find the Marc Antony dagger."

"Thank you, I know you will. And I know when you do, it will ease Neville's mind." Her face went dark and a little hard. "Unfortunately, I don't think it will help our situation at all."

And so she was seeing another guy on the side because of resentment? And did that have anything to do with the theft? Miranda wasn't sure. But two things struck her hard.

First how human this noblewoman was. And second, despite her professed concerns for her husband's feelings, Lady Davinia seemed almost glad that the dagger had been stolen.

CHAPTER TWENTY-TWO

Parker paced the parquet floor beside Sir Neville's antique desk in the Director's office. He glanced at his watch again, the tension in his temples working into a headache. It seemed Miranda wasn't the only one who'd deserted him this afternoon.

Sir Neville gave him a worried look. "I can't imagine what's keeping Toby, Russell. He's always punctual."

"It's been twenty minutes," Parker pointed out.

The assistant had paged the young man three times. It looked like the intern was avoiding being questioned.

Sir Neville leaned back in his leather chair and studied the copy of the employee schedule. "Perhaps we should go look for him. Though I don't know where he'd be."

He was supposed to be in the storeroom helping to pack an exhibit to be sent to the Louvre, but he wasn't there when Sir Neville had called the supervisor a few minutes ago.

Parker blew out a frustrated breath. The boy might have left the building. If so, it would implicate him further. They would have to track him down at his residence. Perhaps get Inspector Wample involved for a warrant. Not an idea he relished.

Parker was about to ask where the employees signed out when there was a knock on the door.

"Come in," Sir Neville called.

The door opened slowly and a smiling face with wavy red hair to his shoulders appeared. "You wanted to see me, sir?"

"Yes. Come in, Toby," Sir Neville said in the tone of a trusted old friend.

The young man slipped through the opening and stood on the far end of the room, hands behind his back, soldier like. "I'm sorry I didn't see your page before, Sir Neville. I was 'elping Ms. Chopra." His youthful accent was lower class with a thin veneer of polish from his education.

"That's all right. Come in, won't you?" Sir Neville waved for the boy to enter.

Gingerly, he advanced a few steps.

He wore the plain black slacks, blue blazer and red tie at the neck that seemed to be the standard museum uniform. His eyes were bright green and with his red hair, fair complexion and a smattering of freckles across the nose, Parker could see a touch of Ireland in his features. The picture of youthful innocence. For a moment he wondered if his hunch was totally off.

"Toby, this is Mr. Parker. He's conducting an inquiry about the dagger."

"Oh. Is that what this is about?" His high-pitched voice went up a few notes.

If he'd been with Emily Chopra, he knew exactly what this was about, but he seemed surprised. Parker gave him his most ingratiating smile. "I just want to ask a few routine questions, Toby. It won't take long."

"Of course. Anything to help."

"Have a seat."

He settled into the padded leather chair across from the desk, rocking back and forth as if he couldn't find a comfortable position.

Parker sat on the edge of the desk where Miranda had been before, frustrated she wasn't here now. With no understanding of interrogation methods, Sir Neville was a poor substitute for her. But Parker needed a witness.

He began. "You've worked here about two months?"

The young man nodded vigorously and smiled. "Yessir."

"And what do your duties consist of?"

"Oh, well." He rocked some more and wiped his palms over his pant legs. "I'm an 'elper. Mostly in the storeroom. You know. Packing and unpacking deliveries, tidying up. That sort of thing. I also 'elp Ms. Chopra and Mr. Eames with their projects."

"Such as the Marc Antony dagger?"

The rocking stopped. The smile faded. "Yessir."

Parker leaned back. "And do you enjoy working with Ms. Chopra and Mr. Eames?"

The smile came back, as well as the nodding. "Oh, yessir. They're the absolute best. I've learned a lot from them."

Letting a moment pass, Parker got to his feet, picked up the clipboard with the employee names Miranda had used. Her notes were on it. He hoped Sir Neville hadn't read them. "Tell me what happened on the morning the dagger was delivered."

"Thursday morning?" His voice rose in pitch again.

"Yes. Thursday."

He blinked several times. "Well, it was stolen, as you know. Bloody awful, pardon my language."

Parker gave him a patient, fatherly smile. "I mean, tell me chronologically. When did you arrive at the museum that morning?"

"When did I arrive?" His face went blank, as if he couldn't remember. "Oh, around eight, as usual. The presentation wasn't until nine, so I went to Special Exhibits to 'elp out there. Then I went round to the café to get a coffee. Then I went down to the storeroom." As he spoke, he fidgeted in the chair, making it squeak as if it were a rocking horse with a riding-obsessed child as its owner.

It was on one of the forward rocks that Parker noticed the last button on his coat was missing. "Do you have the code to access the storeroom?"

He shook his head vehemently. "Oh, no sir. I wasn't issued the code. Someone has to let me in. Same as any other intern."

"And Thursday morning?"

"Thursday morning? Ms. Chopra and Mr. Eames were already there. One of them buzzed me in." So far, that matched Emily Chopra's narrative.

Parker turned a half step away from the boy and pretended to study the clipboard. He stole a glance at Sir Neville. The confusion on his friend's face told him he didn't see why Parker was asking questions he already knew the answers to. He needed to wrap this up.

"Did you notice anything unusual, Toby?"

"Unusual, sir?"

Parker let his gaze rest on the missing button. "In the storeroom Thursday morning."

Toby wiped his hands on his slacks again. "Oh, well. No. Everything looked in order. I...I mean everything was just as right as rain." He grinned and nodded, but there was fear in his eyes.

"Were you surprised by that?"

"No, I—What do you mean?"

Parker sighed. He set the clipboard down on the desk and moved over to the window. "Mr. Yeats, the security director, thinks someone from the museum let the thief in through the door on the side."

Toby's face went pale. "Really? Blimey. I mean. Who would do a thing like that?"

"It looks like Mr. Eames did."

Toby shook his head with even more vigor. "I don't believe that. Not for one minute. There's nobody more upstanding than Mr. Eames."

Parker pretended to study one of the potted plants on the windowsill. "And yet, he'll no doubt go to prison for this crime."

The boy fell silent, pondering that thought.

"All the evidence points to him. He's already in custody as you know."

The young man fidgeted, wiped a finger under his nose, glanced about the room as if looking for an escape. "I heard that. I—I don't know what to say."

"He'll get at least five years. Perhaps more since Buckingham Palace seems to want to make an example of him. When he gets out, he'll never be able to work in a museum again. I don't know how he'll survive. Or who will take care of his mother. Then again, he might not survive the incarceration. Can you imagine what prison will be like for a man like Mr. Eames?"

Parker risked another glance at Sir Neville. The poor man looked perfectly aghast. Parker gave him an almost imperceptible shake of his head. He returned a silent nod.

Then Parker turned back to Toby.

The boy's mouth was open. His green eyes, filled with shock, were spilling over with tears. They ran down his face and dripped onto the coat of his museum outfit. He stared at Parker a long moment, his shoulders shaking.

Parker stood, waiting, trying not to feel sorry for the lad.

At last, he lurched forward, thrust his head into his hands. "Oh, God! What 'ave I done? What 'ave I done?"

Parker moved to the boy, put a steadying hand on his shivering back. "Just tell us what you know." He glanced over at Sir Neville.

The man's eyes were wide, his mouth also gaping. He stared at Parker as if he were looking at the eighth wonder of the world.

Sir Neville got to his feet and hurried to Toby's side. Parker was afraid his friend would tell the boy not to say anything more. But he didn't.

"Toby," Sir Neville said softly. "This must be so hard for you, lad. But you must help Mr. Eames if you can."

The boy nodded. Slowly he raised his head. His eyes were red, and his face smeared with tears.

Parker reached into a pocket and gave him a handkerchief.

The boy snatched it and dabbed it under his cheek as he began to babble. "There's this bloke I used to know. Name's Malcolm. Malcolm Shrivel. Tough guy. We went to school together. Up until level ten. He dropped out after that. I heard he joined a gang in the area. Tottenham, where I grew up. My sister still lives there."

He was rambling. "What about this Malcolm?"

"Well, I hadn't seen 'im for years. Forgot about 'im, really. I wanted to get out of that area. Better myself, you know?"

"Of course, you did, Toby," Sir Neville soothed.

"About three weeks ago, I went round to Tottenham and popped into The Winkin' Owl for a pint with some of me old mates."

"The Winking Owl?" Parker asked.

"It's a pub off Broadwater Road. Me sister Winnie's a barmaid there. She'd called me and told me they'd be there, and she really wanted me to come. Said she had something to tell me."

"I see. What happened?"

"Well, Winnie was busy, so I took a table with me mates. After a pint or two and a bit of catching up, everyone decided to go home. Most of 'em had to be up for work the next day. Meself included. That was when Malcolm walked in. he's a tall one. Muscular. He'd been working out. He was all in chains and black, with his hair dyed and all spiked up. You know, tough guy look." Toby took a few quick hyperventilating breaths as if the very thought of this Malcolm was too much for him.

Parker waited for him to settle.

"So's I go over to Winnie and ask 'er what did she want to tell me. She says it's Malcolm who wanted to talk to me. And he wants to talk in the back room." He stopped, face white, breathing like a diver running out of air in his tank.

"Steady, Toby," Sir Neville purred, his hand still on the lad's shoulder.

Toby gave a quick nod. "I shouldn't 'ave gone, but I didn't 'ave much choice. I stepped back there with him. This tiny little place with no windows. He got me up against the wall and told me he was dating Winnie and what a…what a fine lay she were." He closed his eyes and took more breaths. "He said it would be a shame if anything were to happen to 'er. Like if she were to get beat up really bad and couldn't work. He said that wouldn't 'appen if I cooperated and gave 'im what he needed."

Parker narrowed his eyes with anger. "What did he need?"

Toby rubbed his hands over his slacks again and shook his bowed head from side to side. "I shouldn't 'ave done it. I shouldn't 'ave."

Sir Neville nearly shook him. "Toby, what did you do?"

The lad lifted his head with a boyish pout, his freckled cheeks wet with tears. "I gave him a keycard to the outside door and the access code to the storeroom."

Sir Neville was aghast. "How did you get the code?"

"Mr. Eames was always complaining about learning a new one every month. He mentioned he 'ad to write it down. I—I snuck into his rooms. He doesn't lock the door during the day. I found it on a slip of paper on 'is desk. Labeled and everything. I would never have done it if it weren't for Winnie."

"And the keycard?" Parker asked.

"I gave Malcolm mine and told Mr. Eames I'd lost mine. He got me a new one."

And Eames hadn't even mentioned it. Yeats didn't either, because he thought Eames to be innocent. But the police might know. And that would be the nail in the coffin of the case against him. No wonder they hadn't released him.

Parker leaned over and picked up the hem of the lad's coat. "Does this missing button mean anything?"

The boy's face went red, and he closed his eyes in pain. "That night at the pub, Malcolm tore it off me coat. I'd worn it to show off in front of me mates. Stupid. That morning. The morning the dagger was to be presented, I saw the button on the floor right next to the cart holding the crate. I thought it was some sort of message from Malcolm. A warning I had better keep quiet about all this. I kicked it under one the shelving units before anyone could see it."

And now the police had the button, too.

All at once the boy lunged forward, head in hands panicking. "Oh, God. What's going to happen to me, Sir Neville? What's going to happen to Winnie? I'm so ashamed of meself after all you've done for me. I swear I'd never 'ave done such a thing if it weren't for Winnie."

"We know, lad. We know." Sir Neville looked up at Parker with glassy blue eyes. "What are we going to do, Russell?"

There was only one thing to do. "Toby," Parker said with as much kindness in his tone as he could muster. Despite the chaos the boy had caused, his heart went out to him. "I'm afraid we have to ask you to tell your story to Inspector Wample."

Slowly the lad raised his head and stared helplessly at Parker. Then after a long moment, he nodded.

CHAPTER TWENTY-THREE

Miranda watched Lady Davinia's lips go tight with annoyance as she studied her watch before glancing anxiously around the restaurant. "Thirty-five minutes. I can't imagine what's gotten into Gabrielle."

The waiter came by with the teapot and she shook her head.

He nodded but looked annoyed.

Davinia speed dialed her phone for about the fifth time and held it to her ear. After a few moments she shook her head. "Still going to voicemail."

Miranda tapped her foot and eyed the emptying café. Someone was going to kick them out of here pretty soon.

She took a deep breath. "Why don't we try to go look for her?"

Davinia considered that a moment. "Do you think we can find her?"

Miranda shrugged. "She said she was going around the corner. Can't be far." She hoped.

"Very well." Davinia paid the bill, leaving Gabrielle's uneaten cake and the two of them headed back out to the street.

They picked their way over the cobblestones, past shoppers, bike riders, an iron barrier filled with flowers. At last, they reached the spot where Gabrielle had parked her white Mercedes. A red Peugeot sat in its place.

Lady Davinia uttered a dignified moan. "This was where we parked, wasn't it?"

"If not exactly here, it was near here. I don't see a white Mercedes anywhere."

"She drove off somewhere." Davinia sounded like a lost child. A stately, well-mannered one, but still lost.

Miranda chewed her lip. This wasn't good. It had all the earmarks of foul play. But wasn't she supposed to be the victim of some devious plot here? Maybe she'd had it all wrong. Anyway, with someone as fickle as Gabrielle, for all they knew, she was back at Selfridges trying on more dresses.

She huffed out a breath. "Let's keep looking."

They plowed across the street and trudged down the next sidewalk. Miranda was glad this block had normal cement rather than the cobblestone. They marched under multicolored flags waving overhead, past quaint bistros with colorful awnings, through outdoor cafes where people sat, having their tea under umbrellas.

Miranda eyed the patrons, peered into the store windows, especially the dress store window. But she didn't see Gabrielle Eaton's red-gold curls anywhere.

The sky was clouding over, and the temperature was dropping. Miranda wished for a coat and hoped it wouldn't rain. Especially now that she had Lady Davinia to take care of. The aristocrat might melt in a downpour.

They stepped off another curb to cross the next street.

Davinia looked up at the sky. "Our brollies are in the car, of course." She sounded like she wanted to curse. When they reached the opposite corner, she came to a halt and Miranda saw the strain on her face.

"Perhaps we should ring the police?" The woman was losing her nerve.

Miranda folded her arms and thought about it. She wasn't eager to have Inspector Wample or one of his ilk involved in this hunt. What if Gabrielle was off chatting with a friend somewhere like she'd said? It would be embarrassing.

But she knew Davinia was more worried than she showed. "I'll call Parker," she said at last, hoping that would satisfy her.

Davinia nodded and Miranda stepped into a nearby niche for some privacy and dialed.

"Parker," he answered being unnecessarily formal. It was still comforting to hear his voice.

"It's me. Can Sir Neville hear what I'm saying?"

"No. What's wrong?"

"Lady Gabrielle's missing."

"What do you mean?" The stiffness in his voice turned to concern.

"We were having tea. She got a call and said she had to step out for a few minutes and would be right back. It's been over half an hour, and we haven't seen her."

"Where are you?"

"It's probably nothing. She probably just forgot the time."

"Where are you?" he repeated in his firmest take-charge voice.

"Soho." She looked up at the street signs and gave him the crossroads.

"I'll be right there."

"We'll be in the area. We're going to keep looking."

"I'll find you." He clicked off.

She stepped out of the recess and gave Davinia a forced grin. "He's coming to help look."

The woman exhaled. "That's a relief. What should we do?"

It started to mist. Miranda considered the options and pointed left. "Let's try down that way."

They made their way down another block and a half until they reached a Tudor style building that looked like it had stood there since the Middle Ages.

Between it and the next building a low tunnel had been wedged. It had a sinister air to it.

"Let's try down here," Miranda said, plowing forward.

"All right," Davinia replied as if she had a choice and followed her down the sloping sidewalk.

The tunnel was undecorated and damp smelling. Raw brick and bare pipes lined its close walls. It was short, maybe twenty feet long. Still a good place to get rid of an enemy in the middle of the night. But it was daylight now.

Maybe she was imagining things.

At the end of the tunnel, they turned a narrow corner and were hit by a mishmash of multi-cultural food scents flavoring the air. Hispanic, Asian, Lebanese. Once again Miranda peered into the eating establishments as they went along.

No Gabrielle.

They passed a movie theater, a storefront with a "We Buy Gold" sign in the window, an import and export wholesaler, a place with a gunmetal facade and Asian and English characters. The ones she could read spelled out "Bar Shu."

Chinatown.

Could Gabrielle have gone this far? For all they knew, she could be back at the restaurant where they'd had tea, fussing at the waiters for letting them leave.

Miranda stopped. She looked up the road they were on, then down it. The sky was getting darker, the mist heavier.

"What is it?" Davinia wanted to know.

"Try Gabrielle's cell one more time."

Davinia's frown was skeptical, but she took out her phone and dialed again. They waited.

It rang. Once, twice. Softly, somewhere in the distance synthesized tones with a funky, syncopated beat played. Then stopped.

"Voicemail." Davinia's eyes went wide. "Where did that ringtone come from?"

"Dial her again."

She did and the music played once more. Miranda followed it, a hound on a scent. The sound stopped. "Dial again," she barked.

"Yes, yes." Davinia trotted after her.

The music started again. She hurried down the sidewalk to a narrow side street. The tone got louder. She rounded the corner—and let out a gasp.

There in front of an empty storefront with Asian characters over a window nobody had bothered to translate, sat the Mercedes.

Miranda hurried to it. The car had been pulled up on the sidewalk. The passenger side had been rammed into the wall. The driver's door hung open. The cell phone lay on the pavement.

She ran up to the vehicle, peered inside.

Nobody there.

She rushed around the front fender. And stopped.

Damn.

Her whole body began to quake at the sight on the pavement, as if of their own accord the stones were cracking and breaking into pieces beneath her feet like in some end-of-the-world horror flick. Her lungs felt like they were suddenly flooded with the smothering mist in the air. The crab she'd had for lunch cracked through her stomach lining and clawed its way up her spine, scraping her nerve endings as it went.

No, it wasn't the crab. It was that damn, annoying sensation she'd been feeling. The one she hadn't been paying enough attention to. The one she thought she could do without on this case. The one that always led her to scenes like this. She'd thought this case would be boring, unchallenging, not worth the effort. Hardly.

She stared down at the clump of white silk with the silver bangle-bling that lay tangled over the body. The long arms and legs in distorted positions seemed to pool over the pavement along with the blood. Lots of blood.

Her face was turned in an unnatural way, the green eyes that had glittered with life not an hour ago were now open, unseeing, a look of horror frozen on them. And in the middle of her back, the source of all that blood was—the Marc Antony dagger.

Guilt suddenly flooded her. Because she'd thought this case would be boring, unchallenging, not worth the effort, Gabrielle Eaton was dead.

She heard bells ringing. Big Ben clanging out the time. Gradually she became aware of a whining sound beside her. Slowly it grew louder. Louder. Turned into audible words.

"This can't be happening. This can't be happening. This can't be happening."

Lady Davinia.

Miranda forced herself to snap out of her stupor and her lungs to suck in air. She tiptoed around the body, avoiding the blood, trying not to contaminate the scene. She bent down and laid two fingers along the neck for good measure. For the dictates of her training. She knew what she'd feel.

Nothing.

She glared at the open car door. Gabrielle had been driving. Maybe she'd gotten jacked. She tried to escape by ramming the Mercedes into the wall. Then she jumped out and ran for her life. But the killer caught her.

One scenario. But what was a random carjacker doing with the Marc Antony dagger?

She got up, made her way back to Davinia, and grabbed the hysterical countess.

"Why? I don't understand."

"I don't either." Forcibly, she turned the woman around so she wasn't facing the scene any longer.

That was when she saw the man. And the woman beside him.

"Who the hell are you?" she barked.

"We saw you run down here. Has there been an…accident?"

Somehow Miranda managed to shake her head in answer. "There's been a murder."

CHAPTER TWENTY-FOUR

The man, or somebody, called 911. It wasn't really 911, it was 999 or something like that. Miranda didn't know.

All she knew was that she felt almost giddy when Parker showed up just before the police. He broke through the crowd of gawkers that had gathered, his face as hard as iron.

He took in the scene and turned toward where he'd emerged. "Stay back," he barked. But he wasn't addressing the crowd.

Then she saw Sir Neville coming up behind him. That's who he was talking to.

Ignoring Parker's command, Sir Neville took a few steps toward the scene and stopped. His face turned as white as the vehicle. "Merciful Heavens! What on earth happened?" There was heartbreaking terror in his gentle voice.

Miranda was afraid the frail man might have a heart attack on the spot.

Davinia burst forward and threw herself into her husband's arms. "Oh, Neville, Neville. What are we to do? It's our Gabby? Our Gabby."

Blinking in confusion, "Gabby? Is that Gabby?"

He must not have seen it was her on the ground. Miranda was glad for the gawkers blocking the view.

"Yes. Oh, God. Yes." Davinia pressed her face into his chest and sobbed.

As if he didn't know what to do, Sir Neville gingerly wrapped his arms around his wife, stroked her back to soothe her, though that was impossible for either of them. "What happened?" he asked again, his voice empty and lost.

Miranda gave Parker a steady gaze. Up to her to explain. "Lady Gabrielle got a call when we were having tea," she told him. "She said she was going to see a friend for a few minutes, but she didn't come back. We went to look for her and found…this."

"Stand back. Let us through." The police were here, thank God.

Officers began pushing back the crowd and cordoning off the crime scene. It wasn't until then that Miranda noticed a redheaded young man dressed in the museum uniform, bracing himself against a wall with one hand. His mouth gaped open, and his face was smeared with tears. He bent forward, holding the other hand to his middle as if he had a bad stomachache.

And then she realized his jaw was moving and she heard his screams. "All my fault. All my fault."

Was that the intern they were going to interview? She looked at Parker.

He read the question on her face and nodded. "We got a break in the case. Unfortunately, it seems to have come too late."

She wanted to know what he'd learned, but there was too much commotion.

"You should take Lady Davinia back to the car," Parker said quietly to Sir Neville.

He nodded and began guiding his wife back through the crowd. Just as they disappeared a team of CSIs—or whatever they were called here—showed up. They assembled around the gory scene and began to examine the car and the body.

There was more shouting. Behind them the crowd parted, and tall, lean Inspector Wample appeared with Assistant Chief Officer Ives in tow, both of them wearing the same raincoats she'd met them in.

Miranda felt Parker tense beside her.

Wample gave them a look of indignation when he spotted them and marched over. "You two sticking your noses in where they don't belong again?"

Resisting the urge to punch the guy in the stomach, Miranda repeated her story about the tea, the call, and the hunt for Lady Gabrielle.

Wample nodded. "I'll need a statement from you."

"Be happy to give it."

Without making a move, Parker gave the man a cold, steady gaze. "Perhaps now, Inspector," he said, "you'll be more willing for us to work with you."

Wample stared at him a moment as if it had suddenly dawned on him that might not be a bad idea. But instead of welcoming them aboard, he spat out a scoff and strode over to the crew to inspect their work.

He peered over the technicians crouched around the body. Miranda watched his thin-lipped mouth drop open. "Is that—?"

"Yessir," said a young woman snapping a photo of the blood on the pavement. "It's Lady Gabrielle Eaton."

"I heard who the victim is." He jerked his hand at the body. "Is that the relic that was stolen from the museum?"

"It appears to be, sir."

Miranda leaned close to Parker to whisper. "He's going to call this case closed. Parker, we have to find out who did this whether Wample wants our help or not."

He didn't say anything. He only gave his head one quick determined nod.

"Let me through. For heaven's sake, let me through!" It was Sir Neville. He was back without Davinia this time.

Miranda hoped he'd taken her to the car. The poor woman was beside herself with agony.

He fought his way over to the inspector. "My wife told me…she said…the dagger?" He couldn't see it before for the gawkers.

Wample turned and regarded him with both frustration and compassion. "Yes, Sir Neville. It seems we've recovered it."

An officer tried to keep him back, but Sir Neville managed to position himself to get a clear view of the body. "Oh, my God. My God! My God!"

His cries broke Miranda's heart. He shouldn't have to look at that scene. She marched across the pavement to him, took his arm. "Sir Neville, why don't you go back to the car?"

"Yes. Lady Davinia needs you now." With the same intention Parker had come around to his other side.

He shook them both off, glaring down at the dagger, a crazed look in his eyes. "I need to see it. I need to see it."

What was he doing? Trying to punish himself for this? It wasn't his fault. Not one little bit. "You really shouldn't."

Miranda stared down at Lady Gabrielle's lifeless body and realized one of the CSIs was carefully removing the murder weapon from the victim. Its golden hilt, littered with ancient Egyptian markings in exotic blues and greens, glinted in the light. The blade, red with blood, looked razor sharp, despite its age. Would have to be to use it like that.

"I must see it. Inspector, I must insist on examining that dagger."

Inspector Wample rose from where he'd been crouching and regarded the man. He could have called an officer to take Sir Neville away. Instead, he turned to one of the technicians. "Get him a pair of gloves."

Someone responded and Sir Neville pulled on the gloves.

At Wample's direction, the tech cautiously handed the dagger to the museum director. He took it in his hands as if it were a newborn baby. He stared at it a long while then turned it over. He seemed to study every millimeter of the artifact.

"The Marc Antony dagger," he began after steadying himself, "was discovered over two years ago in Cleopatra's mausoleum off the Alexandria coast." Not news to anyone who'd followed this case, but they were all humoring the poor man. "I was there when they recovered it. It was documented in my presence. I wrote the provenance myself."

Miranda looked at Parker. His expression was wary.

With a gentle move, Sir Neville turned the blade over and pointed at the broad piece of gold just below the hilt. "Right here, on the quillon was an inscription in the hieroglyphics of the time. Roughly translated, it read, 'Be victorious in every battle, my love.'"

Wample began to fidget, shifted his weight. He wasn't enjoying the ancient history lesson. "What are you trying to tell us, Sir Neville?"

Sir Neville looked up at him, his eyes as glassy as if he'd just woken out of a dream. Or a nightmare. "The inscription isn't here. This dagger is a fake."

Miranda felt a little dizzy. That wasn't the Marc Antony dagger? Not the priceless piece stolen from the museum's storeroom? She guessed this case wasn't closed after all.

The thought must have struck Wample at the same time. His mouth opened in a distorted gape, and his gaze fixed on Sir Neville as if he were holding a deadly cobra. Whether he saw his position or his pension or just his pride crumbling before his eyes, Miranda couldn't tell.

But he knew this thing was a lot bigger than he'd thought.

Slowly he cocked his head toward her and Parker, the snake look still in his eyes, and spoke in a strained voice through gritted teeth. "Mr. Parker, Ms. Steele, Scotland Yard requests your assistance."

CHAPTER TWENTY-FIVE

While they waited for the inspector to finish up, Miranda and Parker worked their way through the crowd, which had only grown bigger, and helped Sir Neville back to the car. Parker arranged for their things to be brought back to the hotel where they were going to stay in the first place, while she went back to collect Toby Waverly.

The young man was still leaning against the wall in shock.

Miranda took his arm, and he came along meekly as they pushed back through the gawkers and stepped into the street where the heavy mist had turned into fog curling in the air like smoke after a fire. As she hunted for the inspector's car, she wondered what Toby had told Parker.

She was about to ask when a woman in a slick pale business suit stuck a microphone under her chin.

"Well, look who's here," she said in a jaunty, crisp accent. "It's Miranda Steele from America. Ms. Steele, can you tell us what happened here?"

"What?" Miranda glared at the woman as the words "reporter" and "insensitive" registered in her head at the same time.

"We understand there's been an incident here in Soho. Does it bear any resemblance, do you think, to your last case in Las Vegas?"

Miranda's glare turned to shock. How did this person know about her last case? "No comment," she said firmly, suppressing a growl.

The woman looked back at her camera and smiled. "Well, you certainly had a good bit to say at that press conference in America a few weeks ago."

Yeah, it had been on the news. She didn't realize they'd watch it all the way over here. Guess investigating the death of a celebrity gave you the status of a celebrity. Not something she wanted at all.

"I'm sorry. You'll have to speak to Inspector Wample about that." She pointed down the alley and when the woman craned her neck to see the man in charge, Miranda ducked into the police car.

It seemed to take forever before Parker found her and Wample and Ives slid into the front seats, but at last they took off and left the tragic scene behind. Except for the vestiges that followed them, as always.

It took another forty minutes to wind their way through traffic to Victoria Street before they reached the New Scotland Yard building.

They parked in the lot and went in the back way. Instead of using a dank little interrogation room in the bowels of the place, like they had to do when they talked to George Eames, Wample took everyone to his office on the seventeenth floor.

It was a tidy, open space. Fairly large, with just the bare essentials. Desk, chairs, computer screen and keyboard, corkboard on the wall where schedules and data from recent cases were neatly posted.

Wample took a seat behind the big desk, the row of tall windows overlooking the neighboring building at his back, and gestured to the guest chairs.

There were only two, so Ives offered one first to Miranda, then to Parker. They both refused it, preferring to stand.

With a nod Ives sat Toby Waverly down in the other chair while Wample pulled out a recorder and switched it on.

"What do you know about the murder?" Ives said.

The boy shook his head back and forth, a look of terror in his big eyes. "Murder? I don't know about that, sir. I'm here about what 'appened at the museum."

"Go on then."

They watched him fidget like he had a terminal case of hives while he told his story in an accent that betrayed his working-class roots.

As she listened, Miranda felt every nerve in her body tense. She couldn't believe what she was hearing.

A guy, a bloke, Toby had known in high school contacted him through his sister and got Toby to give him the codes to the museum. The scum-wad douchebag threatened his sister with physical harm.

So Parker's hunch about the intern had been right.

"But what does this creep have to do with Lady Gabrielle Eaton?" she wondered out loud.

Wample eyed her over his cup of coffee. "The two cases may be unrelated."

That was true. This Malcolm jerk took the real dagger and someone else killed Lady Gabrielle with a fake dagger because…She had no idea.

She scratched at her hair. "Why would someone murder Sir Neville's daughter-in-law with a fake dagger?"

"And where did they get it?" Parker wanted to know.

"According to my research," Ives replied, "since the story of the dagger's discovery broke, there have been hundreds of cheap counterfeits produced for souvenir, novelty shops."

Miranda wanted to kick something. "You mean anyone could get one?"

Ives lifted his hefty shoulders. "Afraid so."

That really narrowed it down.

Parker wasn't convinced. "A souvenir sharp enough to kill with? Most souvenir daggers barely work as letter openers." Miranda recalled seeing something like that on his desk at home though it wasn't Egyptian.

Ives shrugged. "Apparently this one was better quality than average."

Wample set down his cup and scowled at Ives. "Go access HOLMES and see if this Malcolm arsewipe has a rap sheet."

"Yessir." Ives popped up out of his chair and disappeared out the door.

Miranda turned to Wample. "Holmes?"

Wample smirked at her ignorance. "Home Office Large Major Enquiry System. Our computer system."

"Nice. Hope it's got the answers we want." They wouldn't be so elementary.

Antsy, Miranda paced over to the window and stared out at the droplets forming on the glass. Her gaze focused on the modern-looking building across the street, then downward. The sky had turned dark, and the rain was making umbrellas go up on the street below, as it turned the pavement a deeper gray.

She began to think out loud. "Shrivel might have gotten the fake dagger and killed Lady Gabrielle to take the heat off the theft."

Wample's chair squeaked as he considered the thought. "Targeting the museum director's daughter-in-law? He'd know the dagger would be ID'd as a fake."

"Most criminals aren't that smart." She turned to Toby. "Was this guy bright?"

"I dunno. 'E's not stupid. 'E's mostly scary."

Yeah. And why risk a murder rap?

Miranda let out a long breath. Who else would kill Lady Gabrielle? Sure, she could be annoying, but she didn't seem to have any real enemies. On the other hand, Miranda had only known the young countess a few days. They should ask Sir Neville or Lady Davinia. Maybe after they had a chance to settle in at home.

Home. Miranda thought of Lionel and wondered if he'd been told of his wife's death yet and how he was taking it.

Gabrielle and Lionel Eaton seemed to have a less than ideal relationship. At dinner last night, he'd flirted with Miranda then stated openly he'd married his wife for her position. That must have gone over well. If they fought, if there was a deep-seated animosity between them? Enough to make a husband kill?

She was getting ahead of herself.

Before she could make another comment, Ives was back.

He shoved a photo printout under Toby's nose. "Is this the bloke?"

Toby looked down at it and winced. "Yessir. That's Malcolm."

Miranda stepped over and peered over the young man's shoulder.

Malcolm Shrivel. Twenty-one. Five-nine. Dropped out of school at Level Ten.

Narrow face. Long, knobby nose. Pale face. Sported a punk look. Black spiky hair. Tight black shirt. Silver spike through one earlobe. A sullen look in a pair of dark, sunken eyes.

The kind of guy that would turn someone like Toby into an even bigger quivering lump of jelly than he was at the moment.

"And the rap sheet?" Wample asked.

"He's got one all right. Been arrested a number of times on theft and drug charges. Did time on only one."

Miranda squinted down at the paper. "Says he's purported to be a member of a street gang known as the Stingers."

Toby's eyes went round as he sucked in a gasp. "Blimey. I've heard of those guys. They're terrifying."

"We know them, too." Wample said.

"Their ringleader's a bloke who goes by the name Scorpion. Ever hear of him?"

Toby shook his head.

Ives handed him another picture. "Have you seen this guy?"

Squirming in the chair, Toby studied it, shook his head. "No, sir. Not that I recall. And I think I would recall someone like that."

Once more Miranda peered over the boy's shoulder.

No wonder Toby was squirming.

This guy was older. Early thirties. He'd been around. Stocky, closely cropped dark hair, thick black brows. Almost good-looking. Head tilted in a cocky, what-are-you-lookin'-at-me-for? attitude that said he was as arrogant as he was sure of his power.

"Arrested on suspicion of drug dealing," Ives said. "The hard stuff. 'Eroin and crack-cocaine. We think 'e's an importer. No proof, though. Charges were dropped. Trenton Jewell defended 'im."

Really? Was this Scorpion the mastermind behind the museum theft and Lady Gabrielle's murder? The thought sent an icy chill down Miranda's spine.

Wample got to his feet and gestured to Ives. "Let's go pick up this Shrivel character and bring him in for questioning."

Toby jumped up, both hands stretched, pleading. "Oh, you can't do that. Please, sir. Please."

"Why not?"

"'E'll know I shopped him. 'E'll hurt my sister."

Wample and Ives looked at each other. The police usually didn't have the means for taking care of assaults before they happened.

With a casual gait Parker strolled across the room to Ives from where he'd been standing observing the scene. He took the papers from him, studied them a long moment then turned to Wample. "Why don't you let us look into this?"

Wample's face went dark. "It's an official police matter, Mr. Parker."

"I realize that. But we have methods the police aren't at liberty to use."

Wample smirked. "I imagine you do. And evidence from those methods usually isn't admissible in court."

Parker's slow grin was as casual as his shrug. "Inspector, I haven't stayed in business for over fifteen years by delivering inadmissible evidence."

Touché, Miranda thought.

The Inspector's mouth went back and forth as he considered it. He tapped his fingers on the desk, turned to stare out his window and sighed. "Very well, Mr. Parker. You have twenty-four hours."

Parker put a hand on Miranda's elbow to lead her out of the office. "Then my partner and I had better get busy." At the door, he stopped and turned back. "And I assume, Inspector, you'll be releasing George Eames now?"

Narrowing his eyes, Wample gave him a curt nod.

CHAPTER TWENTY-SIX

They caught a cab to the hotel. In terms of fancy, the suite turned out to be a step down from their rooms at Eaton House, with deep purple brocade curtains on the windows, standard classic furniture and an even more standard-looking bed.

It had a shower, thank God, which pushed it up in the competition in her opinion. But Miranda barely noticed the décor.

She tried out the shower while Parker ordered room service and a rental car. She changed while he took his turn.

"How are we going to find this guy?"

"I've got his address from the rap sheet," Parker called through the open bathroom door. He'd memorized it. "We'll start there."

"What about that pub where Toby met Shrivel?"

"The Winking Owl? If he's not at home, we'll try there." He stepped out of the bathroom, a towel around his waist. His salt-and-pepper hair was tussled and sexy, his muscled body tempting and delicious. If only they could stop a moment and indulge themselves a little.

But there was no time.

"He might have skipped town."

"Perhaps. But I'll wager he feels safe under Scorpion's protection."

She thought about the evidence. "When the police finish processing Gabrielle's phone, I'll bet the last call she got will be from that creep."

"If he was sloppy."

"Right." They could hope, anyway. But if the guy was smart, if the murder was planned, the only evidence to convict would be what they could get out of him.

She pulled on a pair of black jeans and her toughest-looking top and wished for her spiked belt and leather boots. Her dark running shoes would have to do.

Her mind was going a mile a minute. "How did Shrivel know there was a code to the storeroom? How did he know he'd need a keycard to get in?"

"And that there wouldn't be a security camera at that door?" Parker echoed. She looked over at him.

He'd chosen dark jeans and a tight black top that showed off his muscles almost as clearly as when he'd stood before her half naked a moment ago. He looked tough and mouthwatering at the same time.

"What are the police doing with Toby Waverly?" she wondered as she stepped into her shoes.

"Charging him with accessory to the theft, I would think."

"Too bad. He seemed like a good kid. He was just trying to protect his sister."

"Let's hope a lawyer can get the charges dropped once the real thief is behind bars."

"Yeah." She sank down on the end of the bed, the impact of the last few hours sinking in.

It had been a rotten day all around. If they could do just a little tonight to help find the thief, especially if he was also Gabrielle's killer, it would make things a tad better. But it wouldn't bring the young woman back to life.

Parker strolled over to the dresser and slipped his keys into his pocket. As he reached for his cell phone, it went off. He picked it up. "Yes?"

He listened a moment, his face grave. "I'm so sorry. Let me put you on speaker, Neville. I'm in the hotel with Miranda." He hit a button and sat down next to her on the bed.

"How's Lady Davinia holding up?" she asked.

His deep sigh came over the speaker. "As well as can be expected. She took a sedative. She's sleeping now."

Best thing for her, Miranda supposed.

"The thing I wanted to tell you both—" He paused, as if ashamed. "Oh, Russell. What a fool I've been."

Parker frowned with concern. "What do you mean?"

"I'd forgotten about it. It must have been a fortnight ago. Not more than two weeks before the dagger was scheduled to arrive…"

"What?"

"Gabby showed a sudden interest in the dagger. She asked me where it had been found, what it looked like, how it would be delivered. I thought she was maturing. I told her everything. If only I'd thought to ask her why she wanted to know."

Miranda looked at Parker. "Everything?"

"I told her about the inscription, and…" He sounded as if he were about to weep.

"Go on," Parker said gently.

At last, the words came tumbling out. "She asked about where the dagger would be stored. How it would be kept safe. She said she was worried about it. And so I explained how our security system works to her. To reassure her. And…after that she didn't ask any more questions. I thought she had gone on to something new that had attracted her attention. She was like that, you know."

"Yes." Parker's face mirrored the pain in Sir Neville's voice. "Is there anything else?"

There was a long pause as the poor man collected himself. "No. I just wish...I had thought of this earlier."

"It's all right. We know it now. Thank you. Why don't you get some rest?"

"Yes. Yes, I should. Thank you for your help, Russell. And you, too, Miranda."

"You're very welcome," she told him, meaning it with all her heart.

"Good night." He clicked off.

They both were silent a long while. Then Miranda turned to Parker. "Surely Lady Gabrielle Eaton didn't hang out with the likes of a gang member from a bad part of town."

"I'd say that's unlikely."

"So how did that information get from her to Malcolm Shrivel?"

"Perhaps we'll discover that at The Winking Owl tonight."

Would they find Shrivel there? Maybe. Probably Toby's sister would be there, Miranda hoped. Could they find out what they needed to know and keep the sister from harm, too? Miranda wasn't sure. Guys like that didn't have to wait around for a reason to use their girl's face for a punching bag. She knew that firsthand.

Room service arrived and Miranda's mouth watered at the delicious odors. Coffee, a couple of thick burgers and a pile of fries. "Universal comfort food." Relieved she'd finally have something normal to eat, she sat down and dug in.

After letting her get halfway through the meal, Parker set down his cup and regarded her steadily.

She swallowed the bite she had in her mouth. "What?"

"Before I put him on speaker Sir Neville said he'd told Lionel about what happened. He arrived home shortly after they did and hadn't heard anything."

"How'd he take it?" She snagged a fry and put it in her mouth.

"Not well. Blames himself. Says he treated her badly."

She picked up her coffee cup. Couldn't contradict that, but it didn't make him the cause of her death. Unless...She put the cup back down. "Do you think he had anything to do with it?"

"There isn't anything to indicate that at this point."

"Or not indicate it." They knew so little about these secretive people.

Parker let out a deep sigh. "Sir Neville told me when Lionel went to pieces tonight, Davinia began screaming at him about the dagger. She said if it wasn't for the dagger none of this would have happened."

"She's hysterical."

"Yes."

"Poor Sir Neville. Poor lady." She picked up the burger and chewed thoughtfully, imagining what it was like at Eaton House now with the endless halls echoing with grief and tears. After her afternoon with Davinia, she was beginning to like the woman. "I don't think she and Sir Neville have a very good marriage."

"No. It doesn't seem so."

"I overheard them arguing last night before dinner. And at the restaurant today Davinia told me she feels neglected."

Parker finished his food and wiped his mouth, his face grim. "Neville told me he thinks she's going to leave him."

Miranda stared at him. "For that Sebastian guy?"

"Probably."

She wished she'd had a chance to ask Davinia about that.

"That might change now," Parker offered.

"You're right." Hard to plan a funeral and a divorce at the same time. Funny how life could sock you right in the gut sometimes.

She stuffed the last bite of burger into her mouth, swallowed, and got to her feet. "We've got to get this guy, Parker."

"We will."

CHAPTER TWENTY-SEVEN

He paced back and forth in his narrow room, his head splitting.

He rarely drank, but tonight he opened a cupboard and poured himself a glass of old English rum. Ten-year-old alcohol. One of the few vestiges of antiquity that would truly be in his possession.

He swallowed down a draught and relished the burning in his throat. He set the glass on his desk and sank down into his chair, stared at his library.

Why could he never have what he wanted? Why did things always go wrong for him? He'd planned everything so carefully. He'd thought he'd had it all under control. He'd thought he'd be happy by now.

He'd thought he could fix things, but he couldn't. He couldn't fix anything. He leaned on the desk and put his head in his hands, guilt chewing his heart to bits. Oh, dear God. Gabrielle Eaton. That poor woman cut down in the prime of her life? How could he have let that happen?

He'd wanted to wound Neville but not like this.

He'd gotten in over his head. He'd been a fool. He should go to Inspector Wample. Confess it all. But how could he? He'd lose everything. What else could he do? His mind searched for possibilities. Go on as if nothing had happened? Leave the country? In the end, he could come up with only one solution that made sense. That would work. He'd thought about ending it before. Perhaps now was the time.

If he wasn't too cowardly to do it.

CHAPTER TWENTY-EIGHT

The ride to Tottenham was nerve-racking.

It was dark. It was rainy. Everything was on the wrong side of the road.

Parker drove—she wasn't getting behind the wheel—but it still made Miranda feel uneasy sitting up front where the driver's side should be.

They sloshed their way down the narrow city streets, zigzagging through roundabouts, past shops, pedestrians and endless rows of old buildings. While the wipers kept time to Miranda's heartbeat, in the distance Big Ben tolled nine.

Twenty-four hours. Less than that now. And thirty minutes or so of that went by before they reached the Tottenham area.

It was a tough-looking spot. No graffiti on the walls or trash on the sidewalks like you'd see in certain places of New York, but it had a tired, rundown look.

Little groups of leather-and-chain types gathered in dark recesses along the streets, smoking and sneering at passersby. From a corner a pale young woman leered at them with a drug-induced stare. In the gutter the glint of what looked like a syringe needle glittered. Miranda wondered how mild-mannered Toby Waverly had survived growing up here.

Parker pulled down a one-way lane lined on either side by a row of tidy brick houses and slowed.

"This is the street." His voice was low and ominous.

Miranda eyed a trio of toughies perched on a brick wall that ran in front of the buildings. They eyed her right back. "Looks like the welcoming committee's here to greet us."

Parker's jaw tightened. He nodded ahead. "Fourth one down. With the blue gate."

It was hard to make out the color in the dim streetlights, but the gate stood open and led to a framed entranceway of a small, two-story house. Homey lights shone through lace curtains hanging in a bay window.

"Maybe lives with his 'mum.'"

"Possibly."

119

And maybe she could tell them whether old Malcolm had been in Soho that afternoon.

Parker slowed as they neared the house, about to pull over when the front door opened and a tall, lanky figure appeared.

Like the others in the area, he was in leather and chains, all black. He had a cigarette in his mouth, its fire lighting up the face and outlining the spiked hair just enough to tell her this was the guy she'd seen in the photo in Inspector Wample's office.

"Follow him?" she whispered as if the guy could hear her.

"Exactly."

The car was pointing the opposite direction, so Parker pulled around the block and they picked up the guy just as he crossed the street at the end of it and headed in the opposite direction. Parker lingered back, let another car pull out in front of them while Miranda kept an eye on the dark figure moving ahead of them.

Two blocks down he rounded a corner. They cruised that way and when they reached it, she spotted a pub at the next light on the far corner. Had to be where he was heading.

Parker waited, followed slowly. As they neared, she read the sign over the door. The Winking Owl.

"That's the place Toby Waverly told us about?" It seemed too nice for a dive.

"Yes. Apparently Shrivel's a regular," Parker said as Shrivel slipped through the corner entrance.

Made sense to be regular if he was after Toby's sister.

The Winking Owl was a smallish place. The Tudor frame, old-fashioned lamps, and the medieval style sign over the door told her it might have stood here for centuries. The place where factory workers of yesterdays stopped in for a pint after a sixteen-hour day.

Tonight it was lit up and crowded. Cars lined both sides of the street, but Parker found a spot down the road and pulled over to the curb.

He turned off the engine and they sat there a moment studying the patrons going in. They needed a plan.

"Maybe we should go in separately," she said.

"Separately?"

"So nobody suspects we're together. Once we spot Shrivel, I can act like I'm cruising. You know, flirt with him. Dance with him."

Parker turned his head to her and slowly raised a brow. He didn't care for that idea at all.

She huffed out a breath. "You know I used to beat up guys in bars for fun."

"I'm sure you're quite capable of taking care of yourself. And your idea has merit."

"But…?"

"It might not be the best approach."

She folded her arms. "Okay, let's hear your idea."

"If Shrivel is our suspect, that means he just committed murder. He's not going to let slip any stray details about his whereabouts this afternoon to a stranger he meets in a bar."

He had a point. The guy couldn't be that stupid. And it would probably take a long time and a lot of beers to get even a little bit of information out of him.

"The better tactic might be observation."

"You mean stay incognito and just see what he does?"

Parker nodded. "For the time being. We can close in at whatever point we feel it's necessary."

Sounded good. Still, if this guy was Gabrielle Eaton's killer, she was hoping for a chance to kick the shit out of him.

She reached for the door handle. "Okay. Let's go then."

The pub was smoky and loud and packed to the gills. Polished wood covered the floor and the walls where green globe sconces and posters of the local soccer team hung. In one corner a jukebox competed with a TV playing some sports station, the jukebox clearly winning. In the opposite corner a group of rowdy young men were tossing darts at a board.

There were dark booths and small tables—all full.

They sidled up to the bar and Parker ordered two bottles of a German beer Miranda didn't recognize.

It took awhile to get the drinks.

There were only three bartenders, each of them dressed in green vests and bowties, each of them humping it, racing around trying to keep everyone served. A young guy with a strained look worked a tap while a dark-haired girl shoved bottles into customers' hands and hurried around the bar to see what the four guys pounding on the table and shouting for service wanted.

Miranda lingered at the bar a moment, studying the third barkeep. Shock of red hair pulled back in a messy bun, freckles across the nose. She'd bet her paycheck that was Winnie Waverly, Toby's sister.

The girl turned to set down a drink and she got a glimpse of her face. Lots of makeup. Too much, especially under one eye. It was hard to tell under the lights, but Winnie might have been hiding a bruise.

Anger boiled in Miranda's gut, but she knew she had to keep her cool.

She followed Parker to a spot at the end of the bar where someone had vacated a stool and sat down. Parker hovered behind her. She could feel his body tense and ready to pounce like a wolf on the hunt.

They scanned the room.

Three couples stuffed into a booth across the way. Four card players at a table next to them. Miranda eyed the faces at each table one by one. When she got to the end of the row of booths, she thought the last one was empty. Until she saw the shape of a booted foot sticking out.

A dark figure leaned forward from the wooden seat and rose.

The leather and chains were almost camouflage in this place. But the spiky hair, the narrow face and nose, the sunken eyes gave him away.

"It's him," she whispered over her shoulder to Parker.

"I see."

Shrivel stuck his thumbs in his belt and sauntered over to the bar like he thought he was a cowboy in an old Western. He pushed the people in front of him away and glared at the redheaded barmaid.

She ignored him.

His fist came down hard on the bar's surface. "Service!" he bellowed.

Alarm in her eyes, she turned and hurried over to him, presumably to shut him up.

As soon as she reached him, he grabbed her by the lapels of her vest and gave her a shake. He pulled her close and muttered something to her.

Miranda went rigid. She felt Parker's body tighten behind her.

"Patience," he breathed.

Winnie took Shrivel's hands and pulled them off her as she replied.

Yeah, patience. But if that jerk did anything else, Miranda was going to have to go over there and bloody his lip. If Parker didn't beat her to it.

The bastard reached for Winnie again, but she ducked away in time. He was about to lunge. Miranda shot up from her stool.

But before she could move someone came up behind the guy and yanked at his arm. He spun around. They spoke just a few words. Then they turned and headed out the door.

"Let's go," Parker said.

But Miranda was already pushing through the crowd.

CHAPTER TWENTY-NINE

As soon as they stepped outside and into the damp night air, Miranda saw Shrivel and his buddy hop on a motorcycle and take off.

"Damn." She turned and scrambled for the rental car with Parker right beside her.

The car was around the corner, down the street. They raced to it as fast as they could. But as Miranda yanked the door open and jumped inside, she feared they'd already lost him.

Parker started the car and tore off down the street and around the corner. Finally, the glow of the cycle's taillights appeared as they halted at a stoplight, and Parker slowed.

"We've got them now," he breathed, and she heard the anxiety in his voice.

"Where are they going?"

"We're about to find out."

They tailed the cycle through a maze of old, narrow streets, the shops growing grimier, the buildings rattier, and the corners darker as they went. At last, the cycle turned down a tiny little road with a brick wall on one side and rows of old rusty warehouses on the other. Chicken wire and chain link fences and locked gates stretched along the properties, all topped with barbed wire to keep out intruders.

The cycle pulled up to one of the gates. Shrivel hopped off the back, opened the entry with a key from his pocket. The bike cruised into the yard. Shrivel shut the gate while his partner leaned the cycle against a wall, and the pair went inside the building through a side door.

The warehouse had a sign boasting batteries and car repairs, but most of the lettering was worn off. Still there were enough service vans and vehicles in its shadowy parking lot to indicate it was still in business.

The heavy garage-type doors were shut, and there were no windows on this side. A dim streetlamp was the only light, and it cast creepy shadows along the walls.

Parker idled near the entrance, a black van parked along the street hiding the rental car from view. He tapped his fingers on the steering wheel.

Miranda eyed the gate. "That barbed wire looks electrified."

"There might be another way in."

"You think we should go in?" She was all for rough and tumble, but they had no idea if anyone else was in there. Or how many of them there were. Or what they were doing.

"Let's see what we can find."

He eased around the block, past houses and hedgerows, a filling station, more houses, until he reached another repair shop that seemed to border the other one. This one was bordered with chicken wire and the enclosure here was lower and didn't have barbed wire.

"We could scale that fence," Miranda said.

But would that lead to the right place? Even if it did what would they do when they were inside? They didn't even have weapons.

Parker studied the grounds for a long moment then pulled off again and headed back around to the first repair shop.

They were just passing it when the side door opened, and several dark figures emerged from the shadows. Two big thug-types. Shrivel. The buddy. And a shorter, stocky guy. If she wasn't mistaken...

"Is that Scorpion?" The guy in the picture Ives had shown her in Wample's office? The leader of the street gang named the Stingers?

"Keep an eye on them." Parker passed by slowly, as if he were heading straight home while Miranda twisted around in the seat to get a better view.

It didn't look like anybody had noticed the car.

The short guy gave Shrivel a hard shove, and he stumbled backward, catching himself on the hood of a car. The guy waved his hands then pointed to the two thugs.

Shrivel made a pleading gesture.

Short guy pointed at the cycle then off in the distance.

Shrivel nodded and headed for the bike while everyone else disappeared again into the repair shop's shadows.

"The leader looks like he's mad at Shrivel about something," she said. "He just sent the jerk away on the cycle."

"Some sort of errand?"

"Doesn't look like he's going for fish and chips."

Parker pulled around the block once again. At the end of the last road, they found Shrivel cruising along.

He slowed at a corner, made the turn onto a main road, and with the rental car tailing right behind, the cycle roared off into the night.

CHAPTER THIRTY

Street after street they followed the cycle's red taillights.

Through a dozen intersections, past parks and shops and government buildings. Miranda was grateful for Parker's superb tailing skills, or Shrivel surely would have made them by now.

"This has to be about the dagger," she said half under her breath.

Parker nodded. "I suspect Shrivel tried to intimidate Toby through his sister again."

"But he's in jail."

"He's probably called and told Winnie where he is by now," Parker surmised.

Miranda blew out a breath. "And if Winnie told Shrivel her brother is in jail, it made him blow his stack. He thinks Toby's ratted him out. But that doesn't explain where he's going now."

Parker turned another corner. "Perhaps to see a fence?"

"And get rid of the real dagger?"

"Perhaps."

That didn't sound right. Why would the seemingly fearsome Scorpion, leader of the Stingers, send a guy like Shrivel out with a priceless relic? Alone? On a bike? "Maybe the fence is holding out."

"Perhaps."

No, Scorpion would have sent more thugs if he thought someone was double crossing him. He'd have gone himself. She let out a long breath. "And what does this have to do with Lady Gabrielle?" She could still see those lifeless green eyes staring out at nothing. They had to find whoever did that to her.

Parker was quiet.

She knew him well enough to know he was putting the pieces together in his mind. Or trying to. Like her, she supposed. But he couldn't make them quite fit.

She looked out the windshield and saw they were heading toward the city. The buildings were getting taller and more modern, the traffic heavier, the pedestrians trendier. Music and laughter echoed from nightspots. Up ahead the strange cone shaped structure loomed, twinkling with a thousand lights from its windows.

They went through more traffic lights. Passed more buses. More pedestrians. Where in the hell was that sonofabitch going?

They plowed through all of it and crossed London Bridge, the waters of the Thames dark and green and gurgling beneath them. The shadow of the Tower loomed in the distance. That place where long ago kings had had their wives' heads cut off when they were through with them.

Her stomach twisted at the thought. There were still men today who thought women could be done away with and discarded like yesterday's trash.

They followed the motorcycle's taillights into another shopping district, down a few side streets and finally into a lane lined with rectangular four-and-five story buildings that looked like apartment dwellings.

In the next block the motorcycle pulled over to the curb, and Shrivel hopped off. His lanky, black-clad legs carried him over the walkway and up the darkened stairs to one of the buildings. Just as Parker eased up beside the cycle, Shrivel disappeared inside.

Adrenaline pumping through her veins, Miranda hopped out of the car and raced up the walkway.

The door was locked, of course. Only residents could enter. Heart pounding, panting with frustration, she glared at the side panel.

An intercom. Access for secure entry. Names of the residents were listed, one for each button.

She scanned the names, and her heart began to beat so hard she thought it might jump out of her chest. She recognized only one of them. In number four-oh-six.

Trenton Jewell.

CHAPTER THIRTY-ONE

It was only a few moments before Parker was at her side. When he trotted up the stairs she pointed to the intercom. "Look."

Parker scowled, his face displaying the same shock she was feeling. "Jewell?"

Miranda waved her hands at the name. "Why is Shrivel visiting the attorney for George Eames?"

"He does represent criminals."

That was true. "Maybe he wants to confess."

Parker's expression grew darker. "Or he's following orders from his boss."

"What orders?"

"Can't be sure. We need to get inside." He studied the door as if sizing up what it would take to pick the lock.

Miranda was about to mention that might not be a good idea in a foreign country, when she heard a bus stop on the corner and laughter spill out as the doors opened. She turned and saw a noisy group of partygoers getting off the bus and coming up the walkway.

She waited and watched them—not too steadily—turn in at the apartment building. They were in luck.

"There we are," Parker murmured in her ear.

As the group neared, he grabbed her and drew her close. For good measure he kissed her. Hard.

He was doing it so as not to look suspicious lingering here at the doorway, waiting for a way in, but it still took her breath away.

His lips pressed against hers and her heart burst into a fiery sizzle. Not something she needed right now, but the reaction was involuntary. As so was her mouth pressing back against his, devouring the warmth of his lips, their comfort. Maybe she did need this. His strength, his fire steadied her. Soothed the ragged edges of the pain she'd been carrying around since this afternoon. Carried her away to the memory of their first kiss on her own porch so many months ago.

And as she drank in his scent, it hit her hard how much she needed this man. How much she loved this man.

The giggling group came up the steps and Parker pressed her against the wall and deepened the kiss. He was making her dizzy, but the partiers were close enough to smell the alcohol on them. Had to keep up the impromptu cover.

"I believe I'm positively bladdered, mates," one of the young men slurred.

A woman made a high pitched hee-hee noise. "Watch yer step, now, Terry."

"Right," a second man chimed in. "Can't have you going arse over tit."

Holding her breath, Miranda unlocked her lips, opened one eye, and peeked over Parker's shoulder in time to watch the woman pull up the man tottering on the last step.

The second man was at the door already, patting his pants. "Now where'd I put me bleeding keys, then?"

The woman hee-heed again. "Other pocket, Luc."

Luc patted the other side of his jeans. "Blimey! You're right." He pulled out his keys and tried several times to hit the keyhole with them before a second young woman took them from him.

"You're absolutely gormless."

Apparently, she was the soberest one in the group. She shoved in the key and got the door open.

At last, the four revelers moved inside.

Keeping his gaze steady on Miranda's face, Parker stretched a hand out behind him and caught the door just before it shut.

"Smooth," Miranda grinned with admiration as they slipped inside.

The two "bladdered" couples turned at the end of a long hall without noticing her or Parker and disappeared. Letting out a tense breath, Miranda took in the space.

A worn carpet ran the length of the passage. The walls were dingy, as if they hadn't been painted since maybe the thirties. There was an old, musty smell in the air to match, mixed with the scent of Middle Eastern cooking. Signs without words indicated the elevator a few doors away. More signs pointed around corners situated at each end for the stairs.

"Which way?" she whispered.

Parker gestured to the stairwell.

Her choice, too. Less noise.

They took the stairs two at a time, ascending side by side, floor by floor, until they reached the fourth floor. There Parker laid a steady hand on the door and opened it without making a noise.

He peered into the hall.

Behind him, Miranda strained to see over his shoulder. "Is he there?"

Parker didn't answer. He simply opened the door the rest of the way and gestured for her to follow.

She stepped into the hall. It was empty.

Unless he'd slipped out while they were coming up the stairs, Shrivel had to be in one of the units. Or lurking somewhere after figuring out he was being followed.

They moved cautiously toward the corner, rounded it. This hall was similar to the one on the ground floor, but the carpet was green, the walls painted a muddy beige, the apartment doors an ugly dark red.

She scanned the units. Which one was four-oh-six?

Just as she began to scan for numbers, shouts came from inside somewhere. She shot Parker a questioning look.

He took a step in the direction of the noise.

Suddenly there was a loud, booming crash. And another. Gunshots.

A door banged open in the middle of the hall, and Shrivel stepped out. "It'll be worse next time," he sneered to someone inside the unit. Then he turned and ran off. The next instant he disappeared around the corner.

Heading for the stairwell.

"Stay here." Parker rushed past her and after Shrivel.

"Wait," Miranda hissed and ran after him. But as she reached Jewell's apartment she stopped. The door was still ajar.

She heard a groan.

"Help!"

Hesitating only an instant, with one last glance at the stairwell, she shoved the door open and stepped inside.

Trenton Jewell's large body lay sprawled on the floor of a narrow living space, one big hand over his stomach, his blood seeping through his fingers and staining the throw rug beneath him.

He groaned loudly and lifted his head with what seemed like impossible effort to look up at her through a glazed stare. "Ms. Steele?"

Quickly she glanced past a shelf of law books and spotted a small kitchen through an open arch. She raced through it, snatched a towel off the counter and returned to Jewell.

He was dressed in a dark suit, the blood staining the crisp white shirt, the coat, the pants as it oozed over his knuckles.

She grabbed his wrist, jerked his hand away and pressed the towel down on the wound hard. "Breathe," she ordered.

He did with a heavy, heaving gasp.

"Goodness gracious, what 'appened?" said a female voice.

Miranda's head snapped around. A woman in curlers and bathrobe stood in the doorway. She looked ghostly pale.

"Go call 911," she barked at her.

The woman tilted her head and frowned.

"Emergency. Ambulance. The police."

Getting it now, the woman nodded and hurried off.

The blood had soaked through the towel and Miranda didn't dare press any harder for fear of injuring an organ.

Jewell groaned again and tried to move.

"Lie still," she snapped. She couldn't have two vics in one day. It couldn't happen. She refused to let it happen. "What the hell was Malcolm Shrivel doing here?"

His eyes flashed as if he was shocked she'd seen the intruder and knew who he was. After a minute he spoke. "He...he thought I had the Marc Antony dagger. The...real dagger."

Her own heart felt like it had just stopped. What did he say? Then her head cleared. What was she doing making him talk? "Never mind. Forget I asked. Just try to relax."

But he raised his large head again, his iron gray hair falling in greasy strings over a brow lined with agony, his large sharp nose pointing at her like an eagle's beak. Now she couldn't shut him up.

"I mean, he thought I knew where the dagger was. Since I...represented George Eames." His eyes rolled back in his head, and he let out a cry of pain.

"Just lie still. EMTs will be here any second." She hoped.

But as soon as the words were out of her mouth, sirens sounded in the distance. Not American sirens. Those funny sounding European ones that made you think the Nazis were coming.

"Any second now," she repeated. "Just hold on."

But the blood kept coming.

CHAPTER THIRTY-TWO

Jewell did hold on.

After an eternity the paramedics, all in green, arrived. They got the bleeding to stop, hoisted Jewell onto a gurney and rolled him out.

Miranda stepped out into the hall and found Parker waiting for her.

"Shrivel got away?"

He nodded grimly, eyeing her. "Are you all right?"

She looked down at herself. She was covered with blood. "Hope the hotel's got a good cleaning service."

He gave her a weary sigh. Before he could say anything else the elevator doors opened and Wample and Ives stepped out followed by a couple of crime techs.

Wample's eyes narrowed when he saw them. "You two certainly know how to keep us busy."

Parker straightened his shoulders. Miranda knew he was in no mood for the inspector's guff. "We found your suspect, Malcolm Shrivel, in Tottenham and followed him here. He shot Trenton Jewell."

Miranda noticed he left out the part about the auto repair shop and Scorpion and his boys.

Wample gestured and Ives and the techs went into Jewell's rooms. "How do you know it was him?" Wample wanted to know.

"We heard two gunshots. Then we both saw Shrivel leave Jewell's flat. He ran down those stairs." Parker pointed toward the stairwell. "I tried to capture him, but when I got outside, he was gone."

Wample's lips curled as he turned to Miranda. "You're a right mess."

She returned his sneer. "I was trying to stop the barrister from bleeding to death."

"My associate saved the man's life, Inspector." Parker's voice was low and cold. She knew that was mostly his frustration talking.

Wample nodded. "I'll need your statements." He strode over to the open door. "Ives, get this scene processed while I take Mr. Parker and Ms. Steele to the car."

"Yessir."

Wample lumbered back to the elevator and pressed the button. "Results from the lab are back from this afternoon's incident," he said grimly.

"And?" Miranda asked as the doors opened.

Wample stepped into the lift, Parker behind him. "No fingerprints. The killer wore gloves, as we suspected."

"What about the call on Lady Gabrielle's cell phone?"

"Her mobile?" he said with a superior air. "Untraceable number."

Miranda's shoulders sagged as she glanced over at Parker. His expression was bleak, and he looked worn out.

The doors opened and they made their way through the entrance.

They descended the front steps, headed for Wample's car and she and Parker got into the back seat while Wample made a call outside.

At last, he slipped into the front, readied his recording equipment and his notepad and turned to them.

"By the way," he said with a face so bland an artist could have used it for a canvas. "I'm sorry to break our agreement, but I've just sent a man out to pick up Malcolm Shrivel."

CHAPTER THIRTY-THREE

Big Ben was tolling one in the morning by the time Miranda and Parker got back to the hotel.

She peeled off her bloody clothes, took a quick shower and sank down on the bed in her T-shirt and panties. If only it were as easy to wash away the emotions of today. Instead, they lingered in her heart, boring into her veins like parasites.

She groaned out loud. "Sometimes this job really…sucks."

"I know." Parker stood at the side of the bed, holding out a glass to her. He was still dressed in his tight shirt and jeans.

She sat up on her elbows and eyed the drink. "What is it?"

"Bacardi. It will help you sleep."

His brand. She sat up and took a sip.

She set the glass down on the nightstand and took a deep breath as the liquid began to warm her insides. It didn't feel like it would be enough. Not even if she drank a whole case.

"I didn't get a chance to tell you what Jewell said," she told him on an exhale.

Parker's dark brows drew together. "When you were in the room with him?"

She nodded. "I shouldn't have let him talk, but I wanted to know what Shrivel was doing there."

"What did he tell you?"

She scratched at her hair, the frustration of the scene playing in her mind. "Shrivel thought Jewell knew where the dagger was because of his connection to George Eames."

"And so he shot him to make him tell?"

"I guess so." Though it didn't seem very effective. She stared down at the design in the purple bedspread. Her mind began to run in another direction. "If Malcolm Shrivel doesn't know where the real dagger is…" She reached for the glass and swigged another swallow as it hit her. "Then his gang leader, Scorpion, doesn't have it."

"No," Parker murmured.

"And if Scorpion doesn't have the real Marc Antony dagger…who does? And who killed Lady Gabrielle with a fake one? And how did…?"

Parker took the glass from her and swallowed his own swig. "There were two thefts."

She stared up at him. Then she took the glass back again, put it down on the nightstand and pressed her head between her hands.

This was crazy. "Two thefts?"

But even as Parker nodded, she knew he was right.

It made perfect sense. "Someone else stole the real dagger and replaced it with a fake before Malcolm Shrivel broke into the museum."

"Yes."

"And so Shrivel ended up stealing the counterfeit dagger instead of the real one."

"Exactly."

It had to be. The wheels in her head began to turn faster. "And somehow the information Lady Gabrielle had about the inscription got to Scorpion and he knew he had the fake."

"And now he wants the real one."

"And thinks Eames has it." She frowned. "Why go after Jewell?"

"Guilty people confess all sorts of things to their attorneys."

She thought about that. "Eames is the only one with access to the dagger after it was delivered to the museum as far as we know," she said, wondering how close Lady Gabrielle was to Sir Neville's friend and colleague. "But why would someone who's dedicated his life to old artifacts, who lives in the freaking museum, steal the dagger? He could just go down and look at it on display every day at his job, for Pete's sake." She got under the covers and gave her pillow a sock. "That dagger meant the world to Sir Neville. How could you work with him so closely, day after day and do something like that to him? Eames is Sir Neville's friend." Or was supposed to be.

She reached for the glass again, downed the rest of it, put it back down with a smack.

Parker rose and removed his clothes while he pondered that. Then he slid into bed beside her wearing only his underwear. If only they could just make love and forget this day, this night. If only they could crack this case.

He took her in his arms and lay back on the pillows. "We've been assuming the dagger was taken for gain."

She shrugged, her head against his shoulder. "It's worth over five million pounds."

He took a strand of her hair, entwined it between his fingers. "Yes, that had to be part of it."

The light went on in her head. "But maybe not the only part."

"Exactly. Perhaps not the main part."

"Someone jealous of Sir Neville?"

"He's been very successful in his field."

And Eames, not so much. He'd been living in Sir Neville's shadow all these years. Had to go to him for a job. She let out a long sigh. "Maybe we haven't looked at George Eames hard enough."

Trouble riddled Parker's expression. "We may have made a few erroneous assumptions in this case."

Because of Parker's attachment to Sir Neville. Because his old friend was so fond of Eames.

She tried to think back over the past two days, this time with more objectivity. Something Parker had pounded in her head when she first started at the Agency.

Suddenly she remembered the photo in Eames' room. "The old picture of the cricket players."

Parker had a faraway look in his eyes. "I was just thinking of that."

"It had four friends. Sir Neville, Eames, Jewell...and somebody else."

"Cedric Swift."

She sat up and turned over to face him, hope rising inside her. "That's right. Didn't Sir Neville say Swift was still at Cambridge?"

Parker nodded again. "He's a professor. Computers."

Must be a bright guy. "Maybe the professor could tell us more about what George Eames is really like."

He broke from his thoughts and turned his head to look at her, a smile on his lips. "I did train you well, didn't I?"

"Yeah," she laughed. "Guess you did."

"Are you up for a road trip tomorrow?"

"Am I ever." She had to smile as she said the words she'd never have believed would come out of her lips. "Parker, take me to Cambridge."

He took her in his arms and gave her a long, slow kiss. "I will."

CHAPTER THIRTY-FOUR

The next morning they had a hearty sausage and egg breakfast in the hotel restaurant, then Parker petroled up the rental, and they headed off to the university town.

The ride to Cambridge took over an hour and was mostly through acres and acres of English farmland. But at last, they hit the town.

Parker eased the car over the narrow cobblestone streets past pedestrians and cyclists, taking in the sights. "The university was founded in 1209 when a group of students left Oxford and came here," he told her with a tour guide's flourish.

"Hmm." Miranda gawked at the castle-like structures, each bursting with lofty spires, never-ending columns and arches, and elegant statuary. The place had a definite thirteenth century feel. Along with an iron-sized academic feel that was making Miranda a little antsy.

"Many famous people have studied here," Parker continued as they rode past another one of the colleges. "Scientists, poets, prime ministers, Nobel Prize winners."

She stared at the gray stone statues of two lions perched in front of a building like little sphinxes. Was that a library or a dormitory? "You trying to intimidate me, Parker?"

"Hardly," he chuckled and turned down another road.

Could have fooled her. But she shook off the discomfort and focused on the reason for their journey into the past.

Since it was Sunday, Dr. Swift was at home, so they followed the River Cam over a winding path to a cozy, fenced-in house made of stucco and red brick with lots of cheery windows and a many-gabled roof.

Miranda got out of the car and marched alongside Parker up the quaint, flower-lined walkway.

He used the lion's head knocker and after a moment a small woman with dark shoulder-length hair dressed in black slacks, top and sweater appeared.

She seemed confused to see two strangers at her door. "May I help you?"

"Mrs. Swift?" Parker asked.

"Yes."

He extended a hand. "I'm Wade Parker of the Parker Investigative Agency in Atlanta, Georgia. We spoke on the phone?"

"Oh, yes. The American detective. I didn't expect you so soon." She took Parker's hand and shook.

"This is my partner, Miranda Steele." Miranda shook the woman's hand as well.

"Good morning, Ms. Steele. Come in, both of you, won't you?" She opened the door and stepped aside. "I suppose you'd like to see Cedric straight away?"

Parker nodded. "If it's not inconvenient."

"Oh, no," she sang out. "He's back here in his study, as usual." She led them through an airy hallway lined with family photos to a back room with the door closed.

She knocked on it softly. "Ceddy? The American detectives are here."

A half-muffled voice came from inside. "Yes, yes. Show them in."

She opened the door and Miranda and Parker stepped into a large, high-ceiling office painted in light creamy tones and lined with the requisite bookshelves of a scholar. But these weren't the ancient history books of George Eames' rooms or Sir Neville's office at the museum. These were sleek technical books about advanced calculus and algorithms and computer languages.

The space smelled of tea and technology.

On the opposite side of the room near the window, hung a whiteboard covered with strange marks. Boxes and lines and angle brackets and words Miranda couldn't understand. A large mug sat on a modern style desk with a big screen computer monitor. Behind the desk was a thin man with a face that, though he was Sir Neville's age, glowed with youthful enthusiasm as he studied the screen. The only hair on his head grew around the edges in a distinguished light gray.

He leaned forward, took a sip from the mug, set it down again. He pointed at the screen with glee. "Now, there's a bugger of a bug."

His wife cleared her throat. "Ceddy?" she said in a gentle tone that told Miranda she'd been handling her husband's eccentricities for many a year.

The professor looked up as if coming out of a pleasant dream. "Say what? Oh, yes. So sorry." He laughed and gestured toward the screen. "I'm testing a video game one of my students turned in. It shows real promise. Still has some flaws though." He turned back to the screen with a frown of concentration.

"Ceddy?" his wife said again. "These are the detectives? About Neville's case?"

"Oh, yes. Of course." He turned away from the screen, his face instantly somber, his receding hairline peppered with lines of concern. "Please. Have a seat. Both of you." He gestured toward chairs.

They made the usual introductions and did another set of handshaking while the professor's wife slipped quietly out, shutting the door behind her.

The professor frowned at Miranda. "Why do you look so familiar? Oh. The telly."

"Really?" She gave Parker an awkward glance.

"The news yesterday about..." His voice went thin. "Dreadful business. Just dreadful. I can't imagine..." Shaking his head, he stared out the window. "Poor Neville."

Miranda felt her neck turning red. On the news? She'd been on the news? If she could find that reporter who'd buttonholed her yesterday, she'd put her shoe up her ass. No time for that now.

She sat forward. "Dr. Swift," she began, eager to get to the chase. "We understand you and Sir Neville Ravensdale went to school together here?"

A wistful smile layered over the anguish on his face. "Yes, we did. A long time ago. We were—are—friends."

"Are you still close?"

He tapped his fingertips together as if the answer took some thought. "Not really. Christmas cards, the occasional alumni function, that sort of thing. We spoke last night, of course. I rang Neville after we heard the news. Only briefly, though. He was inundated with calls...I suppose we'll attend the funeral."

He had that lost look she'd seen on Sir Neville's face yesterday, and her heart went out to him.

He shook himself out of his thoughts and sat up. "Oh, would either of you care for anything to drink? I'm afraid I've forgotten my manners."

"No, thank you," she said.

Parker sat back in his chair, crossed his legs and began a more leisurely approach. "Dr. Swift, tell us about your time as a student. Yours and Sir Neville's."

The professor frowned as if he found the question odd. "I'm not sure what you mean."

Parker shrugged. "Was Sir Neville a good student?"

"Well, of course. He was an excellent student. Rose to the top in his field. But he came from humble beginnings. Did you know he attended here on a full scholarship?"

"No. That's very impressive."

"It is indeed."

"And were the two of you close to anyone else? Any other students?"

He nodded. "Why, yes. There were four of us. Trenton Jewell and George Eames were the others. We were all in Emma—Emmanuel College—together. Used to play on the cricket team twice a week. Great fun." He grew quiet for a long moment, indulging himself in his thoughts of days gone by. Then his mouth opened as if he'd just found a set of lost car keys. "I heard George was arrested for the incident at the museum. Is that correct?"

"He's been released," Parker said.

The professor sank back in his chair. "That's a relief to hear. George would never do such a thing. He was as honest as the day was long."

Miranda slid Parker a sidelong glance. Maybe the four weren't as close as the professor thought.

She picked up the next thread. "So you're saying Sir Neville and Mr. Eames got along well?"

"Better than well. "Neville and Eames were fast friends."

She let herself frown as if she was having a hard time understanding him. "But Eames didn't do as well as Sir Neville. Academically, I mean."

"George was still an above average student. And everyone knows the entrance requirements here are very arduous."

"Yes, but all friends have a falling out at some time or another. Did Mr. Eames ever say anything to you about Sir Neville? Something that indicated anger perhaps?"

His eyes grew round. "What are you saying, Ms. Steele?"

"Was there ever any tension between them? Did they argue? Stop speaking to each other?"

He looked at her as if she were crazy. "No, never. Two peas in a pod, I always called them. Both of them mad for archaeology."

She leaned in a little more. "Mr. Eames never had a reason to be jealous of Sir Neville?"

He blinked at her, completely stunned. "Jealous? No. I really don't understand what this has to do with anything if George has been released."

Miranda was silent, waiting for the impact to sink in.

Parker sat forward and studied the professor a long moment. At last, he threw the punch. "I understand one of Sir Neville's teachers gave him a coin once."

Dr. Swift's brows drew together. He stared down at his keyboard. After a long moment the memory came to him. "Oh, yes. I'd forgotten about that. Professor Kent gave it to him. It was an old Roman coin."

The one Sir Neville still carried in his pocket. The one he'd showed them at the polo match.

He lifted a shoulder. "It didn't mean anything to me, but Neville was absolutely thrilled."

"How did Eames feel about that?"

The professor frowned. "He was very happy for Neville. I think they went out and celebrated. I think Trenton went with them. I didn't go for some reason. Can't remember now."

Miranda scooted forward in her chair. "And Mr. Eames wasn't the least bit jealous?"

"No."

"Didn't he love archaeology just as much as Sir Neville?"

"Of course, he did. But he wasn't jealous. He wasn't the type."

"Mr. Eames didn't think Professor Kent should have given the coin to him instead?"

Dr. Swift's mouth opened in horror. "What on earth are you trying to say, Ms. Steele? Do you think I'm lying? I've told you…Oh." He got that faraway look again.

Parker got to his feet. "What is it, Professor Swift?"

"I see. I'd forgotten that as well. There was an argument. Well, not a bad one. But afterwards he did say it wasn't fair for Neville to get the coin."

Miranda's heart began to race. "Mr. Eames told you that?"

Slowly Dr. Swift shook his head. The minutes ticked by as he connected the memories like a logic problem. At last, he spoke again, his voice more somber than before. "No, not George. Trenton. It was Trenton who was jealous."

She sank back into her chair. Trenton Jewell?

"Are you sure it was Mr. Jewell?" Parker asked.

"Yes. He wanted to be in archaeology like George and Neville. Just didn't have the mind for it. I didn't either of course, but I never cared for the field…Come to think of it. That was when Trenton changed his course of study."

"Changed? Wasn't he a law student?"

"No. He started out in archaeology, too. He turned to law after Professor Kent gave Neville the coin. I suppose he thought it suited him better. Turns out it did. I hear he's very successful as a barrister."

Miranda's head was spinning. She glanced over at Parker and saw him frozen in front of the desk, his jaw tight.

The professor blinked at both of them with a boyish expression very close to guilt. "Have I told you what you came here to learn? I hope I haven't said anything I shouldn't have."

"No, you haven't, Professor Swift." Parker assured him, recovering with a polite smile and a final handshake. "You've been very helpful."

CHAPTER THIRTY-FIVE

Parker drove back to London breaking speed limits all the way. But the whole trip Miranda fidgeted and tore at her hair, wishing they had wings or a police copter or a supersonic jet.

"He lied to me. Right there on his floor bleeding all over me while I was saving his life, that bastard lied to me."

Parker didn't reply, but she heard a low rumble from his chest while he scowled at the road ahead.

Couldn't this car go any faster? "He has the dagger. He has to. Scorpion had been Jewell's client. Jewell must have made some kind of deal with him and then tried to double-cross him."

"But it didn't work."

She waved her hands in exasperation. "No. That's why Shrivel left him alive. If Jewell didn't give up the dagger, it would be worse next time, just like he threatened him. And here I thought Shrivel was just a lousy shot."

Parker held the wheel steady as they sped around a long curve. "Scorpion's not the type to trifle with. If Jewell doesn't give him what he wants, he may not stay alive long."

So they'd have to save his ass again to get the dagger back. That sucked. Her mind began to wander back to yesterday afternoon. "Did Shrivel kill Lady Gabrielle as a warning to Jewell?"

Parker considered that a long moment. "Perhaps. She said he was a friend of her family."

"She said he'd gotten her off on DUIs. And she knew about the dagger's security at the museum from Sir Neville."

Parker's eyes narrowed as it hit him the same time it did her. "She was in on it."

"She passed the information about the code and the keycard to Jewell, who passed it to Shrivel."

"Who threatened Toby Waverly for it."

"Oh, God. That really was Shrivel who called Lady Gabrielle yesterday. He was trying to find out if she had the dagger. And when she said she didn't know, he killed her."

"Or he told her Jewell had it and then she was expendable and knew too much."

Crazy, reckless young woman. If only they could have figured this much out before. If only they could have saved her.

Miranda chewed on her lower lip as her troubled thoughts chewed on her stomach lining all the way back to the city. It was afternoon when they reached the outskirts and Parker headed straight for the hospital where Jewell had been taken last night.

Parker had gotten the name from one of the paramedics and had called and checked on him before they left town this morning. The report was he'd come out of surgery all right and would live. Not if she could get her hands on him.

"They probably won't let us in," she moaned as they hurried through the front door.

"Not if I can help it."

Inside the hospital, Parker worked his magic and got Jewell's room number. But the nurse at the ICU station on the third floor was a different story.

She studied them with a weary gaze and shook her head. "I'm so sorry, Mr. Parker, Ms. Steele, but—."

"We're here on official business," Miranda said, resisting the urge to pound her fist on the counter.

The woman's shoulders sagged. "I'm afraid it isn't that."

Miranda frowned. What new trick was this? "What is it then?"

The nurse pressed her hand to her face and Miranda saw the heavy shadows under her eyes. "Mr. Jewell's dead."

What? "We were told he came through surgery last night and would survive."

"No, that's not what happened. He must have woken up and..." Her gaze shifted to a small waiting area across the hall. She raised her arm and pointed with a ghostlike gesture at the television.

Miranda turned around, stepped across the floor and into the room to get a better look. On the screen the reporter that had attacked her yesterday was standing in a subway station, microphone in hand.

"According to tube officials, the tragedy occurred at 5:02 this morning, just as the first train passed through."

The picture switched to a witness. A middle-aged man in street clothes wearing a look of terror. "It were awful. Bloody awful. The conductor tried to stop but there was no time. The man leapt off the platform right in front of him."

Back to the reporter. "Paramedics tried to revive the man, but his injuries were too great. Unfortunately, he expired on the spot. When police arrived on the scene, they identified the body as London barrister Trenton Jewell."

CHAPTER THIRTY-SIX

They headed back to Scotland Yard. Where else could they go for answers?

Half an hour later they were again in Inspector Wample's office, sitting across from the two haggard-looking officers of the Crown.

The tang of death and defeat hung in the air like the London fog.

"Inspector," Parker began. "We have reason to believe Trenton Jewell was involved—"

Wample raised a hand. "We know, Mr. Parker."

Miranda glared at the man.

He closed his eyes and exhaled, then opened a file on his desk. He took out a sheet of paper and handed it to Parker. "He left a suicide note."

Parker scanned it, passed it to Miranda.

Her breath growing rapid, her gut tense, she dared to look down on it. As she read the neat script-like handwriting and spoke the bone-chilling words out loud, her skin felt as cold as ice.

I, Trenton Bartholomew Jewell, being of sound mind and body—save for the pain from my recent gunshot wounds and surgery—do with this instrument confess my crimes against humanity, against the Crown, against my friends.

For these long decades, I have carried within me a deep, abiding resentment against my university friend, Sir Neville Ravensdale. I tried to deny it, contain it, wrestle with it, but to no avail. Over the years, the resentment grew to jealousy, the jealousy to envy, the envy to hatred.

Neville had everything I wanted. He was favored by professors at school. He was gifted in the profession I longed to follow but had no talent for. He took the woman I secretly loved as his bride. He was knighted for his accomplishments. With each success Neville had, the more my ire for him festered.

Miranda put her fingers to her lips suddenly remembering Lady Davinia said Jewell had proposed to her.

And when he discovered the priceless Marc Antony dagger, my loathing for him bubbled over and broke open like a cancerous boil on my heart.

When I heard Lady Gabrielle Eaton joke at a party that it would be funny if the dagger were stolen, I saw my opportunity.

Miranda looked at Parker. "She was involved."

He nodded. She read on.

I knew Lady Gabrielle. I sought her out and told her if the dagger were to be stolen, Neville's marriage to her mother-in-law would be over in a few months, and it would make her husband happy. And I secretly hoped Lady Davinia might turn to me again.

I knew of Lady Gabrielle's husband's dislike for Neville. Everyone in their circle did. I knew Lionel Halsing, Earl of Eaton had a wandering eye, and Lady Gabrielle would do anything to win back his affections.

But she turned me down. She said she couldn't pull something like that off. I tried to reassure her she could, but she refused.

Miranda ground her teeth. That bastard. That dirty bastard.

And so I turned to my more distasteful connections. I contacted a former client of mine. A man who goes by the name of Scorpion. The police know who he is. He was more than willing to do the deed, plus he knew a fence who would dispose of the dagger. We agreed to split the profit.

A short time later Lady Gabrielle called me. Even though she still couldn't do what I had asked, she had discovered the details of the dagger's security at the museum. I passed the information on to Scorpion.

And then the dagger was stolen.

I saw the look on Neville's face in the newspaper. I expected to feel a surge of triumph. Instead, there was only shame and guilt. What had I done?

And then Scorpion contacted me and said the dagger was a fake. I had double-crossed him. I was terrified. I had no idea what he meant. Then he said the inscription I had described to him was missing. He demanded to know how I knew about it. I panicked and told him Lady Gabrielle had told me about the real dagger's inscription.

Miranda put a hand to her face. "Oh, my God. He signed her death warrant."

"There's more," Parker said gently.

Then I realized she must have changed her mind and taken the dagger herself. I confronted her. She swore she hadn't taken it. I didn't believe her. I threatened her. I told her the American detectives were onto her game and she would be arrested soon.

That was why she tried to injure Ms. Steele at the polo match. Scorpion called and made more threats. I feared for my life. I behaved like a coward. I told him Lady Gabrielle had the dagger. I gave him her mobile number. It's because of me that she's dead.

Damn straight.

Scorpion sent someone after her. I'm responsible. I don't deserve to live.

They're going to kill me anyway.

The script was getting harder to read now. Jewell must have been in horrendous pain. The only way he could have managed to get out of the hospital and to the subway was through a powerful, terror-driven adrenaline rush.

I don't know where the real dagger is. I never saw it. By my barrister's oath, for what it's worth now, I never saw it.

I know I must pay for what I've done. But I will not die at the hand of a criminal. I will meet whatever punishment the afterlife has for me by my own hand. I will end it at daybreak.

Trenton Jewell

Miranda raised her head and found her eyes were full of tears. A confession from the grave. What a travesty. What a waste of life.

She handed the paper back to Wample. "He says he doesn't know where the real dagger is."

Wample's expression turned sour. "We don't believe him. We've learned a hundred thousand pounds was recently deposited into Jewell's bank account."

That was a tidy sum. Still, too small for a priceless dagger. "But how—?"

"Our theory is that Jewell was working with someone in the delivery company. I've had men searching Jewell's flat and his law offices all morning. There's no sign of the dagger. We don't expect to recover the relic," Wample said. "We believe he sold it. After we conclude our routine investigation of Jewell's death, the Marc Antony case is closed."

Parker's face was hard. "What about the murder?"

"We have not yet located our suspect Shrivel. We have men canvassing the area near his residence."

"What about this Scorpion creep?" Miranda wanted to know.

"We can hardly arrest him on the letter of a dead man. The defense would laugh us out of court."

He had a point. Sometimes, she hated the way the law worked.

For a long moment everyone sat in silence.

Finally, Parker spoke again. "Inspector, I'm wondering, with your permission, if we might take a look at some of the evidence in Lady Gabrielle's case."

"I don't see why you need to do that, Mr. Parker."

Parker gave him his most charming smile. "Humor me, if you will. I'm thinking of using this as a case study for trainees at my agency. With your permission."

Wample's mouth went back and forth, but Parker's flattery got the best of him. "Oh, very well, Mr. Parker. Ives, take our guests to the evidence room."

While Parker spent the next hour going over the vehicle and the other things the police had gathered in the street yesterday, Miranda pressed her fingers to her temple and tried to keep the strings holding her insides together from unraveling.

She felt as if she was going insane. She'd never left a case unsolved before. And when Parker said he was finished, she felt crazy with relief.

She couldn't wait to get back to the hotel and hit that Bacardi.

CHAPTER THIRTY-SEVEN

Miranda sank down onto the Queen Anne sofa in the hotel suite and put her head in her hands. She wanted to cry. "We failed, Parker. We failed Sir Neville."

He sat beside her, pulled her into his arms. "We did our best. All we could do."

"There has to be something more. There has to be."

But there was nothing she could think of. She leaned her forehead against his shoulder and let her tears stain his suit.

He rubbed his hands over her back, pressed his lips to her hair, and she knew he was just as broken inside. Wade Parker didn't lose cases. Wade Parker didn't give up. But if Trenton Jewell had sold the real dagger on the black market, how could they ever trace it? It would take years. Decades.

And Malcolm Shrivel? He was probably in France or Spain or Argentina by now.

It was over.

She couldn't stand the thought, couldn't bear the biting sense of futility. She lifted her head. "Kiss me," she said and pulled Parker close.

His mouth took hers like a ravenous lion. He devoured her lips as his hands slid over her body, plundering, possessing, his touch nearly imploding her with sudden desire.

Sharp, thrilling pangs of need burst inside her. She pressed hard against him, dug her fingers into the hard muscles of his back. She let her need for him drive away her need to solve this case. Let her need to solve this case fuel her need for him.

They were sublimating, her shrink would say. Diverting an emotion too painful to face into another. Okay, fine. It would work for the moment anyway. Apparently, Parker felt the same.

Rising, he scooped her up in his arms and carried her into the bedroom. He laid her on the thick brocade and pulled at her clothes while she wrestled his off.

146

They came together, skin to skin, bare flesh to bare flesh and Miranda's heart pumped so hard with tenderness and passion, her mind became a blur. A lovely blur where all she could feel was him.

He plunged into her, making her cry out with pleasure and hunger for more. He gave her more. His hands, his body, his mouth. And she gave in kind. More and more until their bodies fused into a single unit.

A oneness, a bond deeper than any they'd ever had before. A place Miranda never wanted to leave.

If only she didn't have to.

Parker clicked off and put his cell back into his pocket.

He'd crept out of bed when his phone had rung a few moments ago and left Miranda to rest.

He strolled to the window and looked out at the city of London, its craggy world-famous landmarks growing luminous under the glow of the golden late afternoon sun.

He thought of the history of kings and empires. He thought of envy and its power to destroy. Its parasitic nature, how it feeds off those who give into it like a cancer. He thought of love and its power to make people do what they'd never dream of doing, both good and bad. And some things they promised not to do.

He thought of his friend Neville Ravendale's comforting touch on his arm when he was a child grieving over his mother. The man who now grieved over the loss of his daughter-in-law and the lives of his family he thought he'd ruined.

And finally, he thought of Malcolm Shrivel and Scorpion and began to turn a plan over in his mind.

Scotland Yard wouldn't bring in either of them. He'd seen too many criminals disappear into the wind after clumsy police attempts at capture. They'd escape. They'd get away with what they'd done. They'd walk free to steal and kill again.

He couldn't let that happen. He couldn't let things be and go back home empty handed.

Besides, if what he had reasoned out was correct, it would only be a matter of time before Scorpion struck closer. He had to act now. Tonight.

He turned and gazed at the door to the bedroom where Miranda lay sleeping. He refused to put her in danger. He refused to take no for an answer this time. He let out a long sigh. Bringing up the topic would only lead to confrontation. A fight, a breach between them was the last thing he needed now. Better to do it secretly.

Alone.

She would figure it out, he knew. No way around that. But by the time she did, it would be done.

The decision was made. He pulled the cell out of his pocket again and stared down at it. He hated himself for what he was about to do, but it was the only option he had.

He began to punch in the number he'd gotten off Lady Gabrielle's phone in the evidence room. The police couldn't prove who it belonged to, but they must have called it. It hadn't been answered, but it might be if the call came from a different number.

He waited for it to ring. Once. Twice. Three times. Luck was with him.

At last, a hoarse, ugly voice answered. "'Oo is this?"

CHAPTER THIRTY-EIGHT

Miranda opened her eyes and found herself naked under the covers of her bed and Parker standing beside her fully dressed in dark suit and tie.

She rubbed her eyes and sat up. "What time is it?"

"Just before seven. I've ordered some dinner."

She stared at the pillow. "I'm not sure I can eat. I think I just want to sleep until tomorrow."

"We should attend Lady Gabrielle's wake." His voice was tender, a sliver of pain edging his tone. "Sir Neville called a little while ago with the details."

"Oh. Yeah, I guess we should." Her heart broke all over again and whatever residual glow was left from their lovemaking earlier slithered away.

"I filled Sir Neville in about Jewell. Wample had already told him the basic gist of the suicide letter."

"How's he taking it?"

Parker shook his head. "He's in denial. I can't blame him. His whole world is falling apart."

"Yeah." And there wasn't a damn thing they could do to bolster it. She tossed the covers aside and got to her feet, her body feeling as heavy as Big Ben. "I guess I'll go shower."

She did so quickly, then forced down a few mouthfuls of food he made her eat. She found a dark pantsuit and top to wear, dragged a brush through her hair. She curled a lip at her image in the mirror. "I hope this is okay."

"It's perfect." Parker came up behind her and slipped a golden chain around her neck, fastened it at the back.

She smiled sadly. "You always know the artful touches."

"But you provide the canvas." He turned her around, gazed into her eyes a long moment. Then he kissed her with a slow, gentle kiss that nearly broke her heart.

"What's that for?" she laughed.

In the dim light his gray eyes glowed with a strange fervor. "Whatever happens tonight, I want you to know I love you."

149

Her brow rose as her stomach tightened. "What are you up to?"

"Nothing. I just know it's going to be difficult for you tonight and I want you to remember it is for me, too."

Now there was a non sequitur if she ever heard one. But they were late and there was no time to argue.

"I'll remember," she told him with a flat smile as she gave her hopeless hair a final fluff and let him usher her out the door.

CHAPTER THIRTY-NINE

As Parker navigated them through the evening traffic in the rental car, he informed her the wake was being held at Quinton Castle in Camden. The estate of Albert DeVere, Marquis of Camden and Lady Gabrielle's father.

"Is that where she grew up?" Miranda asked.

"As I understand, yes."

Except for the time in boarding school Lady Davinia had mentioned.

Parker eased through a roundabout with a well-lit arch at its center, and they made their way through the narrow streets past old factories and fancy estates and more fancy homes that had been turned into apartment buildings.

They didn't talk much. Parker was lost in his private thoughts and Miranda was focused on getting through the next few hours.

There wasn't much to talk about. She hated funerals and wakes and all the trappings of burying the dead. And she had no idea what to say to Lady Davinia or Sir Neville.

Finally, they reached a sprawling red brick building with the requisite cake frosting decorations along its exterior and light streaming from its rows and rows of windows. The property was barricaded by a high stone wall with a foreboding iron gate. Along both sides of the street that ran in front of the wall cars were parked. People stood on the sidewalk along the barricade holding bouquets of flowers and taking pictures.

Lady Gabrielle was popular.

Parker spoke to an attendant and the gate opened to a long drive that led up to the front of the house. Valets stood on a wide porch beside tall Grecian columns waiting to park the attendees' vehicles. Cars lined both sides of the drive.

A lot of people came when the person was young and high-born. No doubt there'd be some press, too. Whoopie. She might end up choking one of them.

After waiting in the line of cars for several minutes, they reached the porch and a valet opened Miranda's door.

Parker caught her hand. "I don't want to be stuck here when we're ready to leave. I'm going to find a spot on the street."

She frowned at him, suspicion gnawing at her stomach. "What's going on, Parker?"

He looked annoyed and a little distracted. "Nothing. You don't want to stay here all night, do you?"

She didn't. And that wasn't what this was about. But he had that hard-as-iron look of determination on his face.

Maybe she was reading too much into his behavior. She knew he was as distressed as she was over this case. He was a proud man who was proud of his work, and he had every right to be upset. It was hard for him to admit defeat.

She let it go. "Okay. Guess I'll go inside. Don't know what I'm going to say to Sir Neville, though."

His eyes went tender. "He understands. You'll do fine."

She nodded and got out of the car.

But as she turned back on the step to watch him wave the valet away and drive off into the night, a little bird in her gut told her something wasn't right about this.

CHAPTER FORTY

A tuxedoed servant met Miranda at the huge front door to open it for her, and another led her down a long echoing corridor until they turned a corner, and she could hear the sounds of soft funeral-type music and muted voices.

She headed for the tall open double-doors the servant indicated and caught the smell of coffee, finger food, and expensive cologne.

She stepped inside.

The hall was circular, its ivory walls embellished with marble and statuary. High above, a large dome capped the room, its circumference outlined by tall columns and triple arches, its ceiling painted with pastel angels surrounded by gold filigree. Gabrielle would have been pleased with that canopy, Miranda decided.

Down below the space was crowded with dark clad figures, chatting to each other in low tones, while the too-warm air grew thick with grief and gossip.

Miranda recognized a few faces among the gathering. The Lovelaces, the Duchess of Oxham. But most she didn't know.

She made her way around the edges of the room, through the forest of strangers until she reached a green marble fireplace and saw Sir Neville on the other side of it on a settee. He stared at the floor beneath his feet, looking wearier, more lost, more fragile than she'd ever seen him.

This had been such an ordeal for him. Tragedy on top of tragedy.

She still had no idea what to say to him, but she steadied herself, went over and sat down beside him. "Hello, Sir Neville," she said quietly.

He lifted his head and blinked at her in surprise. "Ms. Steele." He reached for her hands. "Thank you so much for coming tonight."

She squeezed his hands and studied his crystal blue eyes, their color vibrant, their rims deep red from too many tears. The emotion spilled out of her. "I—I failed you, Sir Neville. I'm so sorry."

His expression turned to concern. "Oh, no, my dear. You did the best you could. You and Russell both. No one could have expected more."

But this time, her best wasn't good enough. She shook her head.

"No one could have known what Trenton was up to. I—I still can't believe it myself. I had no idea how he felt." The lost look returned to his face. He released her hands and patted her arm. "No, if anyone's to blame it's me. I should have left that dagger where it was."

That was a silly notion. "You were doing your job."

"Yes. My job," he said bitterly and stared out at the guests, not really seeing anyone. "It's funny how something like this makes you stop and look at your life. Makes you see the mistakes you've made, the opportunities you've wasted."

"Yeah," she murmured and wondered if he was talking about Davinia.

"If I had it all to do over again—" He let out a heartfelt sigh. "Ah, but what's done is done. We can't change it." He shook himself as if coming out of a dream. "Is Russell here?"

"Uh—" She glanced around the room, didn't see him. "He's parking the car. He should be in here by now."

"Why don't you go look for him, my dear? I need to steady myself a bit more before I speak to the guests."

"Sure," she said. She understood the need for alone time. Rising she patted his shoulder. "I'll send my husband to find you as soon as I find him."

"Thank you." And he gave her that warm, sad smile that broke her heart.

She turned away and began hunting for Parker among the group. She'd made it all the way to the other side of the room when she caught sight of Lady Davinia.

Draped in a long black gown, with her elegant grace, she floated from group to group. She looked like she knew just what to do and say, though her face was pale and her makeup thick with a futile attempt to cover her red, swollen eyes.

She spotted Miranda, politely finished her conversation and came toward her. "Ms. Steele, it's so good of you to come."

"I felt I had to." That wasn't the right thing to say. She didn't do funerals well. If only Parker were here. He knew how to handle any situation with polish and sensitivity. "I'm so sorry."

Davinia pressed her lips together and nodded, unable to speak for a moment. Then she collected herself. "Let me introduce you to some of Gabrielle's friends."

She presented her to several dukes and duchesses, half a dozen countesses, and other friends and acquaintances of the family. Finally, Miranda met Albert DeVere, Marquis of Camden and Lady Gabrielle's father.

Lord Camden was a large man with an imposing figure and a deep bass voice.

"I'm so sorry for your loss, Lord Camden," Miranda told him as she shook hands.

"Thank you, Ms. Steele." He looked back at the raised platform along the side of the room where the casket had been placed for viewing. "I think she would have been pleased with the turn out. She was such a social gadfly, my little girl."

He was right. Gabrielle would have loved the attention.

"It doesn't seem so long ago that I had to say good-bye to her mother. And now I must to her." His eyes teared up. "Please excuse me." He turned away.

His words tore at Miranda's heart. That bastard Shrivel had taken so much, caused so much pain. How could they let him get away with it?

Beside her Davinia squeezed her hand. "I need to see her, Ms. Steele. Will you come with me?"

To view the body? She didn't think she was up for that. "I wasn't—I'm not—"

But Davinia's face was full of pleading. "Please."

Okay. She could be strong for this woman who suddenly needed her. She couldn't undo what had happened. She couldn't bring Shrivel in. But she could do this.

She nodded. "All right."

Two stairs led up to the platform where the elaborate coffin sat. The family standards hung on poles on either side. Wreaths of roses and lilies and carnations were symmetrically placed in the background and along the steps.

Miranda forced her gaze away from the surroundings and down. At Lady Gabrielle's lifeless form.

She looked peaceful. Much better than when she'd found her yesterday. Undertakers were known for working such magic. But the life that had once brightened her girlish face was missing. The light in her glistening green eyes was gone forever.

Miranda noticed they'd put her in the red lace dress she'd picked out on her final shopping trip.

"I thought she'd want to wear that frock," Davinia said, her grasp still tight on Miranda's hand.

"Yes, she would have."

Then Davinia did the unthinkable. She leaned forward and touched the body's red-gold curls. "Oh, Gabby, Gabby. Why did you have to be so headstrong? Why couldn't you have talked to me? Why did you have to go to—?" She put a hand to her mouth and reached for Miranda as she straightened again. "Oh, Ms. Steele I don't know what we're going to do."

Miranda didn't know either. And she didn't have words for the woman. She didn't have words for herself. All she knew was she couldn't stand here another moment longer looking at the woman she hadn't even known a week ago.

It was as if Gabrielle were blaming her for what had happened. As if she were telling Miranda she "must" find her killer.

If only she could.

"I need to sit down," Davinia said in a whispered gasp.

Miranda nodded. "I need to find a ladies' room." She gave the woman's hand another squeeze and turned away.

As Davinia went in the opposite direction, she hurried down the platform steps, searching for a hall to a bathroom or somewhere she could pull herself together. She couldn't last another minute. As soon as she found Parker and he finished making his condolences, they were out of here.

She passed a circle of young men gathered under a gold framed landscape. They parted as she approached and she saw Lionel on a tufted bench, his head in his hands.

She stopped in her tracks. She didn't even like the guy and her heart went out to him, just like the rest of the family.

Not seeing her, he raised his head and stared at the coffin as if he didn't know how he could ever let it go.

She couldn't run off. She had to speak to him first.

Get this over with and get out of here, Miranda told herself. She took a deep breath, straightened her jacket and strode toward him, hand extended. "I'm so sorry for your loss, Lord Eaton."

He frowned and squinted at her as if he couldn't figure out where she'd come from. Then he came to himself and stood. He knew who she was. "Thank you, Ms. Steele. It's kind of you to be here."

Again, she didn't know how to reply to that, so she just nodded.

The bereaved husband was wearing a meticulously tailored black suit, his Van Dyke beard expertly trimmed. Only his demeanor and the hitch in his perfect British accent told her he was truly grieving.

He let out a long, helpless sigh. "A room full of people and I feel completely alone. Even my best friend has abandoned me tonight."

The dude who had been with Davinia at the polo match. "Isn't his name Sebastian...something?"

His manicured brows rose as if he was surprised she knew the name. "Yes. Sebastian Fairfax. He called earlier and gave me his condolences. He apologized profusely, saying he had to be out of town on business. He's a moody chap. I think he simply couldn't face...all this." He gestured around the room.

Miranda drew in a breath. She didn't want to think about whatever Davinia had been doing with Sebastian. She was tired of secret trysts and betrayals. But still she felt for the man. "I know it must be very hard on you."

"I deserve it. I should have gone to the police."

"What do you mean?"

He cast an uncomfortable look around the room. "It's no secret that I've never approved of my mother's marriage to Neville Ravensdale."

"No." His snide remarks the night they'd had dinner would have told her that if everyone else hadn't.

"Two nights after the Marc Antony dagger was stolen, Gabrielle tried to console me. She told me I'd be happy soon because the theft might make my mother leave him." He closed his eyes. "I brushed off her words. I thought she was being foolish. I was riding in the match the next day and I didn't want to think about it. Then when that incident happened with my horse...I wondered if she could have been involved in the theft somehow. I should have gone to the police and told them. If I had, she might still be alive." He pinched his nose between his fingers to stave off tears.

Miranda reached out and patted the grieving man's arm. She wondered how much he knew about Jewell and his letter. Surely, he was aware the barrister was dead.

"She was already involved," she reminded him as softly as she could. "I'm afraid she got in over her head. I don't think anyone could have saved her at that point."

He nodded, and jutting out his chin with fierce control, slowly turned his head as if he were forcing himself to look at the platform again. "My poor, poor, childish wife. I neglected her. I treated her so badly and she just kept on loving me. Why is it you don't appreciate what you have until it's gone?" He put his hand to his mouth to stifle another sob. Control was fleeting when you were in that much pain. "Please excuse me. I must collect myself." He turned away and marched down a short hall and into a room, closing the door behind him.

The room she'd been heading for.

With a sigh Miranda looked around the chamber again. There was no one left to speak to. She certainly wasn't in the mood for small talk with strangers. Her gaze wandered to an elaborate antique clock against the wall. She blinked.

Was that the right time? It was past nine. Where the hell was Parker? She spun around and circled the crowd, searching for him.

He wasn't at the casket. He wasn't speaking to Lady Davinia or Sir Neville or the Lovelaces or the Duchess of Oxham. She slipped down a few of the adjacent halls where guests had broken away to talk. He wasn't in any of them. She began asking total strangers if they'd seen a good-looking man in a dark blue suit. An American.

No one had.

She left the viewing room and made her way back to the front door where she found a doorman. "Did Mr. Wade Parker come in this way?"

"The investigator from America?"

At least he knew who Parker was. "Yes."

"I say, you're Ms. Steele, his partner, aren't you?"

That damned reporter's story again. "Yes," she snapped. "Have you seen Mr. Parker?"

He blinked at her and pulled at his coat awkwardly. "No, m'um. As far as I know he hasn't arrived yet."

Hasn't arrived yet? Hasn't arrived yet? He'd arrived with her over an hour ago.

She turned away, stomped back down the hall and into the main room, barely seeing where she was going. Her chest started to heave. Her head started to pound. It was all she could do to keep the lid on the rage bubbling over inside her.

Let's see, she thought. Where could Parker be right now? Taking an evening stroll along the Thames? A visit to Westminster? An audience with the Queen?

Hell, no. She knew damn well where he was. He went to Tottenham—without her.

He wasn't going to let this case lie. He didn't think it was over. He didn't think they'd done all they could. No, he felt the same way she did. He was going to see this through. He was going to finish it. He was going after a killer.

He was putting himself in danger and he didn't want her in on it. He was protecting her again, sheltering her, dropping her off in a safe place while he went out to do battle. She didn't know if she could ever forgive him for that.

Her mind a blur, she found Davinia and said goodbye. She hurried back down the hall and told the doorman to tell Mr. Parker where she'd gone if he returned. Then she headed out on foot, down the castle steps, over the century-old walkway, her fury building like a raging wildfire with each step.

How dare Parker leave her behind like this? If Scorpion or Shrivel didn't kill him, she might do it herself.

CHAPTER FORTY-ONE

Parker sat nursing his German lager in the far corner booth of The Winking Owl, his back to the wall, his eyes on the door.

The place seemed darker than the night they'd followed Shrivel here, but definitely not as crowded. The jukebox was off and only the monotonous voice of the soccer announcer contended with the conversations of the patrons under the low green-globed lights.

It was mostly men tonight. Tough-looking workingmen with bitterness in their eyes. And non-working types with even more bitterness. The type he'd seen in the bad parts of almost every city he'd worked in during his career. The type who might slit your throat for a few dollars. Or in this case a few pounds.

But perhaps he was reading too much into the clientele because of the one he'd come here to meet.

The two barmaids on duty looked more worn out tonight, though their workload was lighter. As she wiped down surfaces and cleaned glasses behind the bar, Winnie Waverly seemed particularly tired and distressed.

She hadn't waited on him, but he'd seen the sneer of recognition she'd given him when she thought he wasn't looking. He'd also seen her slip off with her cell phone in hand. Calling Shrivel to tell him he'd arrived and was alone?

He hoped so.

He glanced down at his watch. Winnie had made her call twenty minutes ago, and Shrivel had agreed to meet him ten before that. He was making him wait.

Shrivel was being careful. Or he was getting the money together.

Parker had told him on the phone he had information about the dagger, which he would exchange for a sum he had named. He planned to get him into his car on the pretense of taking him to where the dagger was. He would use the voice recorder on his phone without Shrivel's knowledge and get a confession from him. Then drag him to the nearest police station.

Then back to Quinton Castle, pay his respects, pick up Miranda, head home.

The business with Shrivel would be tricky, though. And risky to get into a vehicle with a man who had just hijacked a car and killed the driver, but he planned to frisk him first. If the young man didn't comply, he'd simply take him into a nearby alley and force him to cooperate. And then drag him to the nearest police station. But he knew he had to keep his head if he wanted to help the courts get an unquestionable conviction.

The door opened and two large men strolled in and found a table. Parker looked down at his watch again. Forty minutes late. Had Shrivel changed his mind? Or was he smart enough to see through this ploy?

Parker took a slow draw from his beer. He wouldn't have thought so.

His cell rang.

He stared at it a moment then picked it up. "Where are you?"

"At home."

"We agreed to meet at the pub."

"Too many customers. I can't afford to show my face."

Parker stiffened, nerves alert. Was he trying to play him? "Should I assume you're not interested then?"

An ugly laugh trickled through the phone. "Oh, I'm interested all right. Meet me 'ere." He gave him the address, not knowing Parker already had it.

"I'll be there in five minutes." He clicked off and set the phone down on the table.

So Shrivel was smarter than he'd thought. But was he really at home when the police hadn't been able to find him there?

This was a setup. The question was what to do with it.

He could get in his car and drive to the local police station without Shrivel. Have them send someone over to pick the murderer up. But if Shrivel was in fact in his house, the sight of police cars would make him run and destroy any further chance of bringing the degenerate in.

Parker got to his feet, tossed a few bills on the table and went out the front door.

He stood in the shelter of the corner entrance, eyeing the street.

A group of about five men in leather and chains loitered across the street to his left. They didn't seem to notice him. He saw nothing on the road to the right where his car was parked.

Shrivel might be at the auto repair shop. He'd drive over to Shrivel's street and ride past the house to see if there were any sign of him there, then give him another call. After that, he'd try the shop.

Eventually he would talk him out of his hiding place and into taking a ride with him.

Parker strode to the rental car and pulled his keys out of his pocket. He bent to put the key into the driver side door.

Just as it clicked open, he felt a body press up beside him. And cold metal against his temple.

"I thought you were at home."

The only reply was a low laugh.

With a well-practiced move Parker twisted, brought up his arm fast, and knocked Shrivel's gun hand away. The swine still held onto the weapon. Parker lunged toward him and gave him a hard jab to the stomach.

Shrivel doubled over with an *oof.*

Parker reached out to take the gun from him. His fingers were inches away when someone caught his arm from behind, gave him a sharp punch to the ribs that took his breath, forced him against the hood of the car with a slam.

He turned his head and caught the outline of a tall, bulky figure. He tried to get an elbow free, to get a foot around his leg to bring him down, but the hulking mass pressed in closer. He had no leverage.

"What the fuck are you doing?" Parker growled.

The big man yanked his arm behind his back. "I wouldn't make any funny moves if I was you, septic."

Parker gritted his teeth at the sudden pain. "I came here to make a deal. What do you want?"

"We wants you to take us for a little drive," the man hissed in a thick accent. Then he reached for the handle and jerked the car door open. "Get in."

CHAPTER FORTY-TWO

This was a hell of a mistake.

After she'd left the castle, Miranda had raced out into the street and had to ask five different people directions, like some lost tourist. They all told her there was only one mode of transportation to Tottenham, so she ended up having to take one of those jolly red buses.

Now she was bouncing along trapped inside while the bus took its sweet time with a winding path that seemed to stop at every corner to let passengers on and off. She checked her watch, glared out the window, counted the passing streets.

"Parker, what were you thinking?" she muttered under her breath over and over. How could he do this to her?

After an ulcer-inducing hour-long ride, the bus finally came to a halt on a street in the Tottenham neighborhood.

Hoping Parker wasn't heading back to Camden by now, she got off and hiked the few blocks to The Winking Owl.

As she walked toward the pub, she scanned the curbs. Several empty parking spots. There weren't as many people out as when they were here before. But she didn't see the rental car anywhere.

She strolled past the pub's corner entrance where a couple was making out in the shadows and tried the side street.

Still no rental.

She went all the way down that street and stopped at the far corner. Shrivel's house was that way. He'd walked here the night they'd followed him. She shook her head. He wasn't at home, or the police would have nabbed him already. That left only one other possibility she knew of.

With a sinking feeling, she realized where Parker was.

She turned around and headed back to the pub. At the corner entrance, she crossed the street and turned the other way, hurrying along, moving as fast as she could without looking vulnerable.

The gold chain Parker had given her felt cold against her skin. Good grief.

Pretending to scratch the back of her neck, she reached behind her, undid the clasp, and slipped it into her pocket. Some people around here would cut your throat for something like that.

She turned left at the next corner. Was this the right way? She wasn't sure, but she kept going and soon passed a dingy little café. With a breath of relief, she recognized the shop's faded green awning. In the next block she sniffed the odor of less-than-fresh grilled lamb coming from a place that boasted kebobs. She remembered that, too.

She was headed the right way. But it seemed ten times farther than it had in the car. Didn't matter. Next block. Next block. Turn. Next block.

She pressed on. Past the buildings that grew darker and more menacing. Over the jagged bricks that made up the sidewalk, hoping a snag in them wouldn't catch her toe and bring her down.

No time for that now. No time.

Here was where even tougher looking gangs of jerks loitered around the corners with their black leather and cigs. As she passed a group across the street, one of them whistled at her like she was a dog.

She gave them her coldest fuck-off look and plodded on. Faster. Faster.

Her heart banged in her chest in time to her footsteps and her breath hitched. She was getting that antsy feeling again, that prickle at the base of her skull. That horrible crawling feeling. Like slimy snakes were slithering up her back and down her arms.

Something bad was going to happen. Or was happening now. Or had already happened.

She all but broke into a run. She had to get there. Had to get there. Had to get there.

She tore around another corner, down another half a block bordered by a brick wall on one side—and there she was.

Shivering in the damp, chilly air she pulled her suit jacket around her and stared through the chain link fence topped with barbed wire at the rusty auto repair shop with its worn sign.

Stingy streetlamps cast eerie shadows across the yard beyond. Dogs barked in the distance. She took a step toward the fence. No windows on this side of the building. Hard to tell if anyone was inside. She peered around an ugly bush and her insides turned to dust.

Her blood pounded in her head so hard, she wanted to throw up. She couldn't breathe. Her skin felt colder than if she were dead.

In the first spot close to the side door where they'd seen Shrivel exit with the other hoods—sat Parker's rental car.

Oh, God. Oh, God! What did he think he was doing in there? Why in the hell had he come here? Why did he come without her?

Wind-chilled tears stung her eyes. She shivered with rage now instead of cold. In the tumult of the angry, panicked thoughts tearing through her brain, only one surfaced.

How in the hell was she going to get in there?

CHAPTER FORTY-THREE

Stay calm, she ordered herself and forced two full breaths of cold damp air into her lungs.

Wait a minute. Hadn't they seen a possible way in on the other side of the block when they followed Shrivel here? But how long would it take to get there on foot? She'd already wasted too much time.

She raised her head and studied the barbed wire atop the fence. It looked old like everything did here. Maybe it wasn't really electrified.

She took a few steps, searching the ground for a stick to test it with when she caught sight of the neighboring yard. Was that an optical illusion? Wishful thinking?

She hurried over to find out. No one around.

Yes, the gate really was open.

Just a tad. Without considering the cons, she slipped through the opening and into the yard.

The building next door was set farther back than the repair shop, the whole front was gravel. Vehicles parked every which way. They made good cover as she picked her way to the side, feeling every stone through the thin soles of her dress shoes.

She squinted into the darkness, her gaze scanning the chain link barrier between her and the repair shop. A few more steps and she made out the form. A burst of joy exploded in her chest.

No barbed wire here.

She hurried to the fence, shoved a pointed toe into a link and pulled herself up.

"Damn, Parker," she grunted under her breath. "Next time do me the courtesy of packing a pair of jeans and tennis shoes."

Up she crawled. Hand over hand. Toe over toe. Until she reached the top.

The fence swayed with her weight as she swung one leg over, and she nearly let out a cry. Hold it together. Hold it together. Somehow, she did.

Other leg over. Now down. Down. Jump.

She was on the ground.

Every nerve alert, slowly she turned around.

A high row of windows stretched along this side of the building. Light flickered through them. Someone was in there. But the windows were too far up to climb through.

There was a door on the other side where the rental car was, she reminded herself. They'd seen Shrivel and the others use it before. Something told her that wasn't the way to go.

She stood for a long moment listening to the sound of her own breathing and backfire in a far away street.

She made her decision.

Hoping a rabid Doberman didn't come barreling around the corner, she headed for the back.

She was there in seconds, peering around the rusty siding into the shadows. In the dim light she could make out a row of unkempt bushes and a worn dirt path leading to a back door.

Bingo.

Three quick steps and she was there.

She laid her palm carefully over the handle. Her heart banging in her ears, she tried it. The door opened. Unlocked.

Luck? Or a trap? Didn't matter. She had to take the chance. But she would take one precaution.

Her breath hitching, she pulled out her cell and dialed emergency. 999 it was here, she'd learned somewhere along the way. As softly as she could she described the place to the dispatcher. The woman on the other end said they'd send someone right out. Yeah, maybe in an hour. She couldn't wait that long.

Hoping that call hadn't been a mistake, she put her fingers back on the handle, inched the door open, peered inside.

Darkness.

She listened hard and heard an odd rumbling sound over her own rapid breathing. In one fluid move she swung open the door, stepped inside, noiselessly shut it behind her.

Light rippled through a low internal window.

She shot down to a crouch, held her breath as her eyes adjusted to the dark.

Old wooden chairs lined up against the wall. A desk. Filing cabinets. She was in some sort of waiting room.

Another door on the opposite wall led into the main area.

She duck-walked to it fast as she could, trying not to choke on the dust and moldy smelling air. The inside window was close to the door. She dared to raise herself a few inches and peek through a grimy corner.

Her arm gripped her stomach as it clenched with horrific pain. She slapped her other hand over her mouth to stifle a cry. She heaved as she fought the panic, the sheer terror scraping through her with razor sharp teeth.

A vehicle, an old van or something, was parked and running in one corner of the shop, not far from the room she was in. Its headlights were on. The only illumination in the large, open space.

Three dark figures stood in the light, their backs to the van. She recognized the body shape of one of them. Shrivel. All three faced a chair where someone was bound.

The prisoner was turned toward the light, so she had no trouble making out his face as he blinked in the glare and glowered at his captors.

It was Parker.

CHAPTER FORTY-FOUR

This couldn't be happening. It just couldn't be.

How the hell did Parker get himself in a mess like this? But she knew the answer. He was being noble. The police would never catch up to Shrivel. So he had to lure him in somehow. He must have nearly done it. It was a miracle he'd even found the bastard. But something had gone wrong.

Now what?

Her head spun with nausea as she fought back the rush of emotion. There had to be something she could do. Something. Anything. She forced herself to think.

In the thirteen years before she met Parker, she'd regularly picked bar fights with men and won. But those were mostly drunken slobs who'd underestimated her. Could she take on three ruthless criminals at the same time?

She had to try. If she could just get to Parker, get him out of here somehow, no matter what happened to her she'd consider it a win.

She scooted over to the inside door and pressed it open.

The engine sound grew louder. Still crouching, she squeaked through the door and into the main repair area. The running van was about three yards away. Breathing in the grease and oil fumes, she crouched along the perimeter.

She heard Parker's cavalier laugh. "You can't want the death of an American on your hands." His voice sounded funny.

"'Oo says it will be on my hands?" Shrivel sneered. "We know how to get rid of bodies."

Dear God.

"You didn't dispose of Lady Gabrielle Eaton's very well."

"That was a message."

A chill went down Miranda's spine. Shrivel had murdered her to send a message to Jewell.

She felt her way along the wall. It was made of big cinder block bricks, cold and clammy. In the shadows, she nearly banged into a table shoved against the wall. She looked at the figures. No one had heard it.

She dared to crane her neck and peer into the light.

Oh, my God. Parker's face was bloody and bruised. Red stains were all over his dress shirt and coat. One of his eyes was swollen shut.

But he acted as nonchalant as if he were in the dining room back at Eaton House. "A message, was it? Apparently, it was unclear."

"Where's the fucking dagger, septic?"

Parker managed another laugh. "Funny, I was going to ask you the same thing."

Shrivel reared back and hit him hard on the face. Blood shot into the air.

Grasping the table leg to steady herself, it was all Miranda could do to keep from lunging forward and beating the daylights out that creep. But that would only get her in the same spot.

Fudoshin. She recalled Parker teaching her to use it the first time they sparred together. Calm and control in the midst of a storm. Serenity. Okay. Good time to review the lesson.

She drew in a deep, motor oil scented breath and gathered her wits.

She looked around. There were all kinds of tools strewn everywhere. Wrenches, tire irons, screwdrivers, hammers, all kinds of machinery. An engine block. Overhead those hoses for oil changes hung from the rafters.

Any of these tools would work as a weapon, but would they be enough?

She studied Parker's three captors. Tall, lean Shrivel with his spiky black hair. He was wild and unpredictable, maybe the easiest to take out. A big guy she hadn't seen before stood beside him.

Following the outline of curly hair that was shaved at the sides, she studied his bulky mass. Maybe two-fifty, three hundred pounds. He'd be tough to beat.

And finally, a shorter, stocky guy. Had to be Scorpion himself. The boss had to be here to oversee things. Maybe he thought Shrivel had screwed up. Maybe he thought Shrivel had tried to screw him over. Maybe Shrivel was screwing with Parker's face to prove to his boss he hadn't.

Didn't matter why. She had to get Parker away from them before they killed him.

Sure. Take down two hoodlums and a notorious London gang leader the cops couldn't bring in, all by herself. Piece of cake.

She had to get closer. Still squatting, she dared to scoot across the front of the long table. Dangling along the floor her fingers touched something that wasn't concrete. Leather. Was that really what she thought it was? She squinted at it, grinning in the dark. Hell, yes. A tool belt.

As quietly as she could she picked it up and pulled it around her waist. It was loaded. Screwdrivers, wrenches, a hammer. If only she could find a nail gun.

She hustled around the table's far edge and turned in at the end of it. She spied a familiar shape in the darkness and sucked in a breath. Now there was a real weapon.

Leaning against the wall was a long, beautiful sledgehammer.

She moved over to it and dared to grasp the handle near the base. Gently she pulled it away from the wall. She glared over her shoulder. No one had noticed her. Testing the hammer, she lifted it an inch or two. Had to be twenty pounds or more.

This was her equalizer.

Summoning all the strength she had, she rose. She grasped the hammer with both hands and turned around.

"Why'd ya tell us you 'ad the dagger, then, you fuckin' Yank?" Shrivel screeched.

"Yeah, why?" The big guy stepped forward and socked Parker in the jaw. Her stomach lurched as she heard him grunt in pain.

You're first, Miranda decided. She hoisted the hammer over her shoulder and crept forward.

The thugs were focused on their prisoner. Didn't see her creeping up in the dark. But she knew that wouldn't last long.

She had to strike now.

She took two long steps, planted her feet, and swung the hammer like she was making a grand slam in the ninth inning of the World Series.

A loud squishy crunching sound rang out as she hit the big guy square on his temple. Blood spewed from his large head, and he crumbled to the floor. He didn't move.

One down for the count. She stepped over the body. Who was next?

Shrivel spun around, the look of shock on his ugly face made her want to laugh. But he didn't give her time.

He lunged forward, screaming like a wild goat in heat.

She swung the hammer at him as hard as she could, but he was already too close. She missed. His palms smacked her hard in the chest and the hammer flew out of her hands, clattering to the ground as she stumbled back and lost her balance.

She hit the floor hard. Ribbons of pain shot through her body. *Keep your head. Keep your head.*

Shrivel was coming at her. She rolled under a nearby table, grabbed onto its frame. She forced herself up, tools clanging and banging to the floor as she hefted the table and swung it at her attacker.

The tabletop struck Shrivel full across the abdomen, the force of the blow swatting him away like a dirty little fly.

He stumbled back but kept his footing. More agile than she'd figured.

Heart pounding, she scanned the floor for the sledgehammer. Couldn't find it. She looked up.

Shrivel had a tire iron in his hand.

His black eyes glowing with rage, he came at her fast as a panther.

She danced away.

Moving faster, he caught up, swung at her head. She ducked. He swung the other way. She ducked again. She was about to throw her leg back for a kick to the face when he lunged, slammed her, knocked her against the hood of the running van.

The blow took her breath. Struggling for air she felt the rumble of its engine ripple through her torso as Shrivel leered over her.

He brought up the tire iron, pressed it against her throat. She caught it with both hands, pushed back.

Blood pumped through her brain as she strained and grunted through gritted teeth. It was just a glorified version of arm wrestling, she told herself. She could hold him off until she got her feet into position.

His fishy breath batted against her face. His long, crooked nose hovered over her like a vulture about to devour its prey. Sweat rolled down the length of it and dripped onto her cheeks.

And suddenly, all she could think of was Lady Gabrielle and how terrified she must have been alone in her car with this crazy bastard.

You sonofabitch, she thought as her foot went between his feet.

She thrust her knee up with all her might. Got him right in the balls.

Yelping like a wounded hyena, Shrivel dropped the iron and hobbled away, cradling his crotch.

More where that came from. But she needed another weapon. She scanned the floor for something, anything…and took a little too long.

Somehow Shrivel'd recovered. He flew at her and knocked her to the ground. Before she could think, his fingers were around her throat.

"Don't need no bloody tool. I'll keel you with me bare 'ands."

And he'd do it, too. His grip was so tight around her neck she could barely breathe. Training had her hands groping at his wrists, trying to break his hold. But they were both too slippery with sweat.

Think. Think. Think.

What could she do? She didn't have a weapon within reach. She hissed in a breath and air must have finally reached her brain.

Of course. What had she been thinking? She'd forgotten all about the tool belt. She reached down, groped at her waist just as Shrivel began to shake her. Her head banged against the concrete. She couldn't last much longer.

Her fingers grasped at the loops, searching for…something. Anything.

Finally, her grip landed on the handle of something. She jerked it from its place. She was seeing stars now. Black spots, bright lights flashing in her head. She felt her eyes roll back.

But she managed to force them open one more time.

She lifted the tool, turned it where she could just see it. It was an awl. Kind of like a dagger. Fitting. This was it.

Summoning all the strength she had she jerked it back then drove the blade into the side of Shrivel's head with all her might.

His grip around her throat loosened. She gasped in air as she watched his mouth open and saw blood pour out of it and onto her shirt, mingling with the stuff gushing out the side of his head.

She pushed him off her and got up. His body rolled over onto the floor.

"That's for Lady Gabrielle," she said, and gave his corpse a kick.

She stood there, head spinning, sucking in air for what seemed like an eternity. Then she heard a funny noise.

Clapping.

She turned and squinted into the lights from the still running van, saw Parker sitting there, still bound to the chair. He hadn't moved, hadn't acknowledged her at all. Was he already dead?

Scorpion stepped into the headlights, batting his hands together. "Quite an entertaining exhibition, Ms. Steele. You're very good."

What?

She stared at his stocky body, his slicked back hair. He had on black slacks and a black dress shirt open to the waist. About three pounds of gold chain hung around his neck.

Shaking his head at the lump on the floor that had been Shrivel, he chuckled. "If only half my men could fight with such passion. But now, I'm afraid it's back to business." Slowly he drew a revolver from his waist. Looked like a .357.

Terror braided her organs into knots as, still smiling, he slowly strolled over to Parker and put the gun to his head.

No. "Are you crazy?" she gasped.

He laughed. "We'll see who's the crazy one. All you have to do is tell me where the Marc Antony dagger is and your partner lives."

She blinked at him, wondering if she were having a nightmare. How could he think she knew where the dagger was? "The police said Jewell sold it on the black market."

He let out a low ugly laugh. "Of course, they did. They're idiots."

Parker must have made Shrivel think he had the dagger somewhere. It was how he got the thug's attention. But that didn't mean she knew where it was. Then she realized Scorpion couldn't know whether she knew or not.

He was taking a gamble, hoping Parker had told her.

It didn't matter what she told him. If she convinced him she didn't know where the dagger was, he'd still kill them both. If she made something up, he'd kill them, too.

There was no way to win.

"You're wasting my time, Ms. Steele." She heard the click as Scorpion cocked the revolver. "I will kill him. You know I will."

Yeah, she did. He was too far for her to try to get the gun away from him. He'd shoot long before she reached him.

She stood staring at the evil man, her chest heaving with terror. Was this the end for them? Failure and defeat? Would she never get home? Never see her daughter again? Never hold Parker in her arms again?

The sound of the van's engine rumbled over her thoughts, ironically annoying her. Damn thing was still running. And then it came to her.

One chance. Only one chance. She had to take it.

As fast as she could, she spun and raced to the van's door. She yanked it open, climbed inside, put the thing in gear, revved the motor.

"Let's play a game of chicken, you slimeball."

She hit the accelerator. The tires squealed and took off. Her gamble paid off. Scorpion was too shocked to pull the trigger. She watched the bastard's face turn to horror as she headed right for him and Parker.

He didn't move. He thought she wouldn't do it, didn't he? But what did she have to lose? At least they'd go out in a blaze of glory.

As she barreled toward the pair, her courage wavered. *Move, dammit. Run.* Could she really run both of them down? Kill the only man who'd ever loved her? The front fender was inches away from its target.

And then he caved.

Scorpion dropped the gun and scampered away from the headlights like a roach crawling under the stove. She swerved, barely missing Parker, the tires crying out in protest.

In the headlights she caught Scorpion running for the far wall. Now that was just perfect. She hit the gas and aimed straight for the concrete.

The van lurched forward, slammed into his body with a loud thud, hit the cement wall with a crash loud as Judgment Day.

Miranda flew forward banged her head against the windshield, cracked the glass. She was slung back again. She must have lost consciousness for a few moments.

When she came to, she was sitting still, the engine sputtering against the wall, a burning smell in her nose. Scorpion's dead eyes stared at her through the shattered windshield.

Outside she heard the whine of a foreign siren. Wample or somebody was on the way.

She touched her forehead. Blood. She couldn't feel any pain. Yet. And then she woke up.

Parker. She had to get to Parker.

She jerked open the van door and ran across the floor, leaping over the debris.

"Parker! Parker! Are you all right?"

She reached him just as someone broke through the window. "Police!"

"Over here. We need an ambulance." She grabbed his shoulders, saw his head roll back. "Parker," she cried again, not daring to shake him. "Parker."

But he didn't answer.

CHAPTER FORTY-FIVE

All hell broke loose.

Suddenly the shop was flooded with people. Police shouting and trying to keep everyone away from the crime scene, officers yelling directions, medics trying to get to the injured.

Total chaos.

Someone found a light and switched it on, and Miranda blinked dizzily at the bloody scene of gory violence and destruction around her.

But all she cared about was Parker.

Three paramedics carefully cut off the duct tape binding him and took him away on a stretcher. Inspector Wample appeared out of nowhere and wanted a statement from her. She told him to fuck off and talk to her later and got in the back of the ambulance with Parker. They raced through the streets, sirens screaming.

Someone slapped a piece of gauze on her forehead, wiped the blood off her face, asked if she was in pain anywhere.

She waved him away and stared at Parker lying there, motionless, strapped to the gurney. While the paramedics hooked him to a monitoring machine, stuck an IV into his arm, treated his wounds, all she could do was watch.

They were speaking in medicalese with British accents, and her ears were still ringing with shock, but she caught snatches of what they were saying. Contusions, facial abrasions, head trauma, subdural hematomas. They were worried about brain damage.

Brain damage? Oh, God. That couldn't be. She couldn't lose him now.

If only he would wake up. Wake up, Parker. Please. But when they reached the hospital, he still hadn't moved.

Inside the hospital, they rushed Parker away while nurses ushered her into a room. They cleaned her up, scanned her head, put a bandage over the cut on her forehead.

What were they doing all that for? She wasn't the one with the problem.

"I want to see my husband," she told a youthful looking girl in scrubs.

The girl nodded, and when they were finished with her, she took Miranda to the waiting room near the trauma unit.

All they could tell her was that the doctors were still working on him, and someone would be out to speak to her as soon as they were finished.

She stumbled into the room, sank down into a chair near a potted plant.

An hour passed. Two. Assistant Chief Officer Ives found her, took down her statement, and she had to live the nightmare all over again. But he did his job quickly, thanked her, said she wouldn't be charged and left.

As she watched his flowing raincoat disappear down the hall, she put her head in her hands and burst into tears.

CHAPTER FORTY-SIX

It must have been an hour later when a blond-haired young man in teal scrubs told her Parker was being taken to a room.

He turned out to be one of the doctors that had worked on him. As he escorted her through elevators and a maze of halls, he explained Parker's injuries.

She wished she had a medical dictionary, but she understood the basics. Two bruised ribs, a dislocated jaw, a concussion. No brain damage.

No brain damage. Tears filled her eyes again. Thank God, thank God. "Can I talk to him now?"

The doctor's face grew grim, but he nodded. "You can see him. He hasn't woken up yet." He turned the knob to Parker's door.

She stepped inside the room.

The lights were low. Parker lay on a standard hospital bed, with its head propped up.

His forehead was bandaged. One eye was dark and purple, puffy and swollen shut. There was a tube up his nose, another in his mouth, an IV in his arm. Machines and monitors blinked softly and beeped away. The air smelled of antiseptic.

Quietly she pulled up a chair and sat down beside him. She took his hand in hers.

No response.

"Parker," she whispered. "I'm here. It's Miranda." He lay still, breathing in and out, in and out. "We got the bad guys."

Nothing.

Tears began to stream down her face. She remembered the doctor telling her concussions were tricky. Couldn't predict what might happen. Would he never wake up? What was she going to do if he didn't?

No, he had to. He had to.

She brushed the tears away from her face and put both her hands on his. She traced the outline of his knuckles with her finger. This strong hand that had helped her out of so many jams. That had trained her, comforted her, soothed her, made love to her.

How could she lose him now? How could she live without him? He meant the world to her. She didn't know what to do. How long would she have to wait before he woke up?

He had to wake up. He had to. She had so many things to say to him. She had to tell him how much she loved him. She had to yell at him for going off on his own and getting himself into this fix.

Off on his own. Like she always did.

Was this what he'd gone through when she was in a coma? No wonder he was always so protective of her. No wonder he always fumed when she went off by herself.

But he'd been the one to do it this time, dammit.

What if their roles had been reversed tonight? What if she'd been the one to go after those thugs? She would have if she had thought of it first. What if she were the one lying there. What if they had done God knows what to her? What if they had killed her?

Parker would feel responsible. He was the one who'd brought her into the Agency, trained her, sparked her passion for this work, come up with the consulting idea. He'd blame himself if anything happened to her. He'd never be able to live with it.

Why hadn't she seen that before? Was it too late to fix that? It couldn't be. It just couldn't be.

She took his hand, squeezed it gently. "Parker, I get it," she told him. "I understand now."

But he didn't move.

Oh, God. She might never get to tell him. She might never get to hear his voice again. Never know the sound of that sexy Southern rhythm. No, she couldn't let that happen. She wasn't going to let that happen. She'd think of something. Something. But right now, fatigue hit her with a sucker's punch and suddenly she was spent. Exhaustion hung over her like a dark cloud.

She had to get some sleep. And when she woke up, Parker would be awake, too. Awake and alert and ready to read her the riot act for going to Tottenham so late at night alone. Yeah, she'd set him straight on that.

Still holding onto Parker's hand, she leaned back in the chair, closed her eyes, and listened to the beeping monitors as she drifted off.

CHAPTER FORTY-SEVEN

When she woke, sunlight was streaming in through the window and a nurse was checking Parker's vitals.

Miranda shot up in the chair, ignoring the pain that shot through her muscles. "Is he awake?"

The nurse shook her head, but she could see that herself. He hadn't moved.

The nurse smiled at her with the standard sympathy. "Why don't you go down and have some breakfast?"

Sure, she thought. Why not? She didn't want to leave Parker's side, but she needed a walk at least. She was as stiff as a brick, and all her muscles were bitching at her for what she'd put them through last night.

She got up, stretched, and headed down the hall.

She wandered the halls for a while, decided she couldn't get breakfast down, and found a vending machine where she could get a cup of coffee.

She stood in an empty waiting room as she drank it, staring through the tall windows at the glorious city with its ancient monuments in the early morning light. She should call someone, she thought. Parker's daughter, Gen. Her father. She was stunned to realize he'd be a comfort to her now.

She'd never have found him if it hadn't been for Parker. Never have found Mackenzie. Her life would be that miserable endless treadmill of mere survival she'd been on when she met him.

She wiped her hand across her eyes. What was she going to tell her father? Gen? Everyone at the Agency?

That they'd gone off in search of a stolen treasure and nearly lost their lives? That they'd come up empty-handed?

Why had they come to this city? Had it been worth it? For a lost dagger that would never be recovered? No, for an old friend. A friend who had also lost.

Old friend. Old friend.

Her mind began to race with the recent events. The polo match. Soho. The wake. Actions, gestures, words. They all played together in her mind like a movie.

And then it clicked. The pieces fell into place. She knew.

Trenton Jewell had been telling the truth.

Damned if she would let this one go.

She had the number. She'd gotten it from Parker when they'd first arrived. She pulled her cell out of her pocket and dialed.

As it rang, she knew she was making the call that would set everything straight. And maybe even make what they'd all sacrificed worth it.

CHAPTER FORTY-EIGHT

Davinia unlocked the door to the flat in Chelsea and stepped inside.

She strode across the wooden floor, drinking in the smell of the place, taking in its details.

The homey pillows on the divan, the roses on the coffee table, the whatnot cupboard with her favorite china. He'd furnished it with a modern look that showed off his creative style, but with her tastes in mind.

Ah, these rooms, this place where they'd spent so many hours of mindless bliss. Talking, kissing, touching. The day they'd almost made it to the bedroom. She'd longed to be with him that way, but she hadn't dared. If she did, she was sure he'd leave her. And the rapturous fantasy she'd indulged in would evaporate like the morning dew.

What was he doing with a woman twice his age anyway?

No, that wasn't the reason she'd turned him away that afternoon they'd almost made love. Deep down she knew she could never betray Neville, no matter what he'd done to her.

But the pretty fantasy she'd lived here was gone now. Everything had changed.

She found him on the balcony gazing out over the square, the wind playing with the thick blond waves of his hair she'd loved running her fingers through. He was wearing a lounge suit of sky blue, a color that accented his fair features. It was cut in a style that made his youthful form all too tempting. His casual posture evoked memories of the plans they'd made together, fingers entwined, hearts full of desperate hope and dreams of a future together.

But everything they'd had was just that. A dream. One that would never come true. One she hadn't really wanted to come true.

She knew that now.

"Davinia." He turned to her with that boyish twinkle in his cobalt eyes that always set her heart aflutter. His face went somber as he reached out for her.

She stepped away and shook her head. "No, Sebastian. Not now."

"As you wish." He straightened himself, obviously displeased.

"You told me on the phone you found Prentis."

He nodded and looked away, leaned his elbows on the balustrade. "He was in Bristol."

She gasped. "So far away?"

"When the story broke out in the news he panicked and went to his mother's. I found him there yesterday."

How close they had come to losing it altogether. "Where did the delivery company think Prentis was?"

"They weren't concerned. Before he left, he called in and quit his job. Right after the police questioned him."

"That didn't arouse suspicion?"

"Apparently there's a high turnover in the security business. Though he had good references and a spotless record. I paid him twice what I said I would when he agreed to do what I proposed." She could hear the guilt in his voice, felt it cutting into her own heart.

So they'd destroyed a career of an innocent friend along with everything else with their foolish scheme. "The poor boy must have been terrified."

"Out of his wits. Still is. The police are reinvestigating the lorry company."

"Oh, dear Lord."

He was quick to comfort her. "But there's no evidence. Everything went as planned. Prentis did everything according to my instructions."

"He replaced it with the counterfeit you bought?"

"Yes."

She let out a breath. "So Trenton wasn't involved."

"Not in our part. Or should I say your part?" There was rancor in his tone now that roused her temper.

That was unfair. "It was your idea, Sebastian," she snapped.

He waved an arm, eyes flashing. "Inspired by your constant complaining over Neville's obsession with the damn thing. And you didn't say no when I suggested it."

That much was true. "I didn't believe you could pull it off."

"But I did."

She turned away, pressed her fingers to her temples. "No, Sebastian. I can't blame you. Everything that's happened is my fault."

He was at her side in an instant, pulling her into his arms. "Oh, my darling, no. Forgive me. I didn't mean what I said. It was I. I'm the one who carried it out. But neither of us could have known what Trenton had done. That there was a gang after the thing."

They should have known every ruthless criminal might have made an attempt to take the dagger, might have killed for it. If they had thought that through...

Gently, she pushed him away. "It isn't that simple, Sebastian. Not anymore."

He stood staring at her, his chest heaving. "Dear God, I wish I'd never heard of that blasted dagger."

She turned away and stared over the balustrade. Two young children were playing beside the fountain of Venus down below, laughing and carefree.

She sighed as if her heart would break in two. "All I wanted was one last chance."

She felt him reach for her arm, spin her around.

He glared at her. "And how's that working out, Davinia?"

His cruel jealousy stung her. She knew he'd only gone through with this to prove Neville didn't care for her any longer. To make her leave him. But he'd hit the right nerve. It wasn't working out at all.

She'd never wanted to ruin Neville's big day, never wanted to cause so much trouble. She never meant for anyone to know anything was wrong but him. She'd wanted him to turn to her. When he got home that day, to confide in her, bare his soul to her, tell her he'd failed in his quest, that he couldn't figure out how it had happened.

And then she would tell him what she had done. Show him she had his cherished prize. And he'd understand at last what lengths she'd go to win back his love, to get his attention.

He would be so stunned and thrilled, he couldn't help falling in love with her again. Filled with relief and joy, he would take her in his arms and kiss her. They would come back together and be just as they were in the beginning. They would take long walks and talk the way they used to. Intimate, close walks. They'd make love. It had been so long since she'd felt his arms around her.

But it had all unraveled before she had a chance to catch her breath.

She inhaled, straightened. She had to get this over with. "Do you have it?"

He gave her a curt nod. "It's in here."

She followed him into the sitting room, watched him stroll to the cupboard, open a drawer. He took out a long black velvet pouch. The kind you kept expensive jewelry in.

He handed it to her. "Here."

"Thank you." She didn't know what else to say. She took it from him and slipped it into her handbag.

"Davinia, I beg of you. Take that thing and toss it in the Thames. Sell it yourself. I don't care how you do it, just get rid of it. Get rid of him. He doesn't love you. I'm the one who can make you happy."

She opened her mouth and stared at him, saw his cobalt eyes were turning dark with tears. Slowly she shook her head. "I can't, Sebastian. I simply can't."

He ran a hand through his hair in frustration. "You can't take the blame for this."

"But I am to blame."

"Don't say that." There was desperation in his voice now as it broke with the words.

His handsome face lost all its ardent expectation. She was crushing him, and she hated herself for doing it. How had she ever let herself get caught between two men? One who'd grown to love her but couldn't have her, and one who had her but didn't love her anymore.

Once more he reached for her, took her hand in his, gently this time. "Stay with me, Davinia. Please."

It would never work between them. She'd been lying to herself all this time. She'd never really wanted it to.

She pulled her hand out of his and strode to the door. With her fingers on the handle for the very last time, she turned back to him. "I'm sorry, Sebastian. I can't stay with you. I have a daughter-in-law to bury this afternoon."

CHAPTER FORTY-NINE

Sir Neville sat alone on the rear portico of Eaton House, staring out at the gardens without seeing them.

He didn't hear the warblers singing in the hawthorns, didn't notice the gardeners trimming the hedgerows. His tea and late breakfast sat before him on the table getting cold. His heart was far too heavy to eat.

Ruminating over the recent events, he ran a hand over his face and felt dizzy with grief. So much had happened. So much tragedy, he thought. So much pain. So many people had been hurt. George, Trenton, Gabrielle. Oh, poor, foolish, foolish Gabby. And Lionel, who was now crushed to powder by her death.

And the phone call he'd received this morning from Inspector Wample. Three of the Stingers gang found dead in an auto repair shop in Tottenham. Including the leader, Scorpion. The man Trenton had dealt with. Including the man named Malcolm Shrivel. The vile hoodlum who had murdered Gabrielle.

And his good friend Russell Parker, kidnapped by those very men and beaten within an inch of his life. And Miranda, who had found him and called the police in the nick of time.

All because of that blasted dagger. All because he couldn't let it go. He couldn't let the police handle it. No, he'd had to call in his friend's son to find the thing. And now?

Russell was still alive, but he hadn't woken up yet. What if he didn't?

It was all his fault, Neville told himself. Every bit of it. He bent his head and pressed his hands to his face, wanting to weep. But there were no more tears left in him.

He'd rung the hospital as soon as he'd heard the news, asked to see him, but they'd told him no visitors. He'd go later, he told himself. Russell would be awake then. Later this afternoon. After…the funeral. The thought of Gabby's burial brought a fresh round of tears.

Apparently, he wasn't done with them after all. He took out a handkerchief and let himself mourn anew.

But after a time, he could weep no more.

Putting the handkerchief back into his pocket, he checked his watch. They would be heading out in an hour. He should get ready. He took several steadying breaths to pull himself together.

He had just risen to his feet when he heard footsteps. He turned in time to see Davinia step onto the portico.

She was dressed in stern dark blue, but the silky fabric of her dress made the classic shape of her body as elegant as ever. Her dark hair piled atop her head revealed that graceful neck he would forever adore. Around it she wore a simple string of pearls. Under her arm she carried a matching handbag.

Her face was lined with sorrow. She'd been crying.

"Neville, we have to talk," she said quietly.

He closed his eyes. Oh, dear Lord, not now.

He reached out for the back of the chair to steady himself. He'd been preparing himself for this speech for longer than he could remember. He'd always known one day she'd come and tell him it was over between them.

But why now? Didn't he have enough grief to bear? Didn't she? He ran a hand over his face. No, it didn't really matter, did it? What was one more sorrow in this battalion of them?

He drew in a tight breath and braced himself. "I suppose we do."

She took a hesitant step toward hm. "I feel...I know...we haven't been quite honest with one another."

His eyes flashed. Honest? Had there ever been a more dishonest couple? He would show her honesty. He would tell her exactly how he felt about what she'd done to him.

As he opened his heart to her his voice was low and full of accusation. "Davinia, you were the love of my life when we met. I thought I had found my perfect match. My soulmate. We used to stroll these very grounds and discuss everything we loved. Rodin and Michelangelo and Etruscan art and the Great Sphinx of Giza. I couldn't have been happier when we were first married. And then—"

She blinked at him in shock. "And then?"

Did she have to ask? "And then you began..." he waved a hand, searching for the words, "burying yourself in social affairs. Dinners and parties and flower shows. There was always something. We were never alone."

Her mouth opened and she turned a little pale. "What on earth are you saying, Neville? I did all that for you."

"For me? For me? How can you say such a thing?"

She took another step closer. "Don't you remember the vicious things Lionel said when we told him we were going to be married? That you were below us, that you'd never be one of us?"

"Of course, I do." Why was she bringing up old wounds? Weren't the fresh ones enough for her?

"It cut you to the quick. It did me, too. I could see how deep that wound went. You felt unworthy of me."

He stared at her. She'd seen how he'd felt?

She turned away and moved to the edge of the portico, rested her hand on its classical banister as she gazed out at the gardens. "The truth was, many of my friends agreed with Lionel. I was determined to prove them all wrong. I held my head high and attended as many social affairs as I could. They would all see I was not ashamed to have you at my side, to call you my husband. On the contrary, I was proud to be Mrs. Neville Ravensdale."

Proud to be his wife? When he'd thought she'd been ashamed of him? He didn't know what to say. He didn't know if he should believe her.

Now her words took on a bitter tone. "But you…you turned away from me, Neville. You were the one who buried yourself in your work. You spent more and more time at the museum. I can't tell you how jealous I grew of that place. We hardly saw each other, except when I nagged you into attending a party or the opera with me."

"Because you didn't want me. Because you'd stopped loving me."

She spun around, her face full of disbelief. "Is that what you thought?"

"That's what I know."

She stood for a long moment, fighting for composure, her eyes growing moist, her chest heaving. He was about to beg her forgiveness for the remark when she regained the ability to speak.

Her eyes shimmering, she half smiled at him. "I have something to show you."

She drew the handbag from under her arm and opened it. Divorce papers. He knew it. It took all his strength not to fall to pieces right there in front of her and beg her not to go on.

Out of the handbag she drew a long black velvet pouch. Odd thing to carry legal documents in. But perhaps she'd been hiding them from Lionel.

"I want you to understand I never meant to hurt you, Neville."

He was already hurting. Wounded beyond repair. He would never recover from this blow.

Slowly, with her long, delicate fingers she undid the drawstring.

He wanted to stop her. Wanted to go back in time to when they had first fallen in love. But no, he wouldn't fight her. How could he? What good would it do? He'd never make her love him again.

She put her hand into the bag and drew something out of it. It wasn't papers, but he couldn't make out what it was. His eyes were suddenly filled with tears.

All at once his resolve crumbled. He broke down, became a sniveling, begging fool before her.

He took her by the arms. "Oh, darling Davinia. Can't you still love me just a little? Couldn't we try to find what we once had together? Please, don't leave me."

"Neville." She stared up at him as if amazed beyond all comprehension. "Are you saying you still love me?"

"How can you ask that? I never stopped." Something flashed through the watery haze of his vision. A golden handle. "What is that?"

She held it up to him with both hands. "Oh, Neville. I'm so sorry."

He wiped the back of his hand against his eyes to stare down at what she was holding. He was suddenly unable to breathe.

There in his dear wife's palms lay the Marc Antony dagger.

Slowly he let go of her and lifted the relic. Its golden blade gleamed in the sunlight. He turned it over, studied the hilt, ran his fingers over the imprint of its colorful design. And finally, he examined the quillon, read the ancient hieroglyphics engraved there so long ago. 'Be victorious in every battle, my love.'

It was real.

"*You* took it?"

"Someone did it for me. We replaced it with a fake. The fake that was stolen." The fake that had killed Gabrielle.

"Oh, my Lord." He handed it back to her, sank into a chair.

Davinia rushed to him, laid the bags and the dagger on the table and took his hands in her own. "I wanted to…get your attention, Neville. You were ignoring me. I had to do something drastic. Take something you loved more than me. It was a test. I—I suppose I'm the one who failed it." She knelt beside him, stroked his hair. "Will you send me to prison? Will you hate me forever?"

He looked into his wife's lovely, yearning face and for the first time in years saw what was truly in her eyes. She wasn't lying. She did love him.

He kissed her hands. "Oh, Davinia. Do you really still care for me?"

Now the tears fell from her eyes to her cheeks, dripped down onto his lap. "Of course, I love you. I love you with all my heart."

Reaching out he took her in his arms and felt the closeness he'd yearned for so long. And he kissed her. The lips that he hadn't tasted in years were sweet and wonderful as she kissed him back.

He couldn't believe it. Didn't know how it had happened. She loved him. He loved her. It was that simple. He didn't know what was going to happen now. He didn't know if the police would arrest her for what she'd done.

But no matter what, all they needed to do was remember that their love was as real as that dagger.

CHAPTER FIFTY

Miranda slouched in the hospital chair, half-formed visions of tire irons and rumbling motors flitting through her dreams.

She felt something tug at her. She moaned and tried to turn over. She felt it again. *Get away.* Something was pulling at her hand.

Wishing it would stop, she opened her eyes—and sat straight up.

Parker was squeezing her hand, looking right at her. "Good morning. Or is it afternoon?"

"Parker. Parker. Are you really awake?" She hoped she really was, too.

"I believe so. The doctor was just in here. I believe he said I'm going to be all right."

"Really? Really?" The stab of relief and joy she felt was almost painful.

"But I have a very bad memory of being in a repair shop. You were there." He looked at her as if he'd just recognized who she was. "You rescued me, didn't you?"

"Damn straight, I rescued your ass." Now that he could talk, now that she knew he was going to be okay, her temper started to flare. "You went to Tottenham without me. What the hell were you thinking, Parker?"

"I'm not sure at the moment." He tried to move and winced. He still looked awful with his bandaged head, his bruised and swollen face, the tubes sticking out of him.

She backed off, but only a little. "You could have been killed. You really pissed me off."

"I'm aware of that." He tried a dignified nod but couldn't manage to move.

She almost let out a laugh. He was probably the only man in the world who could make a slur from a fat lip and pain killers sound sexy.

Refusing to give on this one, she sat back in the chair, folded her arms, tapped her foot on the floor. "Well? What do you have to say for yourself, mister?"

He studied her a long moment with his good eye. Then he spoke. Slowly, so the words were clear and undistorted. "I haven't been wrong many times in my career. But I have to admit this was one of them."

Her mouth fell open. The great and successful Wade Parker was admitting he'd been wrong? On a case?

She began to nod as her lips curved into a smile of victory. "That's more like it."

He reached for her hand again, ignoring the pain the movement caused him. "I'm so sorry, Miranda."

She jumped up and leaned him back in his bed. She didn't want him to hurt himself. Taking his hand again, she shrugged. "All in a night's work."

His sexy gray eyes twinkled at her. Well, the one she could see.

She sat back down, turned his hand over and traced a finger over his palm, thrilling at the feel of it and the giddy knowledge that he was alive and awake.

He was alive. He was going to be okay.

But she had to get her thoughts off her chest. "We have a problem, Parker."

"Oh?" He tried to rise up again.

"Lay back for Pete's sake or I'll never get this out."

"Very well." He lay back on the pillow.

"When I rescued you," she cleared her throat to emphasize the point. "You were unconscious. I rode with you in the ambulance, but when we got here to the hospital they took you away, and nobody would tell me where you were or how you were doing for hours and hours."

He didn't speak, but she could see emotion on his face.

"And then they put you in this room and told me you weren't awake, and they didn't know when you would be. It drove me crazy. I couldn't stand it. I felt like I was going insane." She stared down at his hand. The one she'd held onto for all those long, lonely hours.

"And?" he said softly.

"And I realized what you must have gone through when I was the one in a coma. I finally understood why it upsets you so much when I snub you and go off to do things on my own."

She heard him draw in a breath of shock. She must be astounding him.

"And now, you did the same thing to me."

There was a long pause. At last, he said, "I suppose I did."

"We can't go on like this, Parker. We can't have a real partnership if we can't trust each other."

There was another long silence. "What do you propose?" he finally said.

"I propose…" she took a deep breath and laid out her game plan. The one she'd come up with this morning. "No more lying to each other. No more hiding things from each other. Not you. Not me. We agree not to separate, not to go off alone again. From now on, we stick together, no matter how much we disagree. We back each other up."

He pretended to consider the idea, turn it over in his mind as if weighing the pros and cons. Then his one eye twinkled again. She could tell he wanted to smile but it hurt too much.

"I agree," he said. And he gave her hand a very businesslike shake.

Miranda let out a long breath of relief. He'd agreed. He didn't want to dissolve the partnership as she'd feared he might. They could work together. They could do it.

"Oh." She bounced to the edge of her chair as she remembered. "In the spirit of our new agreement, I have something else to tell you. I was walking the halls this morning, thinking about the case, going over all that's happened, and everything came together. I figured out who took the dagger."

She grinned at him with pride. Then she saw him struggle to look expectant. "Who?"

Her shoulders slumped. "You knew?"

He looked away.

"Didn't we just make an agreement?"

He sighed. "I figured it out before we left the hotel for Camden."

That was when he'd made the arrangement to meet Shrivel, no doubt. She shook her head and laughed. "Guess that's what happens when you're hitched to an ace investigator."

"Guess so."

She leaned in, let him pull her into a half embrace and dared to plant a kiss on his swollen lip. He didn't wince this time. He could wear his wounds like the warrior he was.

"I made a call, and I think everything's going to work out."

"With the dagger?"

She nodded. "And Sir Neville."

Ignoring the pain, he gave her a proud grin. "Excellent work, Detective."

CHAPTER FIFTY-ONE

The next day Parker was ready to get off the IV and onto solid foods, and that evening he took his first walk around the hall, though it was a painful trip with his bruised ribs. Miranda liked that he had to lean on her, even if he acted as if he didn't need to.

Sir Neville and Lady Davinia came to visit to thank them for all they'd done.

While Sir Neville stayed in the room with Parker, Davinia took Miranda aside and told her everything. Including the news that she and Neville had made amends and had returned the dagger to the museum.

Miranda smiled at the understated way she summed up the two monumental events.

Neville, of course, wouldn't press charges, Davinia told her. They weren't sure yet what action the police would take, though. Miranda secretly hoped Inspector Wample had had enough of this case.

"What are you going to do now?" she asked as they strolled past the nurses' station.

Davinia turned to her with her regal air. "Lionel's going abroad. He says he needs to get away to pick up the pieces of his life."

"Oh." She hadn't expected to hear that.

"He's talking about opening another real estate office in Madrid. It will keep him busy."

"I guess it will." She dared to ask the real question. "What about you and Neville?" Could they make it work?

Davinia's look turned wistful. "We're planning a new life, too."

"Really?"

Her eyes grew intense. "I'm tired of my status. The flower shows, the royal regattas, the dinner parties. I'm sick to death of it. Every bit of it."

That was a shocker. Miranda had thought it was her life.

Davinia took Miranda's hands in hers. "If all works out, if I'm freed of the charges, Neville and I are going away."

"Away?"

She nodded. "He's going to give up his position and hand the museum over to George. And we're going to travel."

Miranda had to blink at that. "To where?"

"Everywhere. Paris. Rome. Athens. The excavation sites in Alexandria. We want to see every relic, every painting, every work of art the world has ever produced. It will take us the rest of our lives just to make a start, but....Oh, Ms. Steele. It's what I've always wanted."

Miranda was stunned. But she finally thought she understood Davinia. "And what Sir Neville wanted, too."

"Yes. He's delighted with the plan. After all our recent sorrow, all the pain we put each other through, I simply can't believe we can be so happy."

Miranda squeezed the lady's hands, knowing she might be in the presence of true nobility. And that she was honored to be a part of setting things straight for this couple. For these friends.

"I'm happy, too," she told her. "For both of you."

Two days later, the hospital released Parker and they decided to head home. The flight would be dicey, but it would be a while before he was fully healed, and Parker was anxious to get back.

As they left the hospital, the British newshounds accosted them, demanding a story. They wanted to know details about what had happened with Scorpion, the return of the dagger, how as an American he felt about the crime rate in Britain.

Miranda nearly told them all to go to hell, but Parker managed a dignified, "No comment." Then they got into a cab and headed for Heathrow, while Big Ben rang out for the last time.

For this trip anyway.

CHAPTER FIFTY-TWO

They were home. Time to get back to normal and get Parker back to health.

But after a couple days of playing mother hen and nursemaid to him, Parker kicked Miranda out of the house and told her to take some time for herself. He would have told her to go shopping, but that only would have gotten him a dirty look.

Instead, since the kids were out of school, Miranda called Mackenzie and asked if she wanted to go for a run in Chastain Park.

As they jogged together over the rolling red clay path, the smell of wisteria and Georgia pines in the warm summer air, Miranda thought how good it was to be back in Atlanta. The place she now thought of as home. The place where she had people she thought of as family.

They trotted along slowly since they were still both supposed to be recuperating from old injuries, while Miranda told her daughter about what London was like and the less violent parts of the case.

"That sounds interesting," Mackenzie said as they curved around a duck pond. "I might become a detective some day."

Miranda had to look away and pretended to concentrate on a preening goose near the water. She wasn't sure how she felt about that idea. "You mean it?"

The girl just shrugged. "I'm just toying with the thought."

"Sure." Of course.

Kids imagined themselves in twenty different careers before they settled on one. Or life made the choice for them. There was plenty of time to think about it. Mackenzie was only fourteen.

When they reached the other side of the pond, they slowed to a walk to cool down, and their conversation turned to skating and Wendy and the upcoming Atlanta Open.

Mackenzie wiped her brow with her towel. "Wendy's sit spins are getting better. I think she's got a real chance at finaling."

"That's great." Miranda couldn't help breaking out in a smile. They'd both be proud of her.

They passed a man walking a big white dog. After he was gone Miranda stopped and faced her daughter. "Mackenzie, I want to say something to you."

Her dark brows drew together in that ultra-serious adult look. "What is it?"

"Before I left for London, you mentioned something to me...."

"What?"

Didn't she remember? "About finding your father."

"Oh, that." She turned her head and studied a nearby willow tree. "What about it?"

"Well." Miranda hesitated.

She wasn't sure how to say it, but she thought of the promises she and Parker had made to each other. No more lying. No more hiding things from each other. And what was good for the goose and the gander, was good for the goose and her chick.

"I want to say I wasn't completely honest that day."

Mackenzie turned back to her, eyes glowing. With expectation or anger Miranda couldn't tell. "What do you mean?"

Miranda took a deep breath, sucked up her nerves and spat it out. "I don't know if I could find your father. Maybe I could. The truth is....I don't want to find him. I don't want you to know him. He's a criminal. Probably rotting in prison somewhere." She hoped. "But it doesn't matter what he is or was. You're your own person. You don't have to worry about him. You're going to make your own life."

Mackenzie stared at her as if she couldn't understand where all that had come from. But her deep eyes glistened with tears.

Finally, she swiped at her cheek and shook her head. "That's okay, Mother. I told you before I understand. I really do." Smiling mostly to herself, she looked at the running path. "C'mon. I think I can go a little farther. And I want to tell you about this guy."

"Guy?"

But Mackenzie had already taken off and Miranda had to gather herself quick and catch up to her. "What guy?" she asked when she did.

"I met him in biology class last year. He's been hanging around the skating rink. I think he's cute."

"Cute, huh?"

"I kind of think he likes me."

Uh oh. She wondered what Mackenzie's adoptive mother was going to say to this.

As she listened to her daughter describe the young fellow and the sound of their running shoes pounding against the red clay, Miranda decided the adventure of parenthood might turn out to be more harrowing than facing down a shopful of killers.

Feeling happier and more carefree than she had in months Miranda pulled her car into the drive and hopped up the walkway to the massive front door of the Parker estate.

She'd dropped Mackenzie off at home and now she was back at the big house in Mockingbird Hills. Home. Even though it didn't seem so big now after the museum and all the castles she'd been to. It might even be taking on a homey look. She liked that.

Humming a tune, she stepped inside and smiled at the familiar entrance hall with its not-so-huge crystal chandeliers and its not-so-ancient marble tile. She hurried to the mahogany staircase.

Parker should be napping in bed. Time to check on him and fuss at him if he wasn't.

As she took the first step, her cell buzzed. She pulled it out of her pocket. Text message. Was he turning motherly now and checking on her? She began to read.

Her whole body went cold as she froze on the step.

I know where you are.

What the hell? She'd gotten almost the same message right after their last case. Like that one, this was anonymous. What did it mean?

Stalker was her first thought. She should tell Parker. They should look into it.

Then she shook her head. She'd been on the news. People as far away as London knew who she was. This was a prank. Or maybe someone wanting money. Somebody looking for notoriety or fortune on someone else's coattails.

"Miranda?" she heard Parker call from upstairs.

She hesitated on the steps. No more lying. No more hiding things from each other.

If she told Parker about this, he'd only worry, and he needed to rest. She wasn't going to do that to him. She wasn't going to spoil their evening together because of some jerk who just wanted attention.

"Coming," she called out.

This didn't count. She deleted the message, shoved the phone back into her pocket and hurried up the stairs.

She couldn't wait to give her he-man a great big welcome home kiss.

THE END

ABOUT THE AUTHOR

Linsey Lanier writes chilling mystery-thrillers that keep you up at night.

Daughter of a WWII Navy Lieutenant, she has written fiction for over twenty years. She is best known for the popular Miranda's Rights Mystery series and the Miranda and Parker Mystery series. Someone Else's Daughter has received several thousand reviews and more than one million downloads.

Linsey is a member of International Thriller Writers, and her books have been nominated in several well-known contests.

In her spare time, Linsey enjoys watching crime shows with her husband of over two decades and trying to figure out "who-dun-it." But her favorite activity is writing and creating entertaining new stories for her readers.

She's always working on a new book, currently books in the Miranda and Parker Mystery series (a continuation of the Miranda's Rights Mystery series). Other series include the Maggie Delaney Police Thrillers and the Wesson and Sloan FBI Thriller series.

For alerts on her latest releases join Linsey's mailing list at linseylanier.com or check out her store at store.linseylanier.com.

Edited by

Donna Rich

Editing for You

Gilly Wright
www.gillywright.com

Made in the USA
Coppell, TX
23 April 2024

31625943R10114